Second Skin

John Hawkes

Second Skin

New Directions

SIXTH PRINTING

For Charlotte and Edwin Honig

Second Skin

Naming Names

I will tell you in a few words who I am: lover of the humming-bird that darts to the flower beyond the rotted sill where my feet are propped; lover of bright needlepoint and the bright stitching fingers of humorless old ladies bent to their sweet and infamous designs; lover of parasols made from the same puffy stuff as a young girl's underdrawers; still lover of that small naval boat which somehow survived the distressing years of my life between her decks or in her pilothouse; and also lover of poor dear black Sonny, my mess boy, fellow victim and confidant, and of my wife and child. But most of all, lover of my harmless and sanguine self.

Yet surely I am more than a man of love. It will be clear, I think, that I am a man of courage as well.

Had I been born my mother's daughter instead of son—and the thought is not so improbable, after all, and causes me neither pain, fear nor embarrassment when I give it my casual and interested contemplation—I would not have matured into a muscular and self-willed Clytemnestra but rather into a large and innocent Iphigenia betrayed on the beach. A large and slow-eyed and smiling Iphigenia, to be sure, even more full to the knife than that real girl struck down once on the actual shore. Yet I am convinced that in my case I should have been spared. All but sacrificed I should have lived, somehow, in my hapless way; to bleed but not to bleed to death would have been my fate, forgiving them all while attempting to wipe the smoking knife on the bottom of my thick yellow skirt. Or had my own daughter been born my son I would have remained his ghostly guardian, true to his hollow cheeks and skinny legs and hurts, for no more than this braving his sneers, his nasty eye and the scorn of his fellow boys. For him too I would have suffered violence with my chin lifted, my smile distracted, my own large breast the swarming place of the hummingbirds terrified and treacherous at once. Just as all these years I have suffered with a certain dignity for father, wife, daughter, each of whom was his own Antigone—the sand-scratchers, the impatient sufferers of self-inflicted death, the curious adventurers for whom I remain alive. Perhaps my father thought that by shooting off the top of his head he would force me to undergo some sort of transformation. But poor man, he forgot my capacity for love.

With Hamlet I should say that once, not long ago, I became my own granddaughter's father, giving her the warmth of my two arms and generous smile, substituting for each drop of the widow's poison the milk of my courageous heart. At night what a silhouette I must have made, kneeling, looming beside the child as she sat the always unfamiliar white statuary of the chamber pot. She must have known, I think, what happened to her mother, her mother's mother, her grandfather's father, and that she herself was the final accident in this long line of what I shall call our soft and well-intentioned bastardy. In the mirror our two heads—the bald one, the little silver one—would make faces together, reflecting for our innocent amusement the unhappy expressions worn once by those whom she and I—Pixie and I— had survived. So the all-but-abandoned Pixie, and my daughter, whose death I fought against the hardest, and my weightless wife, a flower already pressed between leaves of darkness before we met—these then are my dreams, the once-living or hardly

2

living members of my adored and dreadful family, the cameo profiles of my beribboned brooch, the figures cut loose so terribly by that first explosion which occurred in my father's private lavatory. I know it was meant for me, his deliberate shot. But it went wild. It carried off instead dear Cassandra and hopeless, hysterical Gertrude. Went wild and left only myself alive.

Yes, my own feet at rest on the rotted window sill. But I am no mere sickened leaf on a dead tide, no mere dead weight burdening some gaudy hammock. In body, in mind, am I not rather the aggressive personification of serenity, the eternal forward drift or handsome locomotion of peace itself? As a walker, for instance, I am a tiger. I have always walked far in my white socks, my white shoes, and the extent and manner of my walking have always been remarked upon, with admiration or maliciousness, in the past. Since childhood I have walked into a room, or out, out into the shadowed greens or dangerous sand lots of the world, holding my chin lifted, my lips pleasantly curved and my eye round, measuring my steps so that they would never falter and keeping my hands in motion at my side, wishing never to appear intimidated by the death of my parents, wishing never to conceal the shame which I thought had left its clear and rancid mark on my breast. Even today I take these same slow-paced, deliberate, impervious footsteps, using the balls of my feet in proud and sensual fashion, driving a constant rhythm and lightheartedness and a certain confidence into my stride through the uninhibited and, I might say, powerful swinging of my hips. Of course there are those who laugh. But others, like Sonny, recognize my need, my purpose, my strength and grace. Always my strength and grace.

In all likelihood my true subject may prove to be simply the wind—its changing nature, its rough and whispering characteristics, the various spices of the world which it brings together suddenly in hot or freezing gusts to alter the flavor of our inmost recollections of pleasure or pain—simply that wind to which my heart and also my skin have always been especially sensitive. Or it may prove to be the stark elongated brutal silhouette of a ship standing suddenly on the horizon of the mind and, all at once, making me inexplicably afraid—perhaps because it is so far off that not one detail reaches the eye, nothing of name, passengers, crew, not even smoke from the stack, so that only the ugly span of pointed iron, which ought to be powerless but moves nonetheless and is charged with all the mystery and in-human distance of the compass, exists to incite this terrible fear and longing in a man such as myself. But for now the wind trails off my fingers, the ship fades. Because I suppose that names must precede these solid worlds of my passionate time and place and action.

There was Fernandez, then, my small son-in-law, who held up his trousers with the feathery translucent skin of a rattlesnake, and who, even in his white linen suit and with Cassandra's hand in his at the altar, continued to look like the hapless Peruvian orphan that he was. A breath smelling of hot peppers, dark and deeply socketed nostrils, flat smoky brown skull that cried for lace and candlelight, in his jacket pocket a Bible bound in white calfskin, and in his hand a bunch of somber crimson flowers—this was Fernandez, who underwent a triumphant and rebellious change of character in the wedding car (it was his own though he could not drive it, a sloping green-roofed sedan with cracked glass, musty seats, bare oily floors rent and jagged so that the road was clearly visible, the car Cassandra drove that day only with the greatest effort and determination), this then was Fer-nandez, who caused me, that day, to smile my most perspiring smile for the loss of my dear blonde-headed Cassandra. But even then, of course, I could not have imagined Fernandez on a bloody hotel room floor. And even now, after the fact of these events—time has worked on them like water on old knots—even now I cannot entirely castigate the memory of that Fernandez who was the groom. His favorite name for me was "good Papa Cue Ball." For anyone else—except Cassandra, except me—that nick-name would have been warning enough. But I would have wel-comed Fernandez then, Fernandez with his menacing green car, his piles of tattered ration booklets, his heaps of soft smooth tires piled in the black wooden structure where the chickens scratched, even had he threatened me with the little hook-shaped

4

razor blade he carried next to his Bible in an Edgeworth tobacco tin. Welcomed him with opened arms, I am sure.

But two more names will complete this preliminary roster of persons whose love I have lost or whose poison I happily spent my life neutralizing with my unblemished flesh, my regal carriage, my impractical but all the more devoted being. After Fernandez there was Miranda. I hear that name—Miranda, Miranda!—and once again quicken to its false suggestiveness, feel its rhapsody of sound, the several throbs of the vowels, the very music of charity, innocence, obedience, love. For a moment I seem to see both magic island and imaginary girl. But Miranda was the widow's name—out of what perversity, what improbable desire I am at a loss to say—and no one could have given a more ugly denial to that heartbreaking and softly fluted name than the tall and treacherous woman. Miranda. The widow. In the end I was Miranda's match; I have had my small victory over Miranda; as father, grandfather, former naval officer and man, I found myself equal to this last indignity; to me her name means only ten months during which I attempted to prolong Cassandra's life, ten subtle months of my final awakening. Rawboned and handsome woman, unconventional and persistent widow, old antagonist on a black Atlantic island, there she was—my monster, my Miranda, final challenge of our sad society and worthy of all the temperance and courage I could muster. Now I think of her as my black butterfly. And now—obviously—the scars are sweet.

With the mention of my mother's prosaic name of Mildred I complete my roster, because there is no place here for Tremlow —my devil, Tremlow—or for Mac, the Catholic chaplain who saved my life. No place for them. Not yet. Of course the mere name of my mother has no special connotation, no significance, but the woman herself was the vague consoling spirit behind the terrible seasons of this life when unlikely accidents, tabloid adventures, shocking episodes, surrounded a solitary and wistful heart. Like my father she died when I was young, and I see her with most of her features indistinct. But she too was tall, stoopshouldered, forever smiling a soft questioning smile. I have no recollection of her voice—some short time after my father's decision in the lavatory she ceased to talk, became permanently mute—and my few visual memories of her are silent and show her only at a great distance off. Wearing her broad-brimmed white hat so immense and limpid it conceals her face and back in waves like tissue paper, she kneels in the garden strip next to the little chipped and tarnished electric sign which is the familiar urban monument of men in my father's profession and which, in my boyhood, identified our private house as the combined residence and working place of an active small-town mortician. I see my mother kneeling, hidden by the hat, inert and sweet and ghostly in the summer sun. She seems to me to be praying rather than gardening, and my imagination supplies the black trowel untouched by her white-gloved folded hands but stabbed upright, rather, into the earth at her knees. And then, in another fragment of memory, I see her seated in the middle of our lawn on one of my father's shellacked folding chairs and still dressed in white, still wearing the hat, while he, bareheaded and balding and in shirt sleeves, stands hosing down the long black limousine which was shabby, upholstered in red velvet except for the stiff black patent leather of the driver's seat, and often smelled of invisible flowers—that worn and comfortable old hearse—when it doubled on Sunday afternoons as our family car. The seated woman, the dripping machine, the man working his wrist in idle circles, this is the vision lying closest to the peaceful center of my childhood. And how much it contains: not only the still day of my youth but also the devotion and modest industry of my parents which gave my early life the proportions of a working fairy tale. For the president of the local bank, an unmarried teacher in the elementary school, two brothers dramatically drowned in a scummy pond at the edge of town, the thin mother of infant twins, three beautiful members of the high school graduating class decapitated in a scarlet coupé, a girl who had sold children's underwear in the five and dime, in our house all of them appeared, all were attended by my father and my mother as well, she in the parlor, smiling, he in the shop below, since she was always his perfect partner, the mortician's muse, the woman who more and more grew to re-

6

semble a gifted angel in a dreamer's cemetery as the years passed and the number of our nonreligious ceremonies increased. A few years only—yet all my youth—were marked by the folding and unfolding of the wooden chairs and sudden oil changes in the hearse, until that day my peace and excitement ended and my mother and I were only brief visitors in another undertaker's home.

At least I was witness to my father's death, in a sense was the child-accomplice of whatever dark phantom might have been materializing by his side that noon hour he finally locked himself in the hot lavatory—it was a Friday in midsummer—and rushed through the bare essentials of taking his life. Witness and accomplice because I was crouched with my ear to the door and because we talked together, curious but welcome conference between father and son, and because I played my cello to him and later fished from the trembling cupfuls of water in the bottom of the toilet bowl the little unused bullet which was companion to the one he fired. At least I knew it was for my sake, despite his confusion, his anger, his pathetic cries, and received the tangible actuality of his death with shocked happiness, grateful at least for the misguided trust implicit in the real staging of that uncensored scene.

How like my mother, on the other hand, to spare me: to disappear, to vanish, gone without the hard crude accessories of sweating water jug, pulmotor, stretcher, ambulance summoned from the City Hospital; gone without vigil or funeral, without good-bys. I missed her one morning and that was all. It makes little difference now that she died only twenty miles away and in the care of a half brother. It makes no difference to me. Because I missed her, I knew at once what had happened, I was alone, I could do nothing but alternate my days between the lavatory—endless brushing of teeth, plastering down of hair—and the back of the hearse where I instinctively stretched out to await my final vision of that experience denied me in space but not in time.

And in time it came, the moment when at last I sat up like a miniature fat corpse in the back of the solemn old limousine and found the cobwebs, the streaming motes, the worn velvet carpeting and various bits of silver and thin lengths of steel—the casket runners—all turned to dense geometric substances of light—orange, yellow, radiant pink—and in that blaze, and just as I clenched my hands and shut my eyes, knew that my father had begun my knowledge of death as a lurid truth but that my mother had extended it toward the promise of mystery—this at the instant I saw her, saw her, after all, in the vision which no catastrophe of my own has ever destroyed or dimmed.

She appears from a doorway in a large white house on a hill; clouds are banked heavily behind the house and hill and a deep morning sun appears to lie buried inside the enormous unmoving range of clouds; there is no one else in the great house with all its white chimneys and shuttered windows, silent, breeze-swept, filled with untouched tinkling crystal and dusty sleigh bells strung on long strips of dried and moldy leather, and my mother steps from under the portico, raises a gentle hand to the hat trembling with a motion all its own, and lifts her face, turns it left and right with the benevolent questioning glance of the royal lady prepared to greet either prince or executioner with her lovely smile which, from where I hide down the hill in a bush, is either innocent or blind. Then she is moving, skin and veils and featureless face—except for the smile—reflecting the peach and rose color of the filtered sun, descends one lichen-covered step and then another, sways and climbs up beside the driver of a small open yellow machine with wooden wheels, white solid tires and brass headlamps. The car is thumping up and down, but silently, and behind the single high seat is strapped a little white satin trunk, and the driver, I see, wears a white cap and driving coat, great eyeless goggles and a black muffler wrapped about his throat and hiding his mouth, nose, chin. With one gloved hand he grips a lever as tall and thin as a sword, and there is a sudden flashing when he contracts his arm; with his other hand he is squeezing the black bulb of the horn, though I hear nothing, and is sitting even straighter against the wind; and now he is gripping the steering wheel, holding it at arm's length; and now he turns his head and takes a single long look into my

mother's face, and I see that she is admiring him—or pitying him
—and I quiver; and then the tires are rolling, the trunk swaying,
the muffler beating the air, and suddenly the white coat is brown
with the dust of the road and the vehicle, severe and tangled
like a complicated golden insect, is gaining speed, and I see that
my mother is quite serene, somehow remains unblown, unshaken
as the downward ride commences, and is merely touching her
fingers to the crown of her familiar hat and raising a soft white
arm as if to wave.

A waxen tableau, no doubt the product of a slight and romantic
fancy. Yet I prefer this vision to my father's death. And by way
of partial explanation, at least, I should make note of one concrete circumstance: that my mother, unable to bear the sound of
the death-dealing shot—it must have lodged in her head like a
shadow of the bullet that entered my father's—deafened herself
one muggy night, desperately, painfully, by filling both lovely
ears with the melted wax from one of our dining room candles.

But on now to the erratic flight of the hummingbird—on to the
high lights of my naked history.

Agony of the Sailor

She was in my arms and lifeless, nearly lifeless. Together we stood: the girl, young mother, war bride in her crumpled frock, and I in my cap and crumpled uniform of white duck—it was damp and beginning to soil after these nights awake, was bunched at the knees and down the front spotted with the rum and Coca-Cola from poor Sonny's upset glass—I hardly able to smile, perspiring, sporting on my breast the little colorful ribbon of my Good Conduct Medal and on my collar the tarnished insignia of my rank, and unshaven, tired, burned slightly red and lost, thoroughly lost in this midnight Chinatown at the end of my tour of duty and still wearing in my forgetfulness the dark blue armband of the Shore Patrol, and so protected, protecting, I holding the nearly lifeless hand and feeling her waist growing smaller and smaller in the wet curve of my arm, feeling even her cold hand diminishing, disappearing from mine and wondering how to restore this poor girl who would soon be gone. I looked around, trying to catch sight of Sonny where he sat in the booth with Pixie. And suddenly I was aware of the blind, meaningless, momentary presence of her little breast against my own and I, regretting my sensitivity but regretting more the waste, the impossibility of bringing her to life again—there in the small fleshed locket of her heart—I wished all at once to abandon rank, insignia, medal, bald head, good nature, everything, if only I might become for a moment an anonymous seaman second class, lanky and far from home and dancing with this girl, but felt instead the loose sailors pressing against us, all of them in their idiotic two-piece suits and laced up tight, each one filling me with despair because she and I were dancing together, embracing, and there wasn't even someone to give her a kiss. Here then was our celebration, the start of adventure and begining of misery—or perhaps its end—and I kept thinking that she was barelegged, had packed her only pair of stockings—black market, a present from me—in the small tattered canvas bag guarded now between Sonny's feet.

There should have been love in our dark and nameless China-town café. But there was only an hour to spare, only the shot-glasses flung like jewels among the sailors—each provided with his pocket comb, French letters, gold watch and matching band —only the noise, the smoke, the poster of the old national goat-faced man over the bar, the sound of the record and torch singer, orchestra, a song called "Tangerine," only the young boys with their navy silk ties and Popeye hats, crowded elbows and bowls of boiled rice; only this night, the harbor plunging with battle-ships, the water front blacked-out, bloody with shore leave and sick with the bodies of young girls sticking to the walls of moist unlighted corridors; only our own café and its infestation of little waiters smiling their white-slave smiles and of sailors pulling down their middies, kicking their fresh white hornpipe legs; only ourselves—agitated eccentric naval officer, well-meaning man, and soft young woman, serious, downcast—only ourselves and in the middle of no romance.

So in the shame and longing of my paternal sentiment, flushed and bumbling, I felt her knee, her hip, once more her breasts—they were of a child in puberty though she was twenty-five—and touched the frock which I had found tossed over the back of the hotel sofa. I glanced down at her head, at the hair pinned up and her neck bare, at her face, the beautiful face which reminded me suddenly of a little death mask of Pascal. From one wrist she carried a dangling purse, and when it swung against my ribs—dull metronome of our constrained and hollow dance—I knew it was an empty purse. No stockings, no handkerchief, no lipstick or keys; no love, no mother, no Fernandez. There among all those sailors in the smoke, the noise, I pulled her to me, wincing and lunging both as I felt imprinted on my stomach the shape of hers, and felt all the little sinews in her stomach banding together, trembling. It was midnight—Pacific War Time—and I tried to collect myself, tried to put on a show of strength in my jaw.

"I've never been afraid of the seeds of death," I said, tightening my arm, staring over her head at the litter of crushed cherries and orange rind wet on the bar, "and if I were you I wouldn't blame Gertrude for what she did." We executed a fairly rakish turn, bumped from the rear, blocked by the tall airy figure of a bosun's mate—the uniform was stuffed against his partner in an aghast paralysis of love, bell-bottoms wrapped tight around the woman's ankles, the man's white face swaying in an effort to toss aside the black hair drenched in rum—and I looked down into my own partner's eyes which were lifted to mine at last and which were as clear as sea shells, the pupils gray and hard, the irises suddenly returning to sight like little cold musical instruments. I sighed—my sigh was a hot breath on her dry lips—I blushed, I got my wind again, and it was a mouthful of smoke, mouthful of rum, fragrance of salty black sauce and yellow plague.

"As you know," I said, "I grew up very familiar with the seeds of death; I had a special taste for them always. But when I heard about Gertrude something happened. It was as if I had struck a new variety. Her camel's-hair coat, her pink mules, her cuticle sticks scattered on the floor, her dark glasses left lying on the unmade bed in the U-Drive-Inn, I saw the whole thing, for that moment understood her poor strangled solitude, understood exactly what it is like to be one of the unwanted dead. Suddenly Gertrude and I were being washed together in the same warm tide. But in our grief we were casting up only a single shadow—you."

Quickly, artfully, I gave the bosun's mate a shove with my sea-going hip and, heavy as I was, stood hovering, sagging in front of Cassandra. I held her, with a moistened finger I touched her dry mouth, I raised her chin—unsmiling dimple, unblemished curve of her little proud motherhood—I watched her gray eyes and I waited, waited for the sound of the voice which was always a whisper and which I had never failed to hear. And now the eyes were tuned, the lips were unsealed—moving, opening wide enough to admit a straw—I was flooded with the sound of the whisper and sight of a tiny golden snake wriggling up the delicate cleft of her throat—still no smile, never a smile—and curling in a circle to pulse, to die, in the shallow white nest of her temple.

"I think you would like to know," she began, whispering, spacing the words, "you would like to know what I did with the guitar. Well, I burned it. Pixie and I burned it together." And in her whispered seriousness, the hush of her slow enunciation, I heard then the snapping of flames, the tortured singing of those red-hot strings. Even as I dropped her hand, let go of her waist, brought together my fat fingers where the Good Conduct Ribbon like a dazzling insect marked the spot of my heart in all that wrinkled and sullied field of white, even as I struggled with the tiny clasp—pinprick, drop of blood, another stain—and fastened the ribbon to the muslin of her square-collared rumpled frock, even while I admired my work and then took her into my arms again, hugging, kissing, protecting her always and always, and even while I gave her the Good Conduct Medal—she the one who deserved it; I, never—and shook long and happily in my relief: through all this hectic and fragile moment I distinctly heard the gray whisper continuing its small golden thread of intelligence exactly on the threshold of sound and as fine and formidable as the look in her eye.

"Pixie and I were alone, mother and daughter, and we did what we had to do. I think she disapproved at first, but once I got the kerosene out of the garage she began to enjoy the whole thing immensely. She even clapped her little hands. But you ought to have known," taking note of the ribbon, touching it with the tip of her pinky—no other sign than this—and all the while whispering, whispering those minimum formal cadences she had learned at school and gently moving, turning, arching her bare neck so I should see how she disciplined her sorrow, "you ought to have known the U-Drive-Inn was no place for a child. . . ."

I blushed again, I glanced down at the small bare feet in the strapless shoes—scuffed lemon shells—I welcomed even this briefest expression of her displeasure. "It was no place for you, no place for you, Cassandra," I said, and wished, as I had often wished, that she would submit to some small name of endearment, if only at such times as these when I loved her most and feared for her the most. A name of endearment would have helped. "You were too innocent for the U-Drive-Inn," I said. "I should have known how it would end. Your mother always told me she wanted to die surrounded by unmarried couples in a cheap motel, and I let her. But no more cheap motels for us, Cassandra. We won't even visit Gertrude in the cemetery."

She caught my spirit, she caught my gesturing hand: "Skipper?"—at least she allowed herself to whisper that name, mine, which Sonny had invented for me so long ago before we sailed —"Skipper? Will you do something nice for me? Something really nice?"

She was still unsmiling but was poised, half-turned, giving me a look of happiness, of life, in the pure agility of her body. And hadn't she, wearing only the frock, only a few pins in the small classical lift of her hair, hadn't she come straight from a sluggish bath tub in the U-Drive-Inn to the most violent encounter ever faced by her poor little determined soul? Now she held before me the promise of her serious duplicity, watching and gauging— me, the big soft flower of fatherhood—until I heard myself saying, "Anything, anything, the bus doesn't leave for another hour and a half, Cassandra, and no one will ever say I faltered even one cumbersome step in loving you." I gripped her small ringless hand and fled with her, though she was only walking, walking, this child with the poise and color and muscle-shape of a woman, followed her through the drunken sailors to the door.

In the dark, whipped by pieces of paper—the torn and painted

14

remnants of an old street dragon—a sailor stood rolling and moaning against the wall, holding his white cupcake-wrapper hat in one hand and with the other reaching into the sunken whiteness of his chest, the upturned face, the clutching hand, the bent legs spread and kicking to the unheard Latin rhythm of some furious carnival. But on flowed Cassandra, small, grave, heartless, a silvery water front adventuress, and led me straight into the crawling traffic—it was unlighted, rasping, a slow and blackened parade of taxicabs filled with moon-faced marines wearing white braid and puffing cherry-tipped cigars, parade of ominous jeeps each with its petty officer standing up in the rear, arms folded, popping white helmets strapped in place—led me on through admiring whistles and the rubbery sibilance of military tires to a dark shop which was only a rat's hole between a cabaret —girl ventriloquist, dummy in black trunks—and the fuming concrete bazaar of the Greyhound Bus Terminal—point of our imminent departure—drew me on carefully, deftly, until side by side we stood in the urine-colored haze of a guilty light bulb and breathed the dust, the iodine, the medicinal alcohol of a most vulgar art.

"But, Cassandra," I said in a low voice, flinching, trying to summon the dignity of my suffering smile, all at once aware that beneath my uniform my skin was an even and lively red, unbroken, unmarked by disfiguring scars or blemishes, "look at his teeth, smell his breath! My God, Cassandra!"

"Skipper," she said, and again it was the ghostly whisper, the terrifying sadistic calm of the school-trained voice, "don't be a child. Please." Then she whispered efficiently, calmly, to the oaf at the table—comatose eyes of the artist, the frustrated procurer, drinking her in—and naturally he was unable to hear even one word of her little succinct command, unable to make out her slow toy train of lovely sounds. He wore a tee-shirt, was covered—arms, neck, shoulders—with the sweaty peacock colors of his self-inflicted art.

"There's no need to whisper, lady," he said. Up and down went his eyes, up and down from where he fell in a mountain on his disreputable table, watching her, not bothering to listen, flexing

15

his nightmare pictures as best he could, shifting and showing us, the two of us, the hair bunched and bristling in his armpits, and even that hair was electrical.

She continued to whisper—ludicrous pantomime—without stopping, without changing the faint and formal statement of her desires, when suddenly and inexplicably the man and I, allied in helpless and incongruous competition, both heard her at the same time.

"My boy friend is bashful," she was saying, "do you understand? Let me have a piece of writing paper and a pencil, please."

"You mean he's afraid? But I got you, lady," and I saw him move, saw his blue tattooed hand swim like a trained seal in the slime of a drawer which he had yanked all at once into his belly.

"Father, Cassandra, father!" I exclaimed, though softly, "Pixie's grandfather, Cassandra!"

"No need to worry, Skipper," said the man—his grin, his fiendish familiarity—"I'm a friend of Uncle Sam's."

Yellow and silver-tinted, prim, Cassandra was already sitting on the tattooer's stool, had placed her purse on the table beside her, had forced the man to withdraw his fat scalloped arms, was writing with the black stub of pencil on the back of a greasy envelope which still contained—how little she knew—its old-fashioned familiar cargo of prints the size of postage stamps, each one revealing, beneath a magnifying glass, its aspect of faded pubic area or instant of embarrassed love. Alone and celebrating, we were war orphans together and already I had forgiven her, wanted to put my hand on the curls pinned richly and hastily on the top of her head. I could see that she was writing something in large block letters across the envelope.

She stood up—anything but lifeless now—and between his thumb and finger the man took the envelope and rubbed it as if he were testing the sensual quality of gold laminated cloth or trying to smear her tiny fingerprints onto his own, and then the man and I, the oaf and I, were watching her together, listening:

"My boy friend," she said, and I was measuring her pauses, smelling the bludwurst on the tattooer's breath, was quivering

16

to each whispered word of my child courtesan, "my boy friend would like to have this name printed indelibly on his chest. Print it over his heart, please."

"What color, lady?" And grinning, motioning me to the stool, "You got the colors of the rainbow to choose from, lady." So even the oaf, the brute artist was a sentimentalist and I sat down stiffly, heavily, seeing against my will his display of wet dripping rainbow, hating him for his infectious colors, and telling myself that I must not give him a single wince, not give him the pleasure of even one weak cry.

"Green," she said at once—had I heard her correctly?—and she took a step closer with one of her spun sugar shoes, "a nice bright green." Then she looked up at me and added, to my confusion, my mystification, "Like the guitar."

And the oaf, the marker of men, was grinning, shaking his head: "Green's a bad color"—more muscle-flexing now and the professional observation—"Green's going to hurt, lady. Hurt like hell."

But I had known it, somehow, deep in the tail of my spine, deep where I was tingling and trying to hide from myself, had known all along that now I was going to submit to an atrocious pain for Cassandra—only for Cassandra—had known it, that I who had once entertained the thought of a single permanent inscription in memory of my mother—gentle Mildred—but when it came to rolling up my sleeve had been unable to endure the shock of even a very small initial M, would now submit myself and expose the tender flesh of my breast letter by letter to the pain of that long exotic name my daughter had so carefully penciled out on that greasy envelope of endless lunchroom counters, endless lavatories in creaking burlesque theaters. So even before I heard the man's first order—voice full of German delicacies and broken teeth—I had forced my fingers to the first of my hard brass buttons, tarnished, unyielding—the tiny eagle was sharp to the touch—and even before he had taken the first sizzling stroke with his electric needle I was the wounded officer, collapsing, flinching, biting my lip in terror.

He worked with his tongue in his cheek while Cassandra stood

17

by watching, waiting, true to her name. I hooked my scuffed regulation white shoes into the rungs of the stool; I allowed my white duck coat to swing open, loose, disheveled; I clung to the greasy edge of the table. My high stiff collar was unhooked, the cap was tilted to the back of my head, and sitting there on that wobbling stool I was a mass of pinched declivities, pockets of fat, strange white unexpected mounds, deep creases, ugly stains, secret little tunnels burrowing into all the quivering fortifications of the joints, and sweating, wrinkling, was either the wounded officer or the unhappy picture of some elderly third mate, sitting stock still in an Eastern den—alone except for the banana leaves, the evil hands—yet lunging, plunging into the center of his vicious fantasy. A few of us, a few good men with soft reproachful eyes, a few honor-bright men of imagination, a few poor devils, are destined to live out our fantasies, to live out even the sadistic fantasies of friends, children and possessive lovers.

But I heard him then and suddenly, and except for the fleeting thought that perhaps a smile would cause even this oaf, monster, skin-stitcher, to spare me a little, suddenly there was no escape, no time for reverie: "OK, Skipper, here we go."

Prolonged thorough casual rubbing with a dirty wet disintegrating cotton swab. Merely to remove some of the skin, inflame the area. Corresponding vibration in the victim's jowls and holding of breath. Dry ice effect of the alcohol. Prolonged inspection of disintegrating cardboard box of little scabrous dusty bottles, none full, some empty. Bottles of dye. Chicken blood, ground betel nut, baby-blue irises of child's eye—brief flashing of the cursed rainbow. Tossing one particular bottle up and down and grinning. Thick green. Then fondling the electric needle. Frayed cord, greasy case—like the envelope—point no more than a stiff hair but as hot as a dry frying pan white from the fire. Then he squints at the envelope. Then lights a butt, draws, settles it on the lip of a scummy brown-stained saucer. Then unstoppers the ancient clotted bottle of iodine. Skull and crossbones. Settles the butt between his teeth where it stays. Glances at Cassandra, starts the current, comes around and sits on the corner of the table, holding the needle away from his own face and flesh, pushing a fat leg against victim's. Scowls. Leans down. Tongue in position. Rainbow full of smoke and blood. Then the needle bites.

The scream—yes, I confess it, scream—that was clamped between my teeth was a strenuous black bat struggling, wrestling in my bloated mouth and with every puncture of the needle—fast as the stinging of artificial bees, this exquisite torture—I with my eyes squeezed tight, my lips squeezed tight, felt that at any moment it must thrust the slimy black tip of its archaic skeletal wing out into view of Cassandra and the working tattooer. But I was holding on. I longed to disgorge the bat, to sob, to be flung into the relief of freezing water like an old woman submerged and screaming in the wild balm of some dark baptismal rite in a roaring river. But I was holding on. While the punctures were marching across, burning their open pinprick way across my chest, I was bulging in every muscle, slick, strained, and the bat was peering into my mouth of pain, kicking, slick with my saliva, and in the stuffed interior of my brain I was resisting, jerking in outraged helplessness, blind and baffled, sick with the sudden recall of what Tremlow had done to me that night—helpless abomination—while Sonny lay sprawled on the bridge and the captain trembled on his cot behind the pilothouse. There were tiny fat glistening tears in the corners of my eyes. But they never fell. Never from the eyes of this heavy bald-headed once-handsome man. Victim. Courageous victim.

The buzzing stopped. I waited. But the fierce oaf was whistling and I heard the click, the clasp of Cassandra's purse—empty as I thought except for a worn ten dollar bill which she was drawing forth, handing across to him—and I found that the bat was dead, that I was able to see through the sad film over my eyes and that the pain was only a florid swelling already motionless, inactive, the mere receding welt of this operation. I could bear it. Marked and naked as I was, I smiled. I managed to stand.

Cassandra glanced at my chest—at what to me was still a mystery—glanced and nodded her small classical indomitable head.

Then the tatooer took a square dirty mirror off the wall, held it in front of me:

"Have a look, Skipper," once more sitting on the edge of the table, eager, bulking, swinging a leg.

So I looked into the mirror, the dirty fairy tale glass he was about to snap in his two great hands, and saw myself. The pink was blistered, wet where he had scrubbed it again with the cooling and dizzying alcohol, but the raised letters of the name—upside down and backwards—were a thick bright green, a string of inflamed emeralds, a row of unnatural dots of jade. Slowly, trying to appear pleased, trying to smile, I read the large unhealed green name framed in the glass above the ashamed blind eye of my own nipple: *Fernandez*. And I could only try to steady my knees, control my breath, hide feebly this green lizard that lay exposed and crawling on my breast.

Finally I was able to speak to her, faintly, faintly: "Sonny and Pixie are waiting for us, Cassandra," as I saw with shame and alarm that her eyes were harder than ever and had turned a bright new triumphant color.

"Pixie and I been worried about you. You going to miss that bus if you two keep running off this way. But come on, Skipper, we got time for one more round of rum and coke!"

With fondness, a new white preening of the neck, an altered line at the mouth, a clear light of reserved motherhood in the eye, Cassandra glanced at the little girl on Sonny's lap and then smoothed her frock—this the most magical, envied, deferential gesture of the back of the tiny white hand that never moved, never came to life except to excite the whole ladylike sense of modesty—and slid with the composure of the young swan into the dark blistered booth opposite the black-skinned petty officer and platinum child. I took my place beside her, squeezing, sighing, worrying, aware of my burning chest and the new color of her eyes and feeling her withdrawing slightly, making unnecessary room for me, curving away from me in all the triumph and gentleness of her disdain. I fished into a tight pocket, wiped my brow. Once more there was the smoke, the noise, the sick heaviness of our water front café, our jumping-off night in China-town, once more the smell of whisky and the sticky surface of tin trays painted with pagodas and golden monsters, and now the four of us together—soon to part, three to take their leave of poor black faithful Sonny—and now the terrible mammalian con-cussion of Kate Smith singing to all the sailors.

Duty gave still greater clarity, power, persistence to the whisper: "Has she been crying, Sonny?"

"Pixie? My baby love? You know Pixie never cries when I croon to her, Miss Cassandra. And I been crooning about an hour and a half. But Miss Cassandra," lulling us with his most intimate voice—it was the voice he adopted in times of trouble, always most melodious at the approach of danger—lulling us and tighten-ing the long black hand—shiny knuckles, long black bones and tendons, little pink hearts for fingertips—that spraddled Pixie's chest limply, gently, "Miss Cassandra, you look like you been cashing in your Daddy's Victory bonds. And Skipper," sitting across from us with the child, glancing first at Cassandra and then myself, "you've got a terrible blue look about you, terrible tired and blue." Then: "No more cemetery business, Skipper? I trust there's no more of that cemetery stuff in the cards. That stuff's the devil!"

Cocked garrison cap and shiny visor; petty officer's navy blue coat, white shirt, black tie; two neat rows of rainbow ribbons on his breast; elongated bony skull and black velvet face—he called himself the skinny nigger—and sunglasses with enormous lenses coal-black and brightly polished; signet ring, little Windsor knot in the black tie, high plum-colored temples and white teeth of the happy cannibal; tall smart trembling figure of a man whose only arrogance was affection: he was sitting across from us—poor Sonny—and talking through the Chinese babble, the noise of the Arkansas sailors, the loud breasty volume of mother America's possessive wartime song. Poor Sonny.

"Skipper," once more the whisper of fashion, whisper of feminine cleanliness, cold love, "show Sonny, please."

"What's this? Games?" And casting quick razor looks from Cassandra to myself, shifting Pixie still further away from us and leaning forward, craning down: "What you two been up to anyway?"

I unhooked my stiff collar and worked loose the top brass button and then the next, gingerly, with chin to collar bone trying to see it again myself, through puckered lips trying to blow a cold breath on it, and leaned forward, held open the white duck in a V for Sonny, for Sonny who respected me, who was all bone and blackness and was the best mess boy the U.S.S. *Starfish* ever had.

He looked. He gave a long low Negro whistle: "So that's the trouble. Well now. You two both grieving not for the dead but for that halfpint Peruvian fella who run out on us. I understand. Well now. Husbands all ducked out on us, wives all dead and buried. So we got to do something fancy with *his* name, we got to do something to hurt Skipper. Got to turn a man's breast into a tombstone full of ache and pain. You better just take your baby girl and your bag of chicken salad sandwiches—I made you a two-days' supply—and get on the bus. This family of ours is about busted up."

But: "Hush," I said, done with the buttons and still watching Cassandra—chin tilted, lips tight in a crescent, spine straight—and reaching out for the black angle of his hand, "You know how we feel about Fernandez. But Sonny, you'll find a brown parcel in the back of the jeep. My snapshots of the boys on the *Starfish*. For you."

"That so, Skipper? Well now. Maybe we ain't so busted up after all."

He puffed on his signet ring—the teeth, the wrinkled nose, the fluttering lips, the twisted wide-open mouth of the good-natured mule—and shined it on his trousers and flashed it into sight again —bloodstone, gold-plated setting—and took off his cocked and rakish hat, slowly, carefully, since from the Filipino boys he had learned how to pomade his rich black opalescent hair, and fanned himself and Pixie three or four times with the hat—the inside of the band was lined with bright paper medallions of the Roman Church—and then treated the patent leather visor as he had the ring, puffing, polishing, arm's length examination of his work, and with his long slow burlesquing fingers tapped the starched hat into place again, saying, "OK, folks, old Sonny's bright as a dime again, or maybe a half dollar—nigger money of course. But, Skipper," dropping a bright black kiss as big as a mushmelon in Pixie's platinum hair and grinning, waving toward Cassandra's glass and mine—Coca-Cola like dark blood, little drowning buttons of melted ice—then frowning, long-jawed and serious: "whatever did happen to that Fernandez fella?"

I shifted, hot, desperate, broad rump stuck fast and uncomfortable to the wooden seat, I looked at her, I touched my stinging breast, tried to make a funny grandfather's face for Pixie: "We don't know, Sonny. But he was a poor husband for Cassandra anyway." I used the handkerchief again, took hold of the glass. She was composed, unruffled, sat toying with a plastic swizzle stick—little queen—and one boudoir curl hung loose and I was afraid to touch it.

"Maybe he got hisself a job with a dance band. Maybe he run off with the USO—I never liked him, but he sure was a whizz with the guitar—or maybe," giving way to his black fancy, his affectionate concern, "maybe he got hisself kidnapped. Those South American fellas don't fool around, and maybe they decided it was time he did his hitch in the Peruvian Army. No, sir," taking a long self-satisfied optimistic drink, cupping the ice in his lip like a lump of sugar, "I bet he just couldn't help hisself!"

Then she was stirring the swizzle stick, raising it to the invisible tongue, touching the neckline of her wrinkled frock, once more whispering and informing us, tormenting us with the somber clarity of what she had to say: "Fernandez deserted his wife and child"—hairs leaping up on the backs of my hands, scalp tingling, heart struck with a hammer, fit of coughing—"deserted his wife and child for another person. Fernandez left his wife and child"—I clutched again the handkerchief, wishing I could extricate myself and climb out of the booth—"abandoned us, Pixie and me, for the love of another person. A man who was tall, dark-haired, sun-tanned and who wore civilian clothes. A gunner's mate named Harry. He had a scar. Also, he

23

was tattooed," the whisper dying, dying, the mouth coming as close as it could to a smile, "like you, Skipper."

Then silence. Except for the shot glasses. Except for the tin trays. Except for the moaning sailor and the bay plunging and crashing somewhere in the night. Except for the torch song of our homeless millions. I slumped, Sonny shook his head, threw out suddenly a long fierce burnt-up hand and pure white dapper cuff: "Oh, that unfaithful stuff is the devil! Pure devil!"

The shaft goes to the breast, love shatters, whole troop trains of love are destroyed, the hero is the trumpet player twisted into a lone embrace with his sexless but mellow horn, the good-bys are near and I hear Cassandra whispering and I see the color in her eyes: "There aren't any husbands left in the world. Are there, Skipper?"

But Sonny answered, Sonny who took a shower in our cheap hotel, Sonny whose uniform was pressed dark blue and hard and crisp in a steaming mangle: "Dead or unfaithful, Miss Cassandra, that's a fact. Damn all them unfaithful lovers!"

Bereft. Cool. Grieved. Triumphant. The frozen bacchanal, the withered leaf. Taps in the desert. Taps at sea. Small woman, poor faithful friend, crying child—Pixie had begun to cry—and I the lawful guardian determined but still distressed and past fifty, nose packed with carbonated water, head fuming with rum, all of us wrecked together in a Chinatown café and waiting for the rising tide, another dark whim of the sea. But still I had my love of the future, my wounded pride.

"I think I told you, Sonny, that I'm taking Cassandra and Pixie to a gentle island. You won't need to worry about them."

"That's it, that's it, Skipper. These two little ladies are in good hands. Well now. Well, I understand. And I got a gentle island too if I can just find her. Wanders around some, true enough, but she sure is gentle and she sure just about accommodates an old black castaway like me. Oh, just let Sonny crawl up on that gentle shore!" He was nodding, smiling, with his long smoky five-gaited fingers was trying to turn Pixie on his lap, fondling, probing the fingers, gently feeling for the source of her tiny noise, and all the while kept the two great cold black lenses of his pink and white shell-rimmed sunglasses fixed in my direction. Nodding, at last beginning to croon through his nose —tight lips, menacing cheekbones—holding Pixie and shining all his black love into my heart.

But Pixie was crying. She was crying her loudest with tiny pug nose wrinkled, wet, tiny eyes bright and angry, tiny hands in fists, tiny arms swinging in spasms and doll's dress bunched around her middle, and her cry was only the faint turbulence of an insect trapped in a bottle. Amusing. Pitiful. A little bottle of grief like her mother.

"Pixie don't like this separation stuff," crooning, chucking her under the chin with the tip of his long black finger while Cassandra and I leaned forward to see, to hear: "Pixie don't approve of our family busting up this way." And she bent her rubbery knees, kicked, striking on the table the little dirty white calf-skin shoe that was untied, unkempt, forlorn, and then she was suddenly quiet, appeased, and smiled at Sonny and caught his finger as if to bite it to the bone with all the delight and savagery of the tiny child spoiled and underfed—rancid baby bottles, thin chocolate bars—through all her dreary abandoned days in war-time transit.

"That's the sign, folks! Pixie's ready! Time to go!"

I sat still, I flung my face into the smell of the empty glass, Cassandra took up her purse. And then we were in single file and pushing through the crowd of sailors. First Sonny—flight bag, paper bag stuffed with chicken salad sandwiches, Pixie riding high on his shoulders and thumping his cap—and then Cassandra—small, proud, prisoner of lost love, mother of child, barelegged and desirable, in her own way widowed and silvery and slender, walking now through anchors and booze and the anonymous cross-country passion of the Infantry March—and then in the rear myself—more tired than ever, bald, confused, two hundred pounds of old junior-grade naval officer and close to tears. This our dismal procession with Sonny leading the way. "Step aside there, fella, you don't want to tangle with the Chief!" Pixie was blowing kisses to the sailors; Cassandra was wearing her invisible chains, invisible flowers; and I refused to see, to acknowledge the scampering white-slavers, refused to say good-by to all those little Chinese waiters. Then out the door.

Long steel body like a submarine. Giant black recapped tires. Driver—another mean nigger, as Sonny would say—already stiff and silhouetted behind his sheet of glass and wearing his dark slant-eyed driving glasses and his little Air Force style cap crushed and peaked, ready and waiting to take her up, to start the mission. Concrete pillars, iron doors, dollies heaped high with duffel bags, no lights, crowds of sailors, odor of low-lying diesel smoke, little dry blisters of chewing gum under our feet, and noise. Noise of sailors banging on the sides of the bus and singing and vomiting and crying out to their dead buddies. The terminal. Our point of departure. And the tickets were flying and the SP's were ferocious ghosts, leaping in pairs on victim, lunging slyly, swinging hard with the little wet oaken clubs.

So at last we were packed together in rude and shameless embrace and at last we were shouting: "You go on now, Skipper," tall dancer, black cannon mouth, blow in the ribs, weighing me down with child, provisions, canvas bag, "you go on and get you a nice seat. Take your ladies on off to your island—I'm going to be on mine—no unfaithful lovers on my island, Skipper, just me, now you keeps your island the same. Good-by now, and you remember, Skipper, I'm going to lie me down on my island and just look at them pictures and think of you and Pixie and Miss Cassandra. So long!"

"Sonny!" Crying aloud, crying, bumping against him, bumping and trying to shift the wretched child out of our way, then falling against his tall black twisting form—glint of the buttons, bones of a lean steer, glimpse of a fading smile—then throwing myself and managing at last to kiss the two dark cheeks, warm, oddly soft and dry, affectionate long panther paws, kissing and calling out to him: "Good-by, Sonny. *Bon voyage!*" Then we were flowing on a rough stream toward the bus and he was gone. Poor Sonny.

Soldiers in the Dark

But Sonny was not gone at all. Not yet. The three of us were carried backwards and up into the great dark steel cylinder of our reckless ten-wheeled transport. We joined that monstrous riot for seats—one hundred and three men, a woman, a child, swallowed up for numerous sins and petty crimes into this terrible nonstop belly of ours and fighting hopelessly for breath, for privacy—and were lucky enough to snatch two seats together and to crouch down with flight bag and sandwiches between our legs and my hat askew and the skirt of Cassandra's frock crumpled above her knees. They were slim knees, bare, slender, glistening, disregarded. It was dark, the aisle was heaped high with white duffel bags. And did each of those sagging white canvas shapes represent the dead body of a bantamweight buddy saved from the sea and stowed away in canvas, at last to be lugged or flung aboard Interstate Carrier Number twenty-seven, bound nonstop for the great navy yard of the east? I looked for only a moment at Cassandra's knees and then quickly lifted my granddaughter to the pitch-dark window at my side. Pixie was crying again—insect going berserk in his glass, little fists socking the window—and the sailors were flashing their Zippo lighters and slowly, slowly, we were beginning to move. And then three figures struggled out of the flat gray planes and cumbersome shadows of the concrete, and dashed toward the front of the bus. The tall drunk bosun's mate was waving, Sonny was waving, and between them the moaning sailor was rolling his head, dragging his feet. The tubular door sprang halfway open and, "That's it," helpful, officious, out of breath, "get these fellas inside there . . . that's it!" And then Sonny was alone in the dark and we were backing slowly from the terminal in a wake of oil and compressed air. I pressed my face to the window, against the glass, too tired to make a farewell sign with my hand.

Off to one side, puffing, straightening his coat, Sonny continued to follow us. I saw his imperious arm, saw his slow imperious stride and the long fingers pointing instructions to the driver. Sonny held up his flat hand and we stopped; Sonny began to swing his arm and we started forward, turned, paced his tall backward-stepping shadow—anxious glance over his shoulder, summoning gesture of the long thin arm and flashing cuff—and then he stood aside and waved us on. I smiled, lost him, but even in the blast of the diesel heard what he must have communicated to his mean black brother in the cockpit: "You're OK. Now just keep this thing on the road. . . ."

Then I leaned back heavily and, pain or no pain, shifted Pixie so that she stretched herself flat on my chest and slept immediately. I lay there watching the stars and feeling my hunger grow. The paper bag was between Cassandra's feet, not mine, yet I could see the crushed bulk of it, the waxed paper and wilted lettuce, the stubby wet slices of white meat Sonny had prepared for us on a wobbling card table squeezed into the dirty porcelain lavatory of our cheap hotel. I could taste the white bread—no crusts—I could taste the black market mayonnaise. How many miles behind us now? Five? Ten? The bus was accelerating, was slowly filling with the smell of whisky—thick nectar of lonely travelers—and filled with the sounds of the ukelele, the tuneless instrument of the American fleet, and in her sleep Pixie was sucking her fingers and overhead the stars were awash in the empty black fields of the night. I thought of empty dry docks, empty doorways, empty hotels, empty military camps, thought of him fixing the sandwiches while we slept—pepper, salt, tin spoon and knife— saw him drinking a can of beer on the fantail of the *Starfish* on a humid and windless night. I saw him prostrate on his island of brown flesh, heard the first sounds of returning love.

"Cassandra? Hungry, Cassandra?"

He had diced celery into cubes, had cut olives into tiny green half-moons, had used pimento. Even red pimento. The moonlight came through the window in a steady thin slipstream and in it Cassandra's face was a small luminous profile on a silver coin, the coin unearthed happily from an old ruin and the face expressionless, fixed, the wasted impression of some little long-forgotten queen. I looked at her, as large as I was I wriggled, settled myself still deeper into the journey—oh, the luxury of going limp! —and allowed my broad white knees to fall apart, to droop in their infinite sag, allowed my right arm, the arm that was flung across sleeping Pixie, to grow numb. I was an old child of the moon and lay sprawled on the night, musing and half-exposed in the suspended and public posture of all those night travelers who are without beds, those who sleep on public benches or curl into the corners of out-of-date railway coaches, all those who dream their uncovered dreams and try to sleep on their hands. Suspended. Awake and prone in my seat next to the window, all my body fat, still, spread solid in the curvature of my Greyhound seat. And yet in my back, elbows, neck, calves, buttocks, I felt the very motion of our adventure, the tremors of our cross-country speed. And I felt my hunger, the stomach hunger of the traveling child.

"A little picnic for the two of us, Cassandra?"

She moved—my daughter, my museum piece—and hoisted the sack onto her lap and opened it, the brown paper stained with the mysterious dark oil stains of mayonnaise and tearing, disintegrating beneath her tiny white efficient fingers. Brisk fingers, mushy brown paper sack, food for the journey. She unwrapped a sandwich, for a moment posed with it—delicate woman, ghostly morsel of white bread and meat—then put it into my free hand which was outstretched and waiting. The bread was cold, moist, crushed thin with the imprint of dear Sonny's palm; the lettuce was a wrinkled leaf of soft green skin, the bits of pimento were little gouts of jellied blood, the chicken was smooth, white, curved to the missing bone. I tasted it, sandwich smeared with moonlight, nibbled one wet edge—sweet art of the mess boy— then shoved the whole thing into my dry and smiling mouth and lay there chewing up Sonny's lifetime, swallowing, licking my fingers.

My daughter was safe beside me, Pixie was sleeping on, dreaming the little pink dreams of her spoiled life, my mouth was full, the sailor was moaning. And now the distance threw out the first white skirts of a desert, a patch of poisoned water and a few black rails of abandoned track. I saw the salt mounds, the winding gulch, far off a town—mere sprinkling of dirty mica chips in the desert—and in the pleasure of this destitute world I was eager to see, eager to eat, and reached for another sandwich, stuffed it in. For Sonny.

But then I noticed her folded hands, her silent throat, the sack near empty on her lap, and I stopped in mid-mouthful, paused, swallowed it all down in a spasm: "Cassandra? No appetite, Cassandra?"

She did not answer. She did not even nod. And yet her face was turned my way, her knees tight, elbows tight, on one side not to be touched by thigh of sprawling father, on the other not to be touched by the stenciled name of the seaman whose duffel bag stood as tall as her shoulder and threatened her with reprehensible lumps and concealed designs, and in the thrust and balance of that expression, the minted little lips and nose, the bright nested eye, she made herself clear enough. No appetite. No sensation in a dry stomach. No desire. No orchids sweet enough to taste. Not the sort of woman to eat sandwiches on a bus. At least not the sort of woman who would eat in the dark. Not any more.

But I was alarmed and I persisted: "Join me, Cassandra. Please. Just a bite?"

She waited. Then I heard the firmness of the dreaming voice, the breath control of the determined heart: "My life has been a long blind date with sad unfortunate boys in uniform. With high school boys in uniform. With Fernandez. With you. A long blind date in Schrafft's. A blind date and chicken salad sandwiches in Schrafft's. With little black sweet pickles, Skipper. Horrible sweet pickles. Your sandwiches," the whisper dying out for emphasis, secret, explanatory, defensive, then rising again in the hush of her greatest declamatory effort, "your sandwiches make me think of Gertrude. And Gertrude's dark glasses. And strawberry ice cream sodas. And Gertrude's gin. I can't eat them, Skipper. I can't. You see," now leaning her head back and away, small and serpentine in the moonlight, and watching me with her wary and injured eyes, "nothing comes of a blind date, Skipper. Nothing at all. And," moving her naked fingers, crushing the wax paper into a soft luminous ball, "this is my last blind date. A last blind date for Pixie and me. I know you won't jilt us, Skipper. I know you'll be kind."

I wriggled. I blushed. I took the sandwich. I heard the catgut notes of the ukelele—vision of French letters floating downstream in the moonlight—I heard the black turbine roaring of our diesel engine, beyond this metal and glass heard the high wind filled with thistle and the flat shoe leather bodies of dead prairie rodents. And I was wedged into the night, wedged firmly in my cheerful embarrassment, and chewing, frowning, hoping to keep her feathery voice alive.

Our picnic, our predawn hours together on this speeding bus, our cramped but intricate positions together at the start of this our journey between two distant cemeteries, the nearly physical glow that begins to warm the darkest hour at the end of the night watch—when sleep is only a bright immensity put off as long as possible and a man is filled with a greedy slack desire to recall even his most painful memories—in all the seductive shabbiness of the moment I felt that I knew myself, heart and stomach, as peaceful father of my own beautiful and unpredictable child, and that the disheveled traveler was safe, that both of us were safe. We too would have our candy bars when the sun rose. Sonny had provided the sandwiches but I myself had thought of the candy bars, had slipped them secretly into the flight bag with Cassandra's stockings and Pixie's little fluffy pinafore. We too would have our arrival and departure, our radio broadcast of victory and defeat. In the darkness the driver sounded his horn—triple-toned trumpet, inane orchestrated warning to weak-kneed straying cows and sleeping towns—and my lips rolled into the loose shape of a thoughtless murmur: "Happy, Cassandra?"

"I'm sleepy, Skipper. I would like to go to sleep. Will you try?"

I chuckled. And she smoothed down her frock, brushed the empty paper bag to the floor, pressed her hands together, palms and fingers straight and touching as the child prays, and without glancing at me lay her cheek on her clasped hands and shut her eyes. As if she had toileted, donned her negligee, turned with her face averted and drawn the shade. Modest Cassandra. While I chuckled again, grimaced, rolled my head back to the window, grunted under the weight of Pixie—bad dreams, little pig sounds —then sighed and swung away and dropped to my army of desperate visions that leapt about in the darkness. But safe. Sleeping. Outward bound.

But wasn't Cassandra still my teen-age bomb? Wasn't she? Even though she was a war bride, a mother, a young responsible woman of twenty-five? At least I thought so when at last I awoke to the desert sunburst and a giant sea-green grandfather cactus stabbed to death by its own needles and to the sight of Cassandra begging Pixie to drink down a little more of the canned milk two days old now and pellucid. And wasn't this precisely what I loved? That the young-old figure of my Cassandra—sweet queenly head on an old coin, yet flesh and blood—did in fact conceal the rounded high-stepping baby fat and spangles and shoulder-length hair and dimples of the beautiful and wised-up drum majorette, that little bomb who is all hot dogs and Egyptian beads? Wasn't this also my Cassandra? I thought so and for the rest of the day the emotions and problems of this intensive fantasy saved me from the oppressive desert with its raw and bleeding buttes and its panorama of pastel colors as outrageous and myriad as the colors that flashed in the suburban kitchen of some gold-star mother. Saved me too from our acrobatic Pixie who at lunchtime added smears, little doll-finger tracks and blunt smudges of Nestlé's chocolate to my white naval breast already so crumpled and so badly stained. Smelling the chocolate, glancing at the unshapely humps and amputated spines, thorns, of miles of crippled cacti, I only smiled and told myself that the flesh of the cheerleader was still embedded in the flesh of Pixie's mother and so soothed myself with various new visions of this double anatomy, this schizophrenic flesh. And toward sundown—more chocolate, more smearing, end of a hot and untalkative and disagreeable day—when I was squinting between my fingers at the last purple upheaval of the pastel riot, I struggled a moment—it was a sudden cold sickening speculation—with the question of which was the greater threat to her life, the recklessness of the teen-age bomb or the demure determination of the green-eyed and diamond-brained young matron who was silvery, small, lovable with bare legs and coronet? It was too soon for me to know. But I would love them both, scrutinize them both, then at the right moment fling myself in the way of the ascendant and destructive image. I was still scowling and loving her, suspecting her, when the desert fireworks suddenly ended and the second night came sweeping up like a dark velvet wind in our faces.

"And we don't even have sandwiches tonight, Cassandra. Not one."

I felt the child's tiny knee in my groin—determined and unerring step—I felt her tiny hand return again and again to tantalize and wound itself against my unwashed cheek, absently I picked at the chocolate that had dried like blood on the old sailcloth or cotton or white drill of my uniform. And finding a plugged-up nipple secreted like a rubber talisman or ill omen in my pocket; watching Cassandra stuff a pair of Pixie's underpants into the flight bag; discovering that between my two white shoes there was another, the foot and naked ankle and scuffed black shoe of some long-legged sailor who had stretched himself out at last—in orgasm? in extreme discomfort?—and seeing Cassandra's face dead white and realizing that finally she had scraped the bottom of the cardboard face powder box which I had saved along with her stockings: all of it reminded me of the waxworks museum we had visited with Sonny, reminded me of a statue of Popeye the Sailor, naked except for his cap and pipe, which we had assumed to be molded of rubber until we read the caption and learned that it was made of eight pounds and five different brands of chewed-up chewing gum, and reminded me too that I could fail and that the teen-age bomb could kill the queen or the queen the bomb. The beginnings of a hot and hungry night.

But I must have lain there musing and grumbling for hours, for several hours at least, before the tire exploded.

"Oh!" came Cassandra's whispered shriek, her call for help, and I pinioned Pixie's rump, I sank down, my knees were heaved into flight, Cassandra was floating, reaching out helplessly for her child. In the next instant the rear half of the bus was off the road and sailing out, I could feel, in a seventy-eight-mile-an-hour dive into the thick of the night. Air brakes in full emergency operation. Accidental blow to the horn followed by ghastly and idiotic trill on the trumpet. Diving rear end of the bus beginning to describe an enormous arc—fluid blind path of greatest destruction—and forward portion lurching, hammering, banging driver's black head against invisible wall. Now, O Christopher . . . and then the crash.

Then: "Be calm, Cassandra," I said, and kept my hold on the agitated Pixie but uncovered my face.

And she, whispering, breathing deeply: "What is it, Skipper? What is it?"

"Blowout," I said, and opened my eyes. We were standing still. We were upright. Somehow we had failed to overturn though I saw her naked legs with the knees caught up to her chin and though everywhere I looked I saw the duffel bags lying like the bodies of white clowns prostrate after a spree of tumbling. And in this abrupt cessation of our sentimental journey, becoming aware of moonlight in the window and of the thin black line of the empty highway stretching away out there, and feeling a heavy deadness in my shoulder—twisted muscles? severed nerves?—I was able to glance at my free hand, to study it, to order flexing of my numerous and isolated fingers. I watched them. One by one they wiggled. Bones OK.

"Are you all right, Cassandra? Can you move your toes?"

"Yes, Skipper. But give Pixie to her mother, please."

So we disembarked. We joined the slow white procession of hatless sailors. In the dark and among the angular seventeen-year-olds with ties askew and tops askew, among all the boys red-eyed and damp from cat-napping and too baffled, too bruised to talk, we felt our way up the canted aisle until we reached the listing door, the puckered aluminum steps, the open night. I took her in my arms and swung her down, and out there we stood together, close together, frock and uniform both body-tight in the wind, ankles twisting and shoes filling with sand. The bus was a dark blue dusty shadow, deceptive wreck; our skid-marks were long black treacherous curves in the desert; the highway was a dead snake in the distance; the wind was strong. We stood there with the unfamiliar desert beneath our feet, stood with our heads thrown back to the open night sky which was filled with the tiny brief threads of performing meteors.

The wind. The hot wind. Out there it warmed the skin but chilled the flesh, left the body cold, and though we lifted our faces like startled sun-tanned travelers, we were shivering in that endless night and in the wind that set the long dry cactus needles scraping and made a rasping noise of all the debris of the desert: tiny cellular spines, dead beetles, the discarded translucent tissue of wandering snakes, the offal of embryonic lizards and fields of dead dry locusts. All this rasping and humming; all the night listening; and underfoot all the smooth pebbles knocking together in the hot-cold night. And she, Cassandra, stood there swaying and clasping Pixie awkwardly against her breast, swaying and trying to catch her breath behind Pixie's head; and the pale little fissure of Cassandra's mouth, the pale wind-chapped tissue of the tiny lips made me think of cold kisses and of goose

35

flesh and of a thin dust of salt and of lipstick smeared helplessly on the white cheek. I took her elbow; I put a hand on her back and steadied her; I was surprised to feel the broad band of muscle trembling in her back; I thought of the two of us alone with a hundred and one sailors cut down and left for dead by a pack of roving and mindless Mexicans. Then in our roller-skating stance—hand to elbow, hand to waist—we began to move together, to stagger together in the moonlight, and over my shoulder and flung to either side of the harsh black visible track of our flight from the road I saw the prostrate silhouettes of a dozen fat giant cacti that had been struck head on by the bus and sent sailing. For a moment I saw them, these bloated shapes of scattered tackling dummies that marked the long wild curve of our reckless detour into the dark and milky night. Abandoned. As we were abandoned.

And then the lee of the bus. Clumps of squatting white shivering sailors. A pea jacket for Pixie. Another pea jacket for Cassandra. A taste of whisky for me. Little pharmacist mates clever in first aid and rushing to the sounds of chattering teeth or tidelands obscenity. While the black-faced driver hauls out his hydraulic jack and drags it toward the mutilated tire which has come to rest in a natural rock garden of crimson desert flowers and tiny bulbs and a tangle of prickly parasitic leaves. All crushed to a pulp. Mere pustules beneath that ruined tire.

It was the dead center of some nightmare accident but here at least, crouching and squatting together in the lee of the bus, there was no wind. Only the empty windows, shadows, scorched paint of the crippled monster. Only the flare burning where we had left the road and now the scent of a lone cigarette, the flick of a match, the flash of a slick comb through bay rum and black waves of hair, persistent disappointed sounds of the ukelele—devilish hinting for a community sing—only the cooling sand of the high embankment against which Cassandra and Pixie and I huddled while the sailors grew restless and the driver—puttees, goggles, snappy cap and movements of ex-fighter-pilot, fierce nigger carefully trained by the Greyhound line—bustled about the enormous sulphuric round of the tire. Refusing assistance, removing peak-shouldered military jacket, retaining cap, strutting in riding britches, fingering the jack, clucking at long rubber ribbons of the burst tire: "Why don't you fellows sing a little and pass the time?" But only more performing meteors and this hell's nigger greasing both arms and whistling, tossing high into the air his bright wrenches. In the middle of the desert only this American nigger changing a tire, winning the war.

I unlaced my dirty white buckskin shoes and emptied them. I glanced at Cassandra. I glanced at Pixie who, even though cloaked in her pea jacket, was beginning to play in the sand; I tried to smile but the driver cavorting in the moonlight dispirited me and I wondered where we were and what had become of poor dear Sonny. I hooked one foot onto the opposite knee, gripped the ankle, brushed the sand from the sole of my white sock, repeated the process. I glanced again at the night sky—unmoved by celestial side show—and for some reason, scowling into the salt and pepper stars, gritting my teeth at that silent chaos, the myriad motes of the unconsciousness, I found myself thinking of Tremlow, once more saw him as he looked when he bore down upon me during the height of the *Starfish* mutiny. Again I lived the moment of my degradation. Then just as suddenly I was spared the sight of it all.

Because I had heard a sound. Cassandra's sleeping head lay in my lap—high upturned navy blue collar of the pea jacket revealing only the briefest profile of her worn and lovely little death-mask face—because I was awake and had heard a sound and recognized it. And because suddenly that impossible sound established place, established the hour, explained the tangled bright loops of barbed wire that apparently ran for miles atop the steep rise of our protective sand embankment. I listened, gently pressed the rough collar to her cheek, shivered as I understood suddenly that the wire was not for Indians, not to imprison cows. Listened. And still the impossible sound came to me over the wastes and distant reaches of the blue desert.

Bugle. This mournful barely audible precision of the instrument held rigidly in only a single hand. An Army bugle. Taps. Across the desert the faint and stately and ludicrous sound of taps. Insane song of the forties. And slow, precise, each silvery dim note dragged all the way to the next, the various notes weaving and wafting the sentimental messages into the night air. End of the day—who's listening? who?—and of course lights out. But I listened to the far-away musical moon-howling of that benediction into a dusty P.A. system built on the sands, with a few stomach convulsions heard the final drawn-out bars of that impersonal cinematic burial song meant for me, for every bald-headed indoctrinated man my age. Taps for another bad dream. Brass bugle blown in the desert, a little spit shaken out on the bugler's sleeve.

So I knew that it was eleven o'clock of a hot-cold desert night and that we had come to stop not in the middle of nowhere but at the edge of some sort of military reservation—cavalry post of black horses that would explain the odor of dung on the wind? basic training camp with tequila in the PX and live ammunition on maneuvers? naval boot camp for special instruction in flying the blimp and dirigible?—and knew that whatever I had to guard Cassandra against it was not the Mexicans.

But now I was awake, alert, ready for anything. Hunching over my own daughter and my own granddaughter—outlandish bundles of pea jackets, flesh of my flesh—I became the solitary sentry with quick eyes for every shadow and a mass of moonlit veins scurrying across my naked scalp like worms. Fear and preparedness. Aching joints. Lap beginning to complain. But on the tail of the bugle and also miles away, several unmistakable bursts from a rapid-fire weapon. And I looked for a glow in the sky and tried to imagine the targets—cardboard silhouettes of men? gophers? antiquated armored vehicles?—and I listened and wondered when they would begin to shoot in our direction. Army camp, disabled bus, poor nomad strangers wandering through days and nights and hours that could be located on any cheap drugstore calendar: I took a deep breath, I stiffened my heavy jaw, I waited. In anger I heard a few more snorts of machine gun fire, in anger I nodded once more at the image of Tremlow the mutineer, in anger snapped myself awake.

"Cassandra," whispering, leaning close to her, lifting enormous collar away from her ear, touching the cold cheek, sweating and whispering, "wake up, Cassandra. We've got company. . . ."

Her open eyes, her rigid face and body, the quiver in the breasts and hips, and the outstretched rumpled figure was suddenly alert, half sitting up. And then she had thrust Pixie away, had hidden Pixie in a shadow on the sand. And then side by side Cassandra and I were kneeling together on our hands and knees, waiting with heads raised and red-rimmed eyes fixed on the barbed wire barricade directly above us.

"Men traveling on their bellies," I whispered. "Three of them. Crawling up the embankment to reconnoiter!" We heard the swishing sound of men pressed flat to the desert and, like children making angels in snow, swimming up the steep embankment through loose sand and pebbles and low-lying dried and prickling vines. We heard their concentrated breathing and the tinkling sound of equipment. I recognized the flat fall of carbine with each swing of invisible arm, recognized the uneven sound of a bayonet drumming on empty canteen with each dragging motion of invisible haunch. Then a grunt. Then squeal and scurry of little desert animal diving for cover. Then silence.

And then the heads. Three black silhouettes of helmeted heads suddenly there behind the wire where before there had been only the barbs, the loops, the tight strands and the velvet space and salt and pepper heavens of the whole night sky. But now the heads. All at once the three of them in a row. Unmoving. Pop-ups in a shooting gallery.

And as Cassandra and I knelt side by side in the sand, stiff and exposed and red-eyed in our animal positions, together and quiet but vulnerable, the three heads began to move in unison, turned slowly, imperceptibly, to the right and then to the left, in unison scanning the horizon and measuring the potential of the scene before them. The tops of the heavy helmets and the tips of the chin cups reflected the moon; in the sharp little faces the eyes were white. Soldiers. Raiders. Pleased with the scene. Their whispers were high, dry, choked with sand.

"Lucky, lucky, lucky! Ain't that a sweet sight?"

"Navy to the rescue!"

"Free ride on a Greyhound bus!"

The three of them looked straight ahead—intuitively I knew the driver was still throwing his wrenches into the air, still trying to boss the tire into place, and I groaned—and then in slow motion they began to shift. The heads sank down until the men were only turtle shells and hardly visible on the embankment; the muzzles of two carbines popped into view; the man in the center raised his helmeted head and his white hand and a pair of wire cutters, slipped and tugged and twisted while the wire sang past his face and curled into tight thorny balls. Until they could crawl through. Until they were free.

And then with heads down, shoulders down, rifles balanced horizontally in their hanging hands, they swung in a silent dark green trio over the embankment and down, down, like baseball players hitting the sand and landing not on top of Cassandra and myself but in front of us and to either side. Three sand geysers and Cassandra and I were trapped.

"Company C," panting, whispering, "Company C for Cain," panting and aiming his gun and whispering, "Don't you make a peep, you hear? Either one of you!"

Three small soldiers in full battle pack and sprawled in the sand, gasping, leaning on their elbows, cradling the carbines, staring us down with their white eyes. Web belts and straps, brass buckles, cactus-green fatigue uniforms—name tags ripped off the pockets—paratrooper boots dark brown with oil; they lay there like three deadly lizards waiting to strike, and all of their vicious, yet somehow timorous, white eyes began blinking at once. The middle soldier, the leader, wore a coal-black fingernail mustache and carried his bayonet fixed in place on the end of his carbine. All little tight tendons and daggers and hand grenades and flashing bright points and lizard eyes. Unscrupulous. Disguised in soot. Not to be trusted in a charge.

"Company C for Cain, like I said. But we been in that place for twenty-eight weeks and now we're AWOL. The three of us here are called the Kissin' Bandits and we're AWOL. Understand?"

And the smallest, young and innocent except for his big broken Brooklyn nose—my ghetto Pinocchio—and except for the foam which he kept licking from the corners of his mouth and swallowing, the smallest twitching there in the sand and prodding each word with his carbine and with his nose: "So on your feet, on your feet. No talking, and don't forget the kid."

Slowly, laboriously, indignantly I stood up, helped Cassandra, brushed the seat of my trousers, jerked the creases out of my uniform as best I could, indifferently picked off the cactus burrs, and took little Pixie into my arms.

They marched us to the cactus, in single file herded us thirty or forty feet into the shadow of that old fat prickly man of the desert and out of sight of the bus, the leader at the head of the column and swinging the carbine, slouching along lightly in the lazy walk of the infantryman saving himself, feeling his way with his feet, straggling all the distance of his night patrol—easy gait, eyes down watching for the enemy, back and shoulders loose and buttocks hard, fierce, inseparable, complementary, all his walking done with the buttocks alone—and in the middle Cassandra and myself and Pixie, and in the rear the tinkling dragging sounds of the boys with their cocked carbines and darting tongues and eyes. Raiders. Captives. Firing squad with the cactus for a blank wall.

"Now get rid of your eggs," said the one with the glistening mustache. "Dig your holes deep and bury them."

And there in the safety and shadow of the giant ruptured cactus, while Cassandra and I stood side by side and held hands under cover of her pea jacket, there and in unison the three of them unhooked their rows of dangling hand grenades, helped each other out of their packs and harnesses, freed each other of webbing and canteens and canvas pouches—watching us, watching us all the while—and then with unsheathed and flashing trench knives or bayonets held point down they squatted, dug their three black holes until at last they flung themselves back once more into sitting position and unfastened their boots, unbuttoned their green fatigues and then standing, facing us, watching us, suddenly stripped them off.

41

So the naked soldiers. White shoulder blades, white arms, white shanks, white strips of skin, white flesh, and in the loins and between the ribs and on the inside of the legs soft shadow. But white and thin and half-starved and glistening like watery sardines hacked from a tin. Naked. Still wearing their steel helmets, chin straps still dangling in unison, and still holding the carbines at ready arms. But otherwise naked. And now they were lined up in front of Cassandra, patiently and in close file, while I stood there trembling, smiling, sweating, squeezing her hand, squeezing Cassandra's hand for dear life and in all my protective reassurance and slack alarm.

"Leader's last," came the unhurried voice, "Baby Face goes first."

Lined up by height, by age and height, and each one nudging the next and shuffling, grinning, each one ready to have his turn, all set to go, and one of them hanging back.

"Drag ass, Bud. . . and make it count!"

His round young head was sweating inside the steel helmet, his freckled breast was heaving. I squeezed her hand—be brave, be brave—but Cassandra was only a silvery blue Madonna in the desert, only a woman dressed in the outlandish ill-fitting pea jacket of an anonymous sailor and in a worn frock belonging to tea tray, flowers and some forgotten summer house covered with vines. And in her hand there was no response, nothing. And yet her green eyes were searching him and waiting.

Then he leaned forward, eyes slowly sinking out of focus, tears bright on his cheeks, moon-face growing rounder and rounder under its rim of steel, and caught her behind the neck with a rough childish hand and drove his round and running and fluted mouth against the pale line of her lips. And sucked once, gulped once, gave her one chubby kiss, backed away step by step until suddenly Pinocchio made a wrenching clawlike gesture and threw him aside.

And Pinocchio's kiss: foam, foam, foam! On Cassandra's lips. Down the front of her frock. Snuffling action of the Brooklyn nose. But he couldn't fool Skipper, couldn't fool old Papa Cue Ball. So I squeezed again—brave? brave, Cassandra?—and felt what I thought was a tremor of irritation, small sign of impatience in her cold hand.

And then the third and last, the tallest, and the helmet tilting rakishly, the lips pulsing over the front teeth in silent appeal, the bare arm sliding inside the pea jacket and around her waist, and now the cumbersome jacket beginning to fall, to fall away, and now Cassandra's head beginning to yield, it seemed to me, as I felt her little hand leave mine and saw her returning his kiss—white shoe slightly raised behind her, pale mouth touching, asking some question of the slick black fingernail of hair on his upper lip—and saw my Cassandra raise a finger to his naked underdeveloped chest and heard her, distinctly heard her, whispering into all the shadowed cavities of that thin grisly chest: "Give me your gun, please," hanging her head, whispering, finger tracing meditative circles through the hair on his chest, "please show me how to work your gun. . . ."

But he was gone. All three were gone. They had whirled each to his hole, had flung in boots, carbines, helmets and fatigues, and had refilled the holes. Done with their separate burials they had fled from us in the direction of the unsuspecting sailors and the waiting bus, had run off with their stolen kisses and their crafty plans for travel. At the bus they used judo and guerrilla tactics on the bosun's mate, the moaning sailor and the noxious driver, and dressed like sailors they lost themselves in a busload of young sailors.

I turned and held out my free arm: "Cassandra, Cassandra!" I beckoned her with my fingers, with my whole curving arm, beckoned and wanted to tell her what a bad brush we had had with them, and that they were gone and we were safe at last. And she must have read my smile and my thoughts, I think, because she drew the pea jacket into place once more, thrust her hands carefully into the pockets, glanced soberly across the waste of the desert. And then she looked at me and slowly, calmly, whispered, "Nobody wants to kiss you, Skipper."

From that time forward our driver was dead white and licked a little patch of untweezered mustache all the while he drove. And so we recommenced our non-stop journey, rode with a fine strong

43

tail wind until at last we reached our midnight (Eastern War Time) destination, found ourselves at last on the fourteenth floor of another cheap hotel. Here we stayed two days. Here I lived through my final shore patrol. And here I found Fernandez in this wartime capital of the world.

Be brave! Be brave!

The Artificial Inseminator

And now? And now?

And now the wind and the hammock which I so rarely use. For it is time now to recall that sad little prophetic passage from my schoolboy's copybook with its boyish valor and its antiquity, and to admit that the task of memory has only brightened these few brave words, and to confess that even before my father's suicide and my mother's death I always knew myself destined for this particular journey, always knew this speech to be the one I would deliver from an empty promontory or in an empty grove and to no audience, since of course history is a dream already dreamt and destroyed. But now the passage, the speech with its boyish cadences, flavor of morality, its soberness and trust. Here it is, the declaration of faith which I say aloud to my-self when I pause and prop my feet on the window sill where the hummingbird is destroying his little body and heart and eye among the bright vines and sticky flowers and leaves: *I have soon to journey to a lonely island in a distant part of my kingdom. But I shall return before the winter storms begin. Prince Paris, I leave my wife, Helen, in your care. Guard her well. See that no harm befalls her*. My confession? My declaration of heart and faith? "I have soon to journey to a lonely island. . .guard her well. . . ." Monstrous small voice. Rhetorical gem. And yet it is the sum of my naked history, this statement by a man of fancy, this impassioned statement of a man of courage. I might have known from the copybook what I was destined for.

Because here, now, the wind is a bundle of invisible snakes and the hammock, when empty, is a tangled net-like affair of white hemp always filled with fresh-cut buds, only the buds, of moist and waxen flowers. Because it is time to say that it is Catalina Kate who keeps the hammock filled with flowers for me, who keeps it a swaying bright bed of petals just for me, and that Catalina Kate is fully aware that there must be no thorns among the flowers in the hammock.

But the wind, this bundle of invisible snakes, roars across our wandering island—it *is* a wandering island, of course, unlocated in space and quite out of time—and seems to heap the shoulders with an armlike weight, to coil about my naked legs and pulse and cool and caress the flesh with an unpredictable weight and consistency, tension, of its own. These snakes that fly in the wind are as large around as tree trunks; but pliant, as everlastingly pliant, as the serpents that crowd my dreams. So the wind nests itself and bundles itself across this island, buffets the body with wedges of invisible but still sensual configurations. It drives, drives, and even when it drops down, fades, dies, it continues its gentle rubbing against the skin. Here the wind is both hotter and colder than that wind Cassandra and I experienced on our ill-fated trip across the southwestern wartime desert of the United States, hotter and colder and more persistent, more soft or more strong and indecent, in its touch. Cassandra is gone but I am wrapped in wind, walk always—from the hips, from the hips—through the thick entangled currents of this serpentine wind.

Now I have Catalina Kate instead. And this—Sonny and I both agree—this is love. Here I have only to drop my trousers—no shirt, no undershirt, no shorts—to awaken paradise itself, awaken it with the sympathetic sound of Catalina Kate's soft laughter. And it makes no difference at all. Because I am seven years away from Miranda, seven years from that first island—black, wet, snow-swept in a deep relentless sea—and seven years from Cassandra's death and, thanks to the wind, the gold, the women and Sonny and my new profession, am more in love than ever. Until now the cemetery has been my battleground. But no more. Perhaps even my father, the dead mortician, would be proud of me.

No shirt, no undershirt, no shorts. And from my uniform only the cap remains, and it is crushed and frayed and the eagle is tarnished and the white cloth of the crown has faded away to yellow like the timeworn silk of a bridal gown. But it is still my naval cap, despite the cracks and mildew in the visor and the cockroaches that I find hiding in the sweatband. Still my cap. And I am still in possession of my tennis shoes, my old white sneakers with the rubber soles worn thin and without laces. Some days I walk very far in them. In the wind and on the business of my new profession.

And the work itself? Artificial insemination. Cows. In my flapping tennis shoes and naval cap and long puffy sun-bleached trousers, and accompanied by my assistant, Sonny, I am much esteemed as the man who inseminates the cows and causes these enormous soft animals to bring forth calves. Children and old people crowd around to see Sonny and me in action. And I am brown from walking to the cows in the sun, so brown that the green name tattooed on my breast has all but disappeared in a tangle of hair and in my darkening skin. An appealing sort of work, a happy life. The mere lowing of a herd, you see, has become my triumph.

Yes, my triumph now. And how different from my morbid father's. And haven't I redeemed his profession, his occupation, with my own? I think so. But here, now, this morning, with the broad white window sill full in my view—it is old, thickly painted, cool, something like the bleached bulwark of a ransacked sailing ship—and with the lime tree gleaming beyond the window frame and dangling under every leaf a small ripe lime, here with the hammock a swaying garden in the darkness behind me and the wind stirring my papers, stirring my old naval cap where it hangs from an upright of a nearby black mahogany

47

chair, here I mention my triumph, here reveal myself and choose to step from behind the scenes of my naked history, resorting to this strategy from need but also with a certain obvious pride, self-satisfaction, since now I anticipate prolonged consideration of Miranda. I would be unable to think of her for very long unless I made it clear that my triumph is over Miranda most of all, and that I survive her into this very moment when I float timelessly in my baby-blue sea and lick the little yellow candied limes of my bright green tree. Seven years are none too many when it comes to Miranda, or comes, for that matter, to remembering the death of Cassandra or my final glimpse of Pixie when I left her with Gertrude's cousin in New Jersey. So now I gather around me the evidence, the proof, the exhilarating images of my present life. And now Miranda will never know how many slick frisky calves have been conceived in her name or, on her scum-washed black island in the Atlantic, will never know what a voracious and contented adversary I have become out on mine, on this my sun-dipped wandering island in a vast baby-blue and coral-colored sea. But Catalina Kate, I think, is my best evidence. And having summoned my evidence and stated my position, sensitive to the wind, to the green and golden contours of a country reflected in the trembling and in the fullness of my own hips, sensitive also to the time of cows, I can afford to recount even the smallest buried detail of my life with Miranda. Because I know and have stated here, that behind every frozen episode of that other island—and I am convinced that in its way it too was enchanted, no matter the rocks and salt and fixed position in the cold black waters of the Atlantic—there lies the golden wheel of my hot sun; behind every black rock a tropical rose and behind every cruel wind-driven snowstorm a filmy sheet, a transparency, of golden fleas. No matter how stark the scene, no matter how black the gale or sinister the violence of Miranda, still the light of my triumph must shine through. And behind the interminable dead clanking of some salt-and seaweed-encrusted three-ton bell buoy should be heard the soft outdoor lowing of this island's cows, our gigantic cows with moody harlequin faces and rumps like enormous upturned wooden packing crates.

But the evidence. Earlier this morning she appeared outside my window—Catalina Kate accompanied by little Sister Josie, who attends all our births and who remains faithful to some order that has long since departed our wandering island—appeared outside my window to tell me she was three months gone with child and to give us, Sonny and myself, a present with which to celebrate the happy news, a pound of American hot dogs wrapped up in a moldy and dog-eared sheet of soggy newspaper. Catalina Kate's own child! Her charcoal eyes, her hair plaited in a single braid as thick as my wrist and hanging over one lovely breast; her skin some subtle tincture of eggplant and pink rose, one hand already curved and resting on her belly where it will stay until labor commences, the other hand outstretched with her gift of hot dogs; here this girl, this mauve puff of powder who still retains her aboriginal sweaty armpits and lice eggs in the pores of her bare dusty feet, here this Catalina Kate and beside her the little black-faced nun who vicariously shares the joys of pregnancy and who smiles and who, despite her own youth and her little heavy robes of the order, reveals suddenly a splendid big mouthful of golden teeth. So the two of them stood there, flesh and innocence, until we had expressed our pleasure and Sonny had accepted the package of hot dogs—USA.—on behalf of both of us and I had completed their ritual, their girlish game, by reaching out the window where they stood in the deep sun and lime fragrance and with my fingertips gently touched her where she assured me the treasured life lay growing.

So in six months and on the Night of All Saints Catalina Kate will bear her child—our child—and I shall complete my history, my evocation through a golden glass, my hymn to the invisible changing serpents of the wind, complete this the confession of my triumph, this my diary of an artificial inseminator. At the very moment Catalina Kate comes due my crabbed handwriting shall explode into a concluding flourish, and I will be satisfied. I will be fifty-nine years old and father to innumerable bright living dreams and vanquished memories. It should be clear that

49

I have triumphed over Cassandra too, since there are many people who wish nothing more than to kiss me when the midday heat occasionally sends me to the hammock or when the moon is full, stealing, gliding into the warmth and stillness of Plantation House, or in long silvery lines following me to the edge of a moonlit sea. For a kiss. For a shadowy kiss from me.

I receive the sweet ghostly touch of their lips, I kiss them in return. I stand glancing out over that endless ripple of ocean where we have wandered and will continue to wander, softly I call out a name—Sonny! Catalina Kate!—and watch the endless ribbon of our ocean road and smile. I hear the moving shadows and hear those long-lost words—"I have soon to journey to a lonely island in a distant part of my kingdom"—and I can only smile.

Poor Prince Paris.

The Gentle Island

And so, fresh from the wartime capital of the world, we became her unwitting lodgers, Cassandra and I, Cassandra with her pretended mothering of Pixie, I with my recent and terrifying secret knowledge about Fernandez. Already the fall winds were gathering and every morning from my bedroom window I watched a single hungry bird hang itself on the wet rising wind and, battered and crescent-shaped and angry, submit itself endlessly to the first raw gloom of day in the hopes of spying from on high some flash of food in the dirty undulating trough of a wave. And every morning I stood blowing on my fingers and watching the torn and ragged bird until it flapped away on the ragged wings of its discouragement, blowing, shivering, smiling to think that here even the birds were mere prowlers in the mist and wind, mere vagrants in the empty back lots of that low sky.

Briefly then our new home. White clapboard house, peeling paint, abandoned wasp's nest under the eaves, loose shingles, fungus-like green sludge scattered across the roof. Widow's house, needy but respectable. In front a veranda—the old green settee filled with mice, heap of rotted canvas and rusted springs

—and a naked chestnut tree with incurable disease and also two fat black Labrador retrievers chained to a little peeling kennel. Protection for the poor widow, culprits who heaped the bare front yard with the black fingers of their manure. And in the rear the widow's little untended victory garden—a few dead vines, a few small humps in the frost—and, barely upright and half-leaning against a weed-grown shed, the long-abandoned wreck of a hot rod—orange, blue, white, no tires, no glass in the windows, big number five on the crumpled hood—the kind of hopeless incongruity to be found behind the houses of young island widows. Our new home then, and with its cracked masonry, warped beams, sway-backed floors and tiny old fusty fireplaces packed with the rank odor of urine and white ash, it was just as I had dreamed it, was exactly as I had seen it and even smelled and tasted it during all my exotic hot nights at sea when I suffered each separate moment of my personal contribution to the obscene annals of naval history. This house then, and every bit the old freezing white skeleton I had been hoping for. So on my rickety pine bureau I propped my photograph of the U.S.S. *Starfish* and flung the flight bag in the bottom drawer and hung my uniform in the closet which contained three little seagoing chests made of bone and brass and dried-out cracked turkey skin. Propped up the picture, hung away the spotted uniform, admired the way I looked in a black and white checked shirt and dark blue thick woolen trousers. Ready for gales, ready for black rocks. Everything in order and as I had expected, even to the identical white bowls and pitchers and washstands in Cassandra's room and mine, even to the marble sink, lion claws on the tub and long metal flush chain in the john. Of course I could not have anticipated the black brassiere that dangled as large and stark as an albatross from the tin shower curtain pole. I stared at it a long moment— this first sign of the enemy—and then shut the old heavily varnished ill-fitting door. There was a tap leaking on the other side.

Of all those mornings, darkening, growing colder, dragging us down to winter, I remember most clearly our first in the

widow's house, because that was the dawn of my first encounter with Miranda. Dead brown rotten world, heartless
dawn. Innocence and distraction at half past five in the morning.

I awoke in my strange bed in my strange room in the old
white worm-eaten house and heard Pixie crying her fierce little
nearly inaudible cry and looked about me at the bare sprawling
shadows of monastic antiquity and shuddered, smiled, felt my
cold hands and my cold feet crawling between the camphor-
ridden sheets. It was still dark, as black as the somber mood of
some Lutheran hymn, the flat pillow was filled with horsehair
and the blanket against my cheek was of the thin faded stuff
with which they drape old ladies' shoulders in this cold country.
And the wind, the black wind was rising off the iron flanks of
the Atlantic and driving its burden of frozen spray through the
abandoned fields of frost, across the green jetties, over the gray
roofs of collapsing barns, driving its weight and hoary spray between the little stunted apple trees that bordered the widow's
house and smashing the last of the dead apples against my side of
the house. From somewhere nearby I could hear the tongue
swinging about tonelessly in the bell hung up in the steeple of
the Lutheran church, and the oval mirror was swaying on my
wall, the gulls were groaning above me and Pixie was still awake
and crying.

Stiff new black and white checked shirt of the lumberjack,
dark blue woolen trousers—heavy, warm, woven of tiny silken
hairs—my white navy shoes. I fumbled in the darkness and for
a moment stood at my front bedroom window—silhouettes of
bending and suffering larch trees, in the distance white caps of
hectic needlepoint—for a moment stood at my rear window and
watched the high weeds beating against the screaming shadow
of the hot rod. And then I felt my way down to the cold kitchen
and fixed a day's supply of baby bottles of milk for poor Pixie.

A lone fat shivering prowler in that whitewashed kitchen, I
lit the wood in the stove and found the baby bottles standing in
a row like little lighthouses where Cassandra had hastily stood
them on the thick blond pine kitchen table the night before,
found them standing between an antique coffee grinder—silver-

plated handle, black beans in the drawer—and a photography magazine tossed open to a glossy full-page picture of a naked woman. It was five forty-five by Miranda's old tin clock and noiselessly, listening to the stove, the black wind, the clatter of the apples against the window, I took the bottles to the aluminum sink, primed the old farmhouse pump—yellow iron belly and slack iron idiot lip—discovered a pot in a cupboard along with a case, a full case, of Old Grand-Dad whiskey, and filled the pot and set it on the stove. Then I plucked the nipples from the bottles and washed the bottles, washed the nipples—sweet scummy rubber and pinprick holes that shot fine thin streams of artesian well water into the sink under the pressure of my raw cold thumb—punched two slits in a tin can of evaporated milk—slip of the opener, blood running in the stream of the pump, fingers holding tight to the wrist and teeth catching and holding a corner of loose lip, grimacing and shaking away the blood—and as large as I was ran noiselessly back and forth between the sink and stove until the milk for Pixie's little curdling stomach was safely bottled and the bottles were lined up white and rattling in the widow's rectangular snowy refrigerator. I wiped the table, wiped out the sink, dried and put away the pot, returned the cursed opener to its place among bright knives and glass swizzle sticks, paused for a quick look at a photograph of a young white-faced soldier hung on the wall next to half a dozen old-fashioned hot plate holders. The photograph was signed "Don" and the thin face was so young and white that I knew even from the photograph itself that Don was dead. Squeezing my fingers I tiptoed back upstairs, leaned in the doorway and smiled at Cassandra's outstretched neatly blanketed body and at her clothes bundled on a spindly ladderback rocking chair that faintly moved in the wind. I leaned and smiled, sucked the finger. Pixie had fallen back to sleep, of course, in the hooded dark wooden cradle that sat on the cold floor at the foot of Cassandra's little four-poster bed.

And so I was awake, dressed, was free in this sleeping house and had forgotten the signs—the black brassiere, the naked woman, the full case of Old Grand-Dad—and I could think of nothing but the wind and the shore and a set of black oilskins, cracked sou'wester and long black coat, which I had seen in an entryway off the kitchen. Back down I went to the kitchen and yanked open the door, dressed myself swiftly in the sardine captain's outfit and was shocked to find a lipstick in the pocket. Carefully I let myself out into the first white smears and streaks of that approaching day.

I tried to catch my breath, I socked my hands into the rising and flapping skirts of the coat, I smiled in a sudden flurry of little tears like diamonds, thinking of Cassandra safe through winter days and of a game of Mah Jongg through all the winter nights, and put down my head and made off for the distinct sound of crashing water. From the very first I walked with my light and swinging step and my chin high, walked away from the house ready to meet all my island world, walked actually with a bounce despite the wind, the crazy interference of the black rubber coat, the weight of my poor cold slobbering white navy shoes drenched in a crunchy puddle which I failed to see behind the kennel of the sleeping Labradors. The larch trees with their broken backs, the enormous black sky streaked with fistfuls of congealed fat, the abandoned Poor House that looked like a barn, the great brown dripping box of the Lutheran church bereft of sour souls, bereft of the hymn singers with poke bonnets and sunken and accusing horse faces and dreary choruses, a few weather-beaten cottages unlighted and tight to the dawn and filled, I could see at a glance, with the marvelous dry morality of calico and beans and lard, and then a privy, a blackened pile of tin cans, and even a rooster, a single live rooster strutting in a patch of weeds and losing his broken feathers, clutching his wattles, every moment or two trying to crow into the wind, trying to grub up the head of a worm with one of his snubbed-off claws, cankerous little bloodshot rooster pecking away at the dawn in the empty yard of some dead fisherman . . . . Oh, it was all spread before me and all mine, this strange island of bitter wind and blighted blueberries and empty nests.

I took deep breaths, battling the stupid coat, and I swung down a path of wet nettles, breathed it all in. Breathed in the salt, the scent of frozen weeds, the briny female odor of ripe periwinkles, the stench from the heads of blue-eyed decapitated fish. And the pine trees. The pine trees were bleeding, freely giving off that rich green fragrance which as a child I had but faintly smelled in the mortuary on Christmas mornings. Just ahead of me, just beyond the growths of crippled pine and still in darkness lay the shore, the erupted coast, and suddenly I the only-born, the happy stranger, the one man awake and walking this pitch-black seminal dawn—suddenly I wanted to fling out my arms and sweep together secret cove and Crooked Finger Rock and family burial mounds of poor fishermen, sweep it all together and give it life, my life. Pitching through brier patches, laughing and stumbling under the dripping pines, I hurried on.

And wet, rubbery, exuberant, I emerged into a clearing and stopped short, opened my eyes wide. I saw only a listing hand-made jetty and a fisherman's hut with boarded-up windows, a staved-in dory and a tin chimney that gave off a thin stream of smoke. But beside the dory—gray ribs, rusted oarlock—there was a boy's bicycle propped upside down with its front wheel missing and a clot of black seaweed caught in the sprocket. And though there were days and days to pass before I met the boy— his name was Bub—and met also his fishing father and no-good brother—Captain Red and Jomo—still I felt that I knew the place and had seen that bicycle racing in my own dreams. I could only stop and stare at the useless bicycle and at two squat gasoline pumps pimpled with the droppings of departed gulls and wet with the cold mist, those two pumps once bearing the insignia of some mainland oil company but standing now before the hut and sagging jetty as ludicrous signs of the bold and careless enterprise of that outpost beside the sea. I knew intuitively that I had stumbled upon the crafty makeshift world of another widower. But how could I know that Captain Red's boat, the *Peter Poor*, lay invisible and waiting only fifty yards from shore in its dark anchorage? How could I know that we, Cassandra and I, would sail away for our sickening afternoon on that very boat, the *Peter Poor*, how know about the violence of that sea or about the old man's naked passion? But if I had known, if I had seen

56

it all in my glimpse of Jomo's pumps and Bub's useless bicycle and the old man's smoke, would I have faltered, turned back, fled in some other direction? No. I think not. Surely I would have been too proud, too innocent, too trusting to turn back in another direction.

So I was careful to make no noise, careful not to disturb this first intact and impoverished and somehow illicit vision of the widower's overgrown outstation in the collapsing dawn, and staring at bleached slabs of porous wood and rusted nailheads I restrained my impulse to cup hands against the wind and cry out a cheery hello. And I merely waved to no one at all, expecting no wave in return, and gathered my rubber skirts and swept down the path to the beach.

Overhead the dawn was beginning to possess the sky, squadrons of gray geese lumbered through the blackness, and I was walking on pebbles, balancing and rolling forward on the ocean's cast-up marbles, or wet and cold was struggling across stray balustrades of shale. At my shoulder was the hump of the shore itself—tree roots, hollows of pubic moss, dead violets—underfoot the beach—tricky curvatures of stone, slush of ground shells, waterspouts, sudden clefts and crevices, pools that reflected bright eyes, big smile, foolish hat. Far in the distance I could see the cold white thumb of the condemned lighthouse.

But time, the white monster, had already gripped this edge of the island in two bright claws, had already begun to haul itself out of an ugly sea, and the undeniable day was upon me. I slipped, the coat blew wide, and for some reason I fell back and found myself staring up at a gray sky, gray scudding clouds, a thick palpable reality of air in which only the barometer and a few weak signals of distress could survive. An inhuman daytime sky. And directly overhead I saw the bird, the gray-brown hungry body and crescent wings. He was hovering and I could see the irritable way he fended off the wind and maintained his position and I knew that he would return again and again to this same spot. And against the chopping and spilling of the black water I saw the lighthouse. It was not safely in the distance as I had thought, but was upon me. Black missing tooth for a door, faint sea-discolorations rising the height of the white tower, broken glass in its empty head, a bit of white cloth caught up in the broken glass and waving, the whole condemned weight of it was there within shouting distance despite the wind and sea. I could even make out the tufts of high grass bent and beating against its base, and even through the black doorless entrance way I could feel the rank skin-prickling texture of the darkness packed inside that forbidden white tower, and must have known even then that I could not escape the lighthouse, could do nothing to prevent my having at last to enter that wind-whistling place and having to feel my way to the topmost iron rung of its abandoned stair.

Hovering bird, hollow head of the lighthouse, a sudden strip of white sand between myself and the mud-colored base rock of the lighthouse, little sharp black boulders spaced together closely and evenly in the sand, and then as white as a starfish and inert, naked, caught amongst the boulders, I saw a woman lying midway between myself and the high rock. Vision from the widow's photography magazine. Woman who might have leapt from the lighthouse or rolled up only moments before on the tide. She was there, out there, triangulated by the hard cold points of the day, and it was she, not I, who was drawing down the eye of the bird and even while the thought came to me—princess, poor princess and her tower—I looked up at the bird, still hovering, and then turned to the strip of beach and ran forward. But I stopped. Stopped, shuddered, shut my eyes. Because of the voice.

"So here you are!"

It was deep, low, husky, strong, the melodic tough voice of the woman who always sounds like a woman, yet talks like a man. It was close to me, deep and tempting and jocular, and I thought I could feel that enormous mouth pressed tight to my ear. It sounded like a big throat, shrewd powerful mind, heart as big as a barrel. And I was right, so terribly right. Except for the heart. Her black heart.

"My God. What are you doing down there?"

Somehow I opened my eyes, looked over my shoulder and

raised my eyes from bright pink heart-shaped shell to bunches of weed to jutting hump of the shore to rising tall figure of the woman standing wind-blown on the edge above me. Looked and fought for breath.

Slacks. Canary yellow slacks. Soft thick canary yellow slacks tight at the ankles, cut off with a cleaver at the bare white ankles, and binding the long thighs, binding and so tight on the hips—yellow smooth complicated block of flesh and bone—that she could force only the tips of her long fingers into the slits of of the thin-lipped and slanted pockets. Slacks and square white jaw and great nest of black hair strapped in an emerald kerchief. Great white turtle-neck sweater and trussed white bosom, white breast begging for shields. Shoulders curving and muscular, un-bowed. But yellow, yellow from the waist down, the tall easy stance of a woman proud of her stomach—lovely specimen of broad flat stomach bound and yellow and undulating down the front of the slacks—and staring at me with legs apart and el-bows bent and eyes like great dark pits of recognition in the bony face. A strand of the black hair came loose and there was a long thick silver streak in it.

"Water's about twenty degrees," she said, and I heard the deep voice, saw the mountain of frosty breath, the toss of the hair. "You look like a damn seal. People shoot seals around here." And with one canary stride she was gone.

"Wait," I called, "wait a minute!" But she was gone. And of course when I looked again there was no bird in the sky and no poor white dead thing lying between myself and the blind tower on the rock. So I flung myself up the hump of the shore, knelt for a moment and carefully ran my fingers over the earth where she had stood—the footprints were real, real enough the shape of her large naked foot in the crushed frozen grass—and bewildered, cold, I sped off across those empty fields as best I could; cold and sweating, I found my way back to the sleeping house.

A once-white shutter was banging, the wind was whistling down the halyards of the clothesline, the nose of the hot rod peered at me through the tall grass, all was quiet around the kennel, and the house was sleeping, was only an old wooden structure with a tin mailbox on a post by the gate and crusts thrown out for the birds. Nothing more peaceful than the cord of cherry-wood—ash, spruce, hemlock, whatever it was—piled up for the dogs to foul. But I walked with the woman in my eye, entered the house with the vision of her handsome white face before me. Striking magic. Bold hostility. And I had begun now to suspect that sleeping house and I began to raise a first faint guard in my own defense, approaching the lopsided back storm door with care. But I was too late, of course. Too late.

I entered the darkness, drove the door closed with my shoulder and stood panting and dripping and leaning against the cold rough wall of the entrance way, stood glancing at broken flowerpots, hedge clippers hung from a nail, coil of anchor chain and pile of gunny bags, stared for a moment at a half-empty sack of charcoal briquettes. The place smelled of cold earth and congealed grease, was a wooden bin for the dead leaves and rubbish of the past. Apple cider turned to vinegar. Set of moldy and rusted golf clubs flung in a corner with rakes and a pair of rubber hip boots. But nothing that I could see to fear, and I tore off the sou'wester, pulled off the coat and hung them again where I had found them. Then I put my hand on the old-fashioned glass knob, gave it a gentle turn, and stepped into the kitchen. Cold, trembling, sighing, I was glad to be home. Then I stared at the cruel mess on the kitchen table.

Bottle of Old Grand-Dad. Tall, burnished, freshly opened, bright familiar shape of every roadside bar—there was even a silver measuring device squeezed onto the neck instead of a cap or cork—that oddly professional and flagrant bottle of whiskey stood in the middle of the kitchen table, was a rude incongruous reality in the middle of the mess. And there was the mess itself: all of poor Pixie's baby bottles, all of them, bereft of nipples, emptied, lying flat and helter-skelter on the table in little globs and pools of white baby's milk. I walked to the sink—sides and bottom furiously splashed with the milk poured, shaken, from the bottles—I walked to the table and picked up a bottle, turned it in my hands, replaced it and picked up another, and I could make nothing of this sad vehement litter, merely stood there with my face draining, chin quivering, mouth working and twisting, trying to set itself into the shape, the smile, of my self-sacrifice.

But the nipples. The horror of the nipples. I seized each of them one by one, examined them closely and helplessly until I held five in the palm of my hand, five nipples side by side and each one neatly cut off about a quarter of an inch below the tip. Pair of steel shears spread open near the Old Grand-Dad. Bits of rubber glove made for a midget. I looked and looked and then dropped them—considerable bouncing like wounded jumping beans—and knelt on the floor, felt about under the table for the sixth nipple which I never found.

I was still on my hands and knees and thinking about the pot, the boiling water, the bottles to wash, the extra set of nipples to bring down from my drawer upstairs, thinking of the bottles I had lined up in the refrigerator—had I been watched even then?—when I heard the music. Loud music at eight o'clock in the morning in that sleeping house. I lifted my head, climbed to my feet, and slowly, more slowly than ever, I hitched a little and straightened the front of my trousers, tucked in the checkered shirt, stood listening with jaw jutting and tip of the ears red hot.

Because of course it was not ordinary music. Not that morning, not in that house. It was coming from beyond the dining room—sweet tinkle of cut glass, spindle chairs, ghosts of little old seedless ladies with chokers and gold wedding bands—was coming from the radio-phonograph in the living room. With indignation I recognized the blasting exuberant strains of that brassy music. The *Horst Wessel lied* in full swing, with percussion instruments and horns, trumpets and tubas, and the heavy bass voices of all those humorless young marching men. The *Horst Wessel lied*. I could hear the waves of praise, the smacking of the drums, the maudlin fervor, the terrible toneless racketing of the military snares, could see the muscles of the open mouths, the moody eyes locked front, could feel the rise of their prepos-

61

terous love and bravery, feel the stamping feet, the floating sentiment—blue castles, beer, blood—the catching treacherous rhythm of that marching song. And I was drawn to it, drawn to
it. With scowl and frown and hot wet palms, was nonetheless
drawn to the impossible intensity of that barbaric unity, found
myself leaving the wreck of my efforts for Pixie in the kitchen
and walking toward the sound, the incredible military mass of
that captured phonograph record. I reached the door, stood in
the open door, and those German soldiers were singing the song
of death, the song of the enemy.

Canary yellow slacks, bare feet, a man's white shirt with
open collar and sleeves rolled above the naked elbows. Oh yes,
here was the second glimpse of her and she was on the floor in
front of the fireplace, was kneeling and sitting back on her heels
—wicked posturing, rank mystery of the triangle, bright and
brazen cohesion between the rump and calves and canary
yellow thighs—and her shoulders were thrown back and her
powerful spine was a crescent and her broad hands were cupped
on her knees. Her eyes were turned to the door and fixed on
mine. No smile. Surrounded by leaves of an old newspaper. A
tall glass of whiskey and a box of blue-tipped wooden matches
waiting within reach on the brick apron of the fireplace. She
waited and then jerked her head slightly toward the radio-
phonograph, and I saw the picture of the dead soldier mounted
upright in a silver frame on the cabinet.

"The *Horst Wessel*," she said above the din of the conquering
music. "Don sent me the record." And then listening, abstracted
in the pleasure of the loud marching song, slowly and with level
eyes still on mine, she reached out one white hand, seized the
full glass of whiskey, raised it in a salute in my direction: "Old
Grand-Dad. Bottle's in the kitchen. Help yourself."

She was waiting, watching me, and now I was bracing myself
against the doorjamb, leaning against it, sagging against it,
stood there with one wet shoe tapping time to the march.
"Thanks. But I don't drink."

"Oh. You don't drink. Well then, you can light the fire." And
she tossed the box of matches at my feet, put the glass to her

62

mouth—thick glass, white teeth, burnished whiskey—began to pull at it like a man, and her neck was bare, bold, athletic, and her rump was a yellow rock in the saddle of her calves, and under the white shirt her breasts were crowned with golden crowns. I thought of poor Sonny and his rum and Coca-Cola, I thought of poor Gertrude stealing frantic sips of gin out of her cheap little cream cheese glasses, I thought of poor Pixie's milk curdling in the kitchen sink. But Don's widow was sitting on her heels and drinking, and all the young German men were singing for her, marching for her. I failed to see the spinning wheel and bumped it, that construction of brittle cobwebs five feet high, and thought it was going over. Then I stooped down quickly and stuffed a few leaves of newspaper between the logs and struck a flame.

Iron pot on a hook, iron spit for the impaling and roasting of some headless blue turkey, a little straw broom and dusty heart-shaped bellows, and on the andirons great solid brass balls fit for the gods. Suddenly the tall swallow-tailed flames and crackling puffs of orange and deep green light between the logs threw all these hand-forged or handmade engines into relief, set them in motion, brought them to life, and I smelled the damp bursts of smoke and the widow was warming herself at the witches' fire. Beside the bellows was a coffin-shaped legless duck—faded decoy carved with a knife—that stared me down with two tiny bright sightless chips of glass. Fire in the antique shop. Dead duck. Smoke in my eyes.

"Take off your shoes, for God's sake," she said, and the mellow voice was loud above the chant of the SS men, the firelight landed in yellow lozenges on the slopes and in the hollows of her slacks, "you must be frozen. But go ahead, warm your toes while I tell you about Don."

And I could only nod, tug at the wet laces, free my heels, roll down the socks, wring them out—drops of steam on the hearth—could only make room for her and sit beside her on the cold wide naked planks of that floor with my hands propped behind me and my white feet and hers thrust into the heat. She dropped down on an elbow, crossed her long straight legs at the ankles, held out the whiskey glass—but it was not for me, that whiskey, at least not then—and breathing deeply, straining at the nostrils, shirt binding and slackening across her breasts, she began to wheeze. To wheeze! The big white knuckles of the fingers holding the glass, her crowned breasts, the mighty head of black hair, the stomach girding her in front like the flexible shape of a shield, the fluted weight of neck and arms and legs, all the impressive anatomy of this Cleopatra who could row her own barge, this woman who could outrun horses on the beach or knock down pillars of salt, everything about her revealed perfect health, denied this sudden swirling of mud or rattling of little pits in her chest. But even above the raucous melody of the eager Germans and their impossible military band I heard it: the sound of obstructed breathing, tight low crippling whine in the chest. Yet her eyes on mine were direct and heavy and dark, were large and black and fierce and cracked by spears of silver light. She wheezed on, mocked by the competitive fire, waiting for the steel needle to descend once more into the grooves of plodding Reichstag hysteria, and then whacked herself once on the uppermost yellow thigh and began to talk.

"That's him in the picture," she said without moving, without pointing, merely assuming that I had seen it when I entered the room. I nodded. "That's Don. Young, good-looking boy. He stepped on a land mine, God damn him. In Germany. He took a wrong step and then no more Don. Poof. I met him in South Carolina. There he was, toward sundown standing at a country bus stop in South Carolina. The end of nowhere and burning up at the edges. Nothing but the road, a tree smothered with dust, the little three-sided shed where they were supposed to wait for the bus, a field full of scarecrows. And in front of the shed and surrounded by perhaps twenty cotton pickers, there was Don. I saw him. Short, limber, smile all over his face, head of tight blond curls, overseas cap like a little tan tent on the side of his head. Bunch of tattered damn black cotton pickers out for blood and this wonderful bright little guy with his smile and curly hair. Don. A little angel in South Carolina. So I gave him a lift. Sense of humor? My God, he had a sense of humor." And suddenly she was choking on a snort of laughter, choking, gasping, giving my now toasty bare foot a friendly push with hers. And now her wheezing had found another depth, and each word came out shrouded in its cocoon of gravelly sound, its spasm of spent breath, and there were streaks of moisture at the hairline and on her upper lip. She took another slow drink of whiskey and the silver strand of hair hung down, the voice was deep.

She set down the glass and filled her lungs and said: "Good God, I married him for his humor. Because he was light on his feet and light in his heart. And because he was quick and talented and because he was just a boy, that's why I married him. Why I gave him a lift and followed him to Galveston, Texas, and married him. Don. Three dozen roses, a brand new hot plate, a rented room outside Galveston, and one day Don telling me he had been elected company mascot—what a sense of humor, what a winsome smile—and that night our celebration with a spaghetti dinner and bottle of dago red. I should have known then that it couldn't last. My God. . . ."

The golden foot was struggling against mine, the perspiration was as thick as rain on her lip, her shirt was wet and through it I could see the sloping shoulder, the handsome network of blue veins, the companion to the black brassiere that was still hanging in the john upstairs. Stretched full-length at my side she was wheezing and staring into the light of the fire, and now there were dimples, puckers, unsuspected curves in the canary yellow slacks, and now her chest was maniacal, was as trenchant and guttural and insistent as the upturned German record itself. So I looked at her then, forced myself to return the stare of those vast dark eyes, and she tried to shrug, tried to toss back the thick length of silver hair, but only glowered at me out of her stricken heaviness and abruptly tapped herself on the chest.

"Asthma." Tapping the finger, squaring the jaw, watching me. "I get it from too much thinking about Don. But it's nothing. Nothing at all. . . ."

I nodded. And yet the fire had fallen in and the pot and spit were glowing and her knee was lifting. Her lips were moist, pulled back, drawn open fiercely in the perfect silent square of the tragic muse, and I leaned closer to smell the alcohol and Parisian scent, closer to inspect the agony of the muscles which, no thicker than hairs, flexed and flickered in those unhappy lips, closer to hear whatever moaning she might have made above the racket of her strangulation.

"What can I do? Isn't there something I can do?"

"The secretary," she said. "Bring me the box in the middle drawer. Saucer too. From the kitchen."

So I embarked on this brief rump-swinging bare-and-warm-footed expedition, and with the woolen pants steaming nicely around my ankles and the checkered shirt pressing against my skin its blanket of warm fuzzy hairs, I glided heavily to the little chair, the papers, the oil lamp—God Bless Our Home etched on the shade—and calmly, backs of the hands covered with new warmth, licking my lips and feeling that I might like to whistle —perhaps only a bar or two, a few notes in defiance of the *Horst Wessel*—I returned to the cold kitchen with hardly a glance, hardly a thought for the remnants of poor Pixie's breakfast and lunch and dinner. Solicitous. Professional search for a saucer. Long-faced scrutiny of the cupboards. The hell with the nipples.

And then I was kneeling at her side, leaning down to her again with the box in one hand and the dish in the other, and though she was heaving worse than ever with her eyes still shut, nonetheless she knew I was there and tried to rouse herself. "What next?" I asked, and was startled by the quickness of her reply, shocked by the impatience and urgency of her rich low voice.

"Put some powder in the dish and burn it. For God's sake."

Sputtering match, sputtering powder, glowing pinpricks and smoke enough to form a genie. I tried to fight the smoke, the stench, with my two wild hands. But it was everywhere. And now her voice was coming through the smoke and for a moment I could only listen, breathe in the terrible odor, keep watching her despite my tears.

"I don't really believe in this stuff," drinking in enormous whiffs of greasy smoke, "but sometimes it helps a little. Don told me about it, found an ad in the Galveston paper," filling her lungs with punk and dung and sparks, "he was such a sweet airy little clown. Five months of marriage to Don," swirling, sinking, drifting now on the fumes of the witches' pot, "and then a land mine in Wiesbaden or some damn place and no more Don and me a widow. . . ."

"I'm a widower myself," I said, and I stood up carefully, avoided the large white hand that was reaching for my trouser leg, stared once at the little unmoving face of the dead soldier, and started out of the room.

But just as I approached the door: "Well," I heard her say, "we'll make a great pair."

And when I reached the upstairs hallway Pixie was screaming in her cradle and Cassandra was wrapped in a musty quilt and stood trying to coil up her hair before the oval mirror. I heard the gasping breaths below turn to laughter and for a long while hesitated to enter my icy room. Because of the dressmaker's dummy. Because she had placed the dummy—further sign of industry in the island home, rusted iron-wire skirt and loops of rusted iron-wire for the bold and faceless head, no arms, torso like an hourglass, broad hips and sweeping behind and narrow waist and bang-up bosom all made of padded beige felt, historical essence of womanhood, life-size female anatomy and a hundred years of pins—she had placed this dummy at the head of my bed and dressed it in my naval uniform so that the artificial bosom swelled my white tunic and the artificial pregnancy of the padded belly puffed out the broad front of my official white duck pants which she had pinned to the dummy with a pair of giant safety pins rammed through the felt. Cuffs of the empty sleeves thrust in the pockets, white hat cocked outrageously on the wire head—desperate slant of the black visor, screaming angle of the golden bird—oh, it was a jaunty sight she had prepared for me. But of course I ignored it as best I could, tried to overlook the fresh dark gouts of ketchup she had flung down the front of that defiled figure, and merely shut my door, at least spared my poor daughter from having to grapple with that hapless effigy of my disfigured self.

And moments later, scooping Pixie out of the cradle, tossing her into the air, jouncing her in the crook of my arm, smiling:

"Have a good sleep, Cassandra? Time to start the new day." In the mirror her little cold sleepy face was puffy and pitted, was black and white with shadow, and the faded quilt was drawn over her shoulders and her hair was still down.

"What's burning?" she said. "What's that awful smell?" But in the mirror I put a finger to my lips, shook my head, though I knew then that the noxious odor of grief, death and widowhood would fill this house.

Cleopatra's Car

Shanks of ice hanging from the eaves, the wind sucking with increasing fury at the wormholes, Miranda standing in the open front doorway and laughing into the wind or bellowing through the fog at her two fat black Labradors and throwing them chunks of meat from a galvanized iron basin slung under her arm, the ragged bird returning each dawn to hover beyond the shore line outside my window, empty Old Grand Dad bottles collecting in the kitchen cupboards, under the stove, even beside the spinning wheel in the parlor—so these first weeks froze and fled from us, and Cassandra grew reluctant to explore the cow paths with me, and my nights, my lonely nights, were sleepless. I began to find the smudged saucers everywhere—stink of the asthma powders, stink of secret designs and death—and I began to notice that Cassandra was Miranda's shadow, sweet silent shadow of the big widow in slacks. When Miranda poured herself a drink—tumbler filled to the brim with whiskey—Cassandra put a few drops in the small end of an egg cup and accompanied her. And when Miranda sat in front of the fire to knit, Cassandra was always with her, always kneeling at her feet and holding the yarn. Black yarn. Heavy soft coil of rich black yarn dangling from Cassandra's wrists. Halter on the white wrists. Our slave chains. Between the two of them always the black umbilicus, the endless and maddening absorption in the problems of yarn. It lived in the cave of Miranda's sewing bag—not a black sweater for some lucky devil overseas, nor even a cap for Pixie, but only this black entanglement, their shapeless squid. And I? I would sit in the shadows and wait, maintain my guard, sit there and now and then give the spinning wheel an idle turn or polish all the little ivory pieces of the Mah Jongg set.

And marked by Sunday dinners. The passing of those darkening weeks, the flow of those idle days—quickening, growing colder, until they rushed and jammed together in the little jagged ice shelf of our frozen time—was marked by midday dinners on the Sabbath when Captain Red did the carving—wind-whipped, tall and raw and bald like me, his big knuckles sunk in the gravy and his bulging eyes on the widow—and when Bub waited on table and ate alone with Pixie in the kitchen, and Jomo—back straight, sideburns reaching to the thin white jaws, black hair plastered down with pine sap—sat working his artificial hand beside Cassandra. On Sundays Jomo worked his artificial hand for Cassandra, but I was the one who watched, I who watched him change the angle of his hook, lock the silver fork in place and go after peas, watched him fiddle with a lever near the wrist and drop the fork and calmly and neatly snare the full water glass in the mechanical round of that wonderful steel half-bracelet that was his hand.

Those were long Sunday meals when the Captain spoke only to say grace and ask for the rolls; and Bub stood waiting at my elbow and smelled of brine and uncut boy's hair; and Jomo sat across from me, solitary—except for Cassandra at his side—and busy with his new hand; and Miranda drank her whiskey and cursed the weather and grinned down the length of the table at the quiet lechery that boiled in old Red's eyes; and Cassandra, poor Cassandra, merely picked at her plate, yet Sunday after dreary Sunday grew heavier, more ripe to the silent fare of that cruel board. Dreary and dull and dangerous. So at the end of the meal I always asked Jomo how he had liked Salerno. Because of course he had lost his hand in the fighting around Salerno. A city, as he said, near the foot of the boot. What would I have done without Jomo's hand?

Family and friends, then, gathering week after dreary week for the Sabbath, meeting together on the dangerous day of the Lord, pursuing our black entanglement, waiting around for something—the first snow? first love? the first outbreak of violence?—and saying grace, watching the slow winter death of the oak tree, feeling wave after wave of the cold Atlantic breaching our trackless black inhospitable shores. And then another Sunday rolling around and the sexton rushing to the Lutheran church to ring the bells—always excited, always in a hurry, can't wait to get his hands on the rope—and once again the frenzied sexton nearly hanging himself from the bellpull and another Sunday ringing and pealing and chiming on the frosty air.

So the gray days died away and the hours of my lonely and sleepless nights increased, each hour deeper and darker and colder than the one before and with only the dummy—mockery of myself—to keep me company, to follow me through the cold night watch. Luckily I found an old brass bed warmer in the closet behind the trunks and every night I filled it with the last coals of the fire and carried it first to Cassandra's room, devoted fifteen minutes to warming Cassandra's bed, and then carried it across the hall—hot libation, hot offering to myself—and shoved it between the covers where it spent the night. And I would lie there in the darkness and everywhere, except in my feet, suffer the bruising effects of the flat frozen pillow and the cold mattress, and clutching my hands together and waiting, knowing that even the coals would cool, would remember one of Jomo's phrases spoken when he thought I couldn't hear—blue tit—and in the darkness would begin to say the phrase aloud—blue tit—aware that in some mysterious way it referred to the cold, referred to the way I felt, seemed to give actual substance, body, to the dark color and falling temperature of all my lonely and sleepless nights. Then I would dream with Jomo's incantation still on my lips. And I would dream of Tremlow leading the mutiny, of Gertrude's grave, of Fernandez mutilated in the flophouse, and I would awaken to the sound of the wind and the sight of my white spoiled uniform flapping and moaning on the dressmaker's dummy. Blue tit. And at dawn a hard tissue-thin sheet of ice in the bottom of the basin, big block of ice in the pitcher, frozen splinters like carpet tacks when I stumbled to the bathroom to empty the bed warmer down the john. Standing in that bathroom, shivering, blinking, bed warmer hanging cold and heavy from my hand, I would always lean close to the bathroom mirror and read the message printed in ornate green type on a little square of wrinkled and yellowed paper which was pasted to the glass. Always read it and, no matter how cold I was, how tired, I would begin to smile.

Wake with a Loving Thought.
Work with a Happy Thought.
Sleep with a Gentle Thought.

I would begin to smile, begin to whistle. Because it tickled my fancy, that prayer, that message for the new day, and because it was a talisman against the horrors of blue tit and saved me, at least for a while, from the thought of the black brassiere.

So the changes of those cold days. Until the local children became glum Christmas sprites and the first snow fell at last—sudden soaring of asthma powder stench, dirty little volcanoes smoldering in every room—and the night of the local high school dance loomed out of the fresh wet snow and I, I too, was swept along into the glaring bathos of that high school dance. Kissing in the coatroom. Big business out back in the car. Little bright noses in the snow. Jomo's hook in action. Beginning of our festive end.

"Ready, Skip? Ready yet, Candy? They'll be here any sec. . . ."

Even in the cold and echoing bathroom—lead pipe, cracked linoleum, slabs of yellow marble—and even with the cold water running in the tap and the snow piling against the window and

72

the old brown varnished door closed as far as it would go, still I could hear her calling to us from the parlor, hear the sound of her tread in the parlor. But though her voice rose up to us crisp and clear and bold—a snappy voice, a hailing voice, deeply resonant, pathetically excited—and though I resented being rushed and would never forgive her for daring to invent and use those perky names, especially for shouting up that cheap term of endearment for Cassandra when I, her father, had always yearned hopelessly for just this privilege, nonetheless it was Saturday night and the first snow was falling and I too was getting ready, after all, for the high school dance. So I could not really begrudge Miranda her excitement or her impatience. I too felt a curious need to hurry after all. And perhaps down there in the parlor—kicking the log, sloshing unsteady portions of whiskey into her glass, then striding to the window and trying to see out through the darkness and heavy snow—perhaps in some perverse way she was thinking of Don, though her chest was clear and though from time to time I could hear her laughing to herself down there.

Laughing while I was making irritable impatient faces in the bathroom mirror. Giving myself a close shave for the high school dance. Trying to preserve my own exhilaration against hers. And it was pleasurable. After a particularly good stroke I would set aside the razor and fling the water about as wildly as I could and snort, grind my eyes on the ends of the towel. Then step to the window for a long look at the black night and the falling snow.

Wet hands on the flaking white sill. Sudden shock in nose, chin, cheeks, sensation of the cold glass against the whole of my inquisitive face. Kerosene stove breathing into the seat of my woolen pants, eyes all at once accustomed to the dark, when suddenly it coalesced—soap, toothpaste, warm behind, the cold wet night—and I smiled and told myself I had nothing to fear from Red and saw myself poised hand in hand with Cassandra on the edge of the floor and smiling at the awkward postures and passions of the high school young. I stared out the window, tasting the soap on my lips, watching the snow collect in the black crotch of a tree—slick runnels in the bark, puckered wounds of lopped branches crowned with snow—that grew close to the window and glistened in the beam of the bathroom light, and I felt as if I were being tickled with the point of a sharp knife. Thank God for the sound of the tap and of Cassandra's little thin shoe spanking across the puddles of the bathroom floor. I waited, face trembling with the coldness of the night.

"Skipper. Zip me up. Please."

"Well, Cassandra," I said, and turned to her, held out both hands wide to her, "How sad that Gertrude can't see you now. But your dress, Cassandra, surely it's not a mail-order dress?"

"Miranda made it for me," tugging lightly at a flounce, twisting the waist, "she made it as a surprise for me to wear tonight. It has a pretty bow. You'll see. It's not too youthful, Skipper?"

"For you?" And I laughed, dropped my arms—antipathy toward my embrace? fear for the dress?—and wiped my hands on the towel, frowned at the thought of Miranda's midnight sewing machine, stood while with straight arm and straight fingers she followed the healing needlework on my skin, traced out the letters of her lost husband's name—did she, could she know what she was doing? know the shame I felt for the secret I still kept from her?—then by the shoulders I turned her so I could reach the dress where it hung open down her back. "Of course it's not too young for you, Cassandra. Hardly."

"And we're not making a mistake tonight? We shouldn't just stay home and let Miranda go to the dance alone with Red and Bub and," pausing—moment of deference—whispering the name into the little clear cup of her collar bone, "and with Jomo?"

"Of course not," I said, and reached for the zipper, probed for it, quickly tried to work the zipper. "It's only a high school dance, Cassandra. Harmless. Amusing. We needn't be out late," pulling, fumbling, trying to work the zipper free, "and think of it, Cassandra. The first snow. . . ."

She nodded and plucked at the bodice, fluffed the skirt, put one foot in front of the other, and with each gesture there was a corresponding ripple in the prim naked shape of her back and a corresponding ripple in the dress itself. That dress. That green taffeta. Flounces and ruffles and little bright green fields and cascading skirt. Taffeta. Smooth for the palm and nipped-in little deep green persuasive folds for the fingers. Swirling. Shining. Cake frosting with candles. For a fifteen-year-old. For a cute kitten. For trouble. Green taffeta. And when we went down the stairs together, Cassandra holding up the knee-length skirt, I following, steadying myself against the flimsy bannister, I saw the green bow, the two full yards of fluted taffeta with a green knot larger than my fist and streamers that reached her calves. Bow that bound her buttocks. Outrageous bow!

So I zipped the zipper and in the mirror full of contortion, mirror crowded suddenly with hands, elbows, floating face, I tied my tie and spread a thin even coating of Vaseline on my smooth red scalp—protection for the bald head, no chafing in wind or snow, trick I learned in the Navy—and grinned at myself in the glass and buffed my fingernails and struggled into my jacket and rapped on Cassandra's door—exposure of black market stocking, gathered green taffeta hem of skirt, hairpin in the pretty mouth—and waited and waited and then escorted her down the dark stairs.

"Candy! My God, Candy! She looks like a dream, doesn't she, Skip?"

Before I could reply or smile or make some condescending gesture they hugged each other, hooked arms and crossed the parlor to the fire, in front of the fire held hands, admired each other, babbled, swung their four clasped hands in unison. Girlish. Hearts full of joy. The big night. Miranda was dressed in black, of course—her totem was still hanging in the bathroom—and around her throat she wore a black velvet band. Her bosom was an unleashed animal.

"My God, Candy, we're just kids. Two kids. Two baby sitters waiting for dates! And they'll be here any sec!"

"And me, Miranda?" Squirming, shrugging, raising my chin toward the cracks in the ceiling, "What about me, Miranda?"

"You?" She laughed, showed her big white knees, pretended to waltz with Cassandra in front of the fire. "You're the Mah Jongg champion. Boy, what a Mah Jongg champion you are!"

And suddenly locking Cassandra's face between her bare white hands, and swaying, smiling at Cassandra's little downcast eyes: "My God, I wish Don were here," she said. "I wish Don could see you tonight, Candy."

"Watch out for the asthma," I murmured, but too softly and too late because the dates were stamping on the veranda, banging on the door, and she was gone, was already rushing down the hall and kissing them, throwing herself on the sniffling figures standing there in the cold.

And under my breath, quickly: "First dance, Cassandra? Please?"

"I can't promise, Skipper. I can't make promises any more."

Then the fire shot high again and the black beauty was herding them all into the parlor—Jomo, Bub, Grandma who looked like a little corncob tied up with rags—and they were all blowing on their fingers, kicking the snow off their boots, sniffling. Red ears. Mean eyes. Smears of Miranda's lipstick on each of the faces.

"Have a drink, Jomo?" she said, and hugged his narrow black iron shoulders with her long white arm, ran her other hand through Bub's wet hair. "Just one for the road?"

"Can't. Red's out in the car. Waiting."

The long-billed baseball cap, the steady eyes, the flat black sideburns sculpted frontier-style with a straight razor, pug nose and skin the color of axle grease and little black snap-on bow tie and lips drawn as if he were going to whistle through his teeth —this was Jomo and Jomo was looking at Cassandra, staring at her, with one oblivious snuff of his pug nose expressed all the contempt and desire of his ruthless race. It was the green taffeta bow, of course, and before he could finish his contemplation of that green party favor, green riddle as big as a balloon, I stepped in front of him, and hoping, as I always hoped, that one day he would forget and give me his cold hook of steel, I thrust out my hand.

"Evening, Jomo," I said. "How's the cod? Running?"

He waited. No artificial hand. No real hand. Only the soft light of fury sliding off his face, only one more baffling question

76

to ask his old man about and to hold against me. So he turned to Miranda, jerked his head toward the door.

"Anyways, Red's got a pint in his pocket. Let's go."

But the little old woman, mother of the Captain and grandmother of his noxious sons, was pushing on Bub's sleeve and pointing in my direction and trying to talk.

"She wants to say something," Bub said. "Tell Bub," he said, and stuck his ear down to the little happy bobbing clot of the old woman's face. Crushed once with a clam digger. Dug out of a hole at low tide. Little old woman with love and a sense of humor.

"All right," I said, "what is it? And how is Mrs. Poor tonight?" I smiled and glanced at Cassandra—shining and silent cameo by the hearth—and smiled again, squared my shoulders, leaned my head slightly to one side for Mrs. Poor who was clinging to Bub's arm and pumping with excitement in all the little black muscular valves of her mouth and eyes. Every Saturday Red went down to feed her doughnuts, and on Sundays after grace he would sometimes tell us about her health and happiness. "Well," I said, knowing that she was shrewd, not to be trusted, that the little rag-bound head was stuffed with Jomo's jokes and snatches of the prayer book which she knew by heart, "well, tell us what Grandma wants to say tonight."

Bub looked at me, wiped his nose. "She says all the girls are sweet on you. You're apple pie for the girls, she says. All the girls go after a rosy man like you. Real apple pie, she says." And Bub was scowling and the old woman was nodding up and down, grinning, pointing, and Miranda was kneeling and fixing Cassandra's bow.

"What a nice thing to say," said Cassandra. "Don't you think so, Skipper?"

Jomo leaned over and smacked his thigh. "God damn," he said, "that's good."

And going down the hall toward the open door where I could see the snow driving and sifting—Miranda first, then Cassandra and Jomo and Bub and last, as usual, myself—I noticed Bub's quick ferret gesture, quick fingers nudging his brother's arm, and clearly heard his young boy's voice cupped under a sly hand, in the darkness saw his boy's feet dance a few lewd steps to the fun of his question:

"What's that thing she's wearing on her ass?"

And Jomo, in a dead-pan voice and puppet jerk of the silhouetted head: "Never you mind, Bub. And watch your language. You got a mouth full of rot."

"Maybe. But I'd like to kill it with a stick."

Old joke. Snickering shadow of island boy. Jackknife shadow of older brother. But then the snow, the darkness, the packed and crunching veranda, the dying oak and the picket fence heaped high with snow, and beyond the fence, low and throbbing like a diesel truck, the waiting car. It was a hot rod. Cut down. Black. Thirteen coats of black paint and wax. Thick aluminum tubes coiling out of the engine. And in the front an aerial—perfect even to the whip of steel, I thought—and tied to the tip of the aerial a little fat fuzzy squirrel tail, little flag freshly killed and plump, soft, twisting and revolving slowly in the snow, dark fur long and wet and glistening under the crystals of falling snow. The lights from the house were shining on the windshield —narrow flat rectangle of blind glass already half-buried like the silver hub caps in the heavy snow—and I glanced back toward the house and waved and, blinking away the snow, licking it, thinking of another departure, "*Au revoir*, Grandma," I called softly, "take good care of Pixie." Then I stumbled to the car with wet cheeks and with a smile on my wet lips.

I took hold of the handle. Turned, pulled, shook the handle. "Come on, Bub," I said, leaning down, rapping on the glass, shading my eyes and attempting to peer into the car, "open the door, you're not funny." I squinted, brushed at the snow with a cold hand. I saw the two heads of hair and the knife-billed baseball cap between them in the back, saw Bub laughing, poking at Captain Red who sat behind the wheel holding the pint bottle up to his lip. I saw the pint bottle making the rounds.

"All right," I said, when the door came open at last, "now get out for a moment, Bub. You can sit on my lap."

"Now wait a minute. Just you wait. I got this seat first. Didn't I? If there's any lap-sitting to be done, it's you who's going to do it. Now you want to ride to the dance with us you better just climb into the car and have a seat. Right here." Pointing. Laughter. Bottle sailing out the window. Captain Red—tall man dressed in his Sunday duds, shaved, fit to kill—blowing the horn three times. Three shrill trumpet blasts through the falling snow.

"But, Bub," leaning closer, trying to whisper into his ear, "I'm bigger than you are. I'll be too heavy."

And the shout: "Never you mind about that. I'll do the worrying, you just do what I say. And I say you can sit on my lap or you can walk!"

Then there was the meshing of metal, the hard shower of snow, sparks under the snow, and if I hadn't leapt—puffing, pumping, displaying blind humiliating courage since it's always the fat man who has to run to catch the train—surely I would have been left behind, left standing there with my hopeless breath freezing on the dark night air. An evening at home. Evening with Grandma. Up and down to the lavatory. Smiles. But I did leap, sucked all possible breath into my lungs and desperate, expecting and even willing to be maimed, for five or ten steps plowed along beside the moving car and then jumped, ducked my head, got a grip on the dashboard and back of the seat, hunched my neck and shoulders—presence of mind to save fingers, feet, loose ends of cloth and flesh from the slamming door—and perched there, balanced there absurdly on Bub's tough wiry little lap. Steaming upholstery, six steaming people. Smells of gasoline, spilled whiskey, fading perfume, antifreeze. And Bub. With my head knocking against the roof of the car I knew him for what he was: a boy without underwear, holes in his socks, holes in his pockets, rancid navel, hair bunched and furrowed on the scrawny nape of his neck, and the mouth forever breathing off the telltale smell of sleep and half-eaten candy bars. This country boy, this island boy. Filled with fun. With hate. With smelly self-satisfaction.

"Jingle Bells, everybody," cried Miranda, "sing along with me!" But we were swerving, skidding, sliding through the snow and all at once the lights of the high school were flickering above the tombstones in the cemetery on the hill.

And into the tiny exposed orifice of Cassandra's ear: "I got dibs on the first dance," said Jomo, and I understood the meaning of her downcast eyes and through the snow I heard that the bass drum was out of time with the rest of Jack Spratt's Merry Hep Cats.

But how long, oh my God, how long did I endure that drummer—pimples, frightened eyes, chewing gum under his chair, some kind of permanent paralysis in his legs—how long endure the cornet—begging for alms—or the little girl with the accordion —black and white monster on her bare knees—or the poor stick of a schoolteacher at the upright piano or the paper cups of pop, the wedges of chocolate cake—chocolate on the lips, cheeks, melting all over the hands—how long endure the concrete walls, steam pipes, varnished and forbidding floor, the red, white and blue bunting hung from the nets, how long endure the mothers or the fat old men waiting around for the belly-bumping contest? How long? How long endure all this as well as the sight of Jomo going after Cassandra with his damnable hook? Long enough to be tempted into love once more, long enough to perspire in that cold gymnasium, to win the belly-bumping contest —treachery of my long night—long enough to have my fill of pop and chocolate cake. Too long, oh God, much too long for a man who merely wanted to dance a few slow numbers and amuse his daughter.

"If the power fails," and I startled at the sound of Red's deep voice, glanced at the uncertain yellow glow of the caged lights, glanced at the windows filled with wind and snow, "if it fails there's no telling what all these kids will do. Might have quite a time in the dark. With all these kids." And the two of them, widow in black, Captain Red in black double-breasted suit, swung out to the middle of the floor, towered above that handful of undernourished high school girls and retarded boys. Two tall black figures locked length to length, two faces convulsed in passion, one as long and white and bony as a white mare's face, the other crimson, leathery, serrated like the bald head to which it belonged, and the young boys and girls making way for them, scattering in the path of their slow motion smoke, staring up at them in envy, fear, shocked surprise. From the side lines and licking my fingers, swallowing the cake, I too watched them in shocked surprise, stuffed a crumpled paper napkin into my hip pocket. Because they were both so big, so black, so oblivious. But if this was the father, what of the ruthless son? What of Cassandra? What dance could they possibly be dancing?

I was her guardian, her only defense, and I tossed off my Coke —fifth free Coca-Cola, thoughts of Sonny—crushed the cup, and in my heavy dogtrot ran the whole length of that cold basketball court and in the darkest corner saw a flash of steel, the sheen of bright green taffeta. And paused. Bumped a proud mother. But started out onto the floor anyway. Alone. Breathless. Trying to avoid the dancers.

"Say there," behind me the woman's voice, sound of Sunday supper in the Lutheran church, "that fellow's got a nerve."

"Don't he though? And all these young boys in uniform and men like that going around scot free? Lord God. Ain't it a crime?"

The boys were wearing their white shirts—frayed collars, patches in the sleeves—and their wrinkled ties, the young girls were wearing their jerseys, homemade skirts, glass earrings— hand-me-downs—their cotton socks and saddle shoes. And I was among them and I looked into their frightened eyes, looked through the jerseys, and despite my desperation I was able to keep my wits about me—interesting little blonde, sweet raven head—and was not ashamed to look. Sixteen, seventeen, even nineteen years old and undernourished and undeveloped as well. Daughters of poor fishermen. Daughters of the sea. Anemic. Disposed to scabies. Fed on credit, fed on canned stock or stunted berries picked from a field gone back to brier, prickly thorns, wild sumac. Precious brass safety pins holding up their panties, and then I saw the pins, all at once saw the panties, the square gray-white faded undergarments of poor island girls washed in well water morning and night and, indistinguishable from kitchen washrag or scrap of kitchen towel, hung on a string between two young poplars and flapping, blowing in the hard island wind until once more dry enough and clean enough to return to the plain tender skin, and of course the elastics had been worn out or busted long ago and now there were only the little bent safety pins for holding up their panties and a few hairpins for the hair and a single lipstick which they passed from girl to girl at country crossroads or in the high school lavatory on the day of the dance. Plain Janes, island sirens, with long skinny white legs—never to know the touch of silk—and eyes big enough and gray enough to weep buckets, though they would never cry, and little buttocks already corrupted, nonetheless, by the rhythm of pop melodies and boys on leave. I steadied myself on a thin warm shoulder. "Don't be afraid," I murmured, "it's only Papa Cue Ball," and smelled the soap in her straight shining hair and saw that her skirt had once belonged to Mamma—poor skillful pleats—and that her face revealed the several faint nearly identical faces of a little Dionysian incest on a winter's night.

"You leave Chloris alone," her partner hissed, and I yanked my hand from her shoulder, blushed at the realization that I had been squeezing her little thin rounded shoulder.

"No harm meant," I said under my breath. "Just lost my footing. She's all yours," and I smiled at the relentless black walnut eyes, wheeled and cut in on Jomo, took Cassandra right out of his arms.

"OK, Jomo," I said, "I'm cutting in."

It was the far dark corner of the gym and there was a young marine sitting on top of a pile of wrestlers' mats, and I noticed his mouthful of bright cigar, his crooked smile in the dark, the glint of the bottle he didn't even pretend to hide. Three or four younger boys were hanging around the marine and sharing his bottle, waiting for word from Jomo and talking in lewd tones about Cassandra and me. By the way they turned their heads and covered their mouths and jerked their thumbs at us I knew perfectly well that they were talking in lewd tones about us. Country haircuts—except for the shaved marine—and the country ears and country Adam's apples. Inheritors of the black Atlantic. Boys who talked a lot but never danced. And of course the marine, the pride of the school, the pride of the woman at the piano. Sophomore in uniform. Leather head. Twenty-seven wounds in the rib cage. Telling them how he raped the little

Japanese children. Cocking his knee in the darkness, passing the bottle. Promising to show them all twenty-seven scars in the john.

And glancing to the left, to the right, leaning down as close as I could to Cassandra, and fighting all the while against the current and trying to draw away from Jomo's friends in the corner—but there was no escaping the shadows, the arrogant glow of the cigar—and trying to subdue the electrical field of green taffeta and worrying, apologizing for my graceless steps, "It's a tough crowd, Cassandra," I said, "I don't like the looks of it."

She was stiff, her back was stiff, her arm was suddenly un-supple, she was making it hard for me. And I wanted to see her face—how could she, why did she turn away from me?—and wanted to feel the taffeta yielding, wanted some sign of her happiness. "You aren't having fun, Cassandra?" I said, and squeezed her hand, wondered whether I might not be able to imitate the sons of the sea and whirl her around by that little tapering white hand for our amusement, hers and mine, and whirl her so that her skirts would rise. But there was only the varnished floor, only the stiff shadows of ropes and acrobatic rings looping down from the darkness overhead, only the steam pipes along the walls with their enormous plaster casts like broken legs, and it was discouraging and I wanted to take her to the cloakroom and take her home. "Refreshments, Cassandra? How about some chocolate cake?" And seeing a movement in the vicinity of the indolent marine and talking closer to her ear, more quickly, "Or Coke, Cassandra? Join me in a little toast to Sonny?"

But one of his admirers had taken the marine's peaked cap, had hung it on the side of his head and was sauntering in our direction, swaggering. The cap was flopping against his neck, the pubic hair was curling around his ears, he was whistling—despite the clarion cornet and choking accordion—and he was advancing toward us casually, deliberately, shuffling our way from the darkness of giggling drinkers and lolling marine. Then a punch on my arm, jab in my ribs, and a boy's brogan landed

83

in a short swift kick just above my ankle and Bub was saying, "Come on, Sister, let's dance," and threw his arms around her and hopped from side to side, snorting and snuffling happily into the green. Proud of his rhythm. Proud of the hat. Bub acting on orders. Bub determined to work his hands under the green bow. And Cassandra? Cassandra's eyes were closed and she was resting her palms lightly on the heavy wooden humps of his boyish shoulders. As I started away I saw them converging on her—Jomo, Red—saw the menacing horizontal thrust of the baseball cap, the bright arc of the swinging hook, the enormous black figure of Captain Red with his tie pulled loose. They began cutting in on each other, spitting on their hands or giving her up without a word, standing by and serving as outriders for each other, and at once I understood that they were taking turns with her and that this then was their plan, their dark design.

"Me?" I said. "Someone wants me? Outside?"

She grinned, a tiny girl, messenger with bobbed hair, and said she would show me the way. Mystery. Trap set by the marine? Cruel joke? But I decided that Miranda must be having asthma out in the snow and that my little girl guide—spit curls, washed and fed, eyes like a little mother cat, and plump, liberal with her own lipstick, well-mannered and ready for the juice of life —must surely be the daughter of the frenzied sexton who was so dead set on hanging himself from the bell ropes of the Lutheran church. So I followed her.

"Like the dance?"

"Why, yes," I said, startled, trying to keep up with her, to keep in close behind her, "yes, I do. It gives me an idea of what my own high school reunion might be like," and I was using the back of my hand, then my handkerchief, trying to catch the scent of her.

"I bet you were popular," she said. She was not giggling, spoke with no discernible mockery in her voice, this child of chewing gum kisses and plump young body sweetly dusted with baby talc, "I bet you'd have fun with the kids in your school or with your classmates even after thirty or forty years or whatever it is. You don't look like a kill-joy to me." And leading me into a cold dark corridor, concrete, bare lead, whistling with the cold wind of my own distant past: "You know what?" speaking clearly, matter-of-factly, while I joined her hastily at the dead weight of a metal fire door and the snow began driving suddenly through a narrow crack and into our faces, "I bet all the girls go for you. Am I right? Aren't you the type all the girls go after?"

"Well, Bubbles," I said, and like Carmen's her black hair was curled into little flat black points, "you're the second person to mention this idea tonight. So perhaps there's something in what you say."

"I knew it," she said, and we were pushing together, forcing the wrinkling door to yield, small plump girl and tall fat man straining together, beating back the snow, smelling the cold black night of the silent parking lot and breathing together, testing the snow together, "I knew you were the shy unscrupulous type. The type of man who might get a girl in trouble. A real lover."

"No, no, Bubbles, not in trouble. . . ." But I was shivering, smiling, setting straight the core of my boundless heart. A real lover. I believed her, and I lifted my broad white face into the wet tingling island snow. We had been able to open the door about a foot and so stood together hand in hand just outside the building. Together, the two of us. Blood under the skin and alone with Bubbles, scot free again.

A pale lemon-colored light from the gymnasium windows lay in three wavering rectangles on the snow. Pale institutional light coming down from the high school wall. And beyond the cold wall, beyond the tenuous light stretched the parking lot with its furry white humps of buried automobiles and, at the far edge, the black trees tangled like barbed wire. Behind the trees was the cemetery, and I could just make out the crumbling white shapes of the tombstones, the markers of dead children, the little white obelisks in the island snow. It was the place of rendezvous for the senior class, of passion amongst the fungus and the marble vines, of fingernail polish on the lips of the cherubim. So I felt that Bubbles and I were alone in some cheap version of limbo, and I chuckled, warmed the fingers of my free hand, and loved the trees, the perfect star-flashes of the snow, the nearness of the little cold cemetery, the buried cars, and at my side the small wet girl. But where, I wondered, was the heavy wolfish shadow of Miranda? Where the shadow of the woman who should have been clutching her chest and wheezing out there in the middle of that field of enchanted snow?

"I don't see anyone," I said. "Are you sure you've got the right person?"

"You're supposed to meet her in the cemetery. Lucky you."

I nodded. "But it looks so far."

"Don't be silly," smiling up at me, shining her curls and eyes and earrings up at me through the snow, "it isn't far. So good-by for now."

"All right then," I said. I dropped her hand, licked my chapped lips, tried and failed to imitate the bright promise of her young voice. "Good-by for now."

Then I put down my head and started across the lot—six feet and two hundred pounds of expectant and fearless snowshoe rabbit—and wondered how many couples there were in the cars and whether or not I would dare to ask Bubbles for a kiss. I wondered too what Miranda could possibly be doing in the cemetery. And at that moment I had a vision of Miranda leaning against a lichen-covered monument in her old moth-eaten fur coat and signaling me with Jomo's flashlight, and I hurried, took large determined strides through the trackless snow.

But I stopped. Listened. Because the air seemed to be filled with low-flying invisible birds. Large or small I could not tell, but fast, fast and out of their senses, skimming past me from every direction on terrified steel wings and silent except for the unaccountable sharp noise of the flight itself. One dove into the snow at my feet—nothing but a sudden hole in the snow— and I stepped back from it, raised my hands against the un-predictable approach, the irregular sound of motion, the blind but somehow deliberate line of attack. Escaped homing pigeons? A covey of tiny ducks driven berserk in the cold? Eaglets? I found myself beating the air, attempting to shield my eyes and ears, thought I saw a little drop of blood on the snow. And I was relieved with the first hit. It caught me just behind the ear—crunching shock at the base of the head—and still it might have been the ice-encrusted body of a small bird, except that despite the pain, the vigorous crack of the thing and my loss of breath, and even while I reached behind my ear and discovered my fingers covered with ice and blood, I was turning around, stooping, trying and of course failing to find the body. With the second hit—quite furious, close on the first, snowball full in the face—my relief was complete and I knew that this time at least I had nothing to fear from any unnatural vengefulness of wild birds.

Tremlow, I thought, when the hard-packed snowball of the second hit burst in my face, Tremlow, thinking that only Tremlow's malice—it was black and putty-thick, a curd incomprehensibly coughed up just for me—could account for the singular intensity of this treachery intended to befall me in the parking lot, could account for the raging meanness behind this ambush. I stood my ground, spitting snow, shaking the snow out of my eyes, dragging the snow away with my two hands and feeling the sudden purple abrasions on my cheeks, trying to dodge. Not a shadow, not a curved arm, not a single one of them in sight. But the barrage was slowing, though losing none of its power, none of its accuracy, and I could see the snowballs now and they were winging at me from all angles, every direction. I swung at them, growled at them, helpless and wet and bleeding, and still they came. The third hit—blow in the side, sound of a thump, no breath—sailed up at me slowly, slowly, loomed like a white cabbage and struck me exactly as I tried to step out of its path. Tracer bullet confusion of snowballs. Malevolent missiles. From every corner of the lot they came, and from the vicinity of the all-but-hidden cars—lovers? could this be the activity of island lovers? nothing better to do?—and even, I thought, from as far as the cemetery.

I fought back. Oh, I fought back, scooping the snow wildly, snarling, beating and compressing that snow into white iron balls and flinging them, heaving them off into the flurry, the thick of the night, but I could find no enemy and it was a hopeless sweat. "Tremlow!" I shouted, raising my head though I felt in tingling scalp and quivering chin the unprotected condition of that bald head as target, "Tremlow! Come out and fight!" A hoarse shout. Unmistakable cry of rage addressed to the phantom bully, the ringleader of my distant past. Perhaps from somewhere, from some dark corner of the world, he heard.

Because it ceased. I saw no one, heard no human sound, no laughter, and the last of the discharged snowballs fell about me in a heavy but harmless patter like the last great duds of a spent avalanche. Final lobbing to earth of useless snowballs. Irregular thudding in the snow. Then safe. Then silence. Only the gentle puffing fall of the now tiny flakes, only the far-off wind, only the muffled sound of Jack Spratt's Merry Hep Cats commencing once again in my ears. Only the yellow light on the snow. And of course the blood and snot on the back of my hand.

I waited. And slowly I controlled my temper and my pain, controlled my breathing, brushed the palm of my hand over my scalp and regained my usual composure. I was wet and chilled, but I smiled when I saw what an enormous ring I had trampled all about me in the snow. The great stag that had been at bay was no longer at bay. Tremlow, if he had ever been there, was gone. As I walked slowly back along the deep path I had cut from the fire door to the center of the parking lot I forgot about the demon of my past and began to muse about that enemy of the present who was, I knew, only too real. How was it possible, I wondered, for a man to throw snowballs with an artificial hand?

But it was my night of trials and when I returned to the gymnasium, blinking, wiping face and hands with my handkerchief, trying to reset the sparkle in my watering eyes, I saw the two of them at once—Jomo, Cassandra—saw that the hook was buried deep in the bow, that the two of them were dipping together to the strains of a waltz—Jomo leading off with a long leg thrust between her legs—and that Jomo was panting and that his trousers were sopping wet up to the knees. Poor Cassandra like a green leaf was turning, floating, waltzing away out of my life, a green leaf on the back of the spider. My teen-age bomb and her boy friend. And I might have charged him then and there, might have struck him down when two little white roly-poly women cut me short, caught my arms, hung a numbered placard around my neck, pushed me forward like little tugs—dirt in the girdles, dough in the dimples, mother's milk to spare—and the music stopped, girls giggled, someone stood on a Coca-Cola crate and shouted: "Take your places, belly-bumpers! Gather about now, folks, for the contest!"

And another voice: "Make them take off their belts, hey, Doc! Buckles ain't fair!"

And the first: "Ladies, pick your bumpers . . . bumpers in place . . . come on now, fellows, we got to start!"

Laughter. Calls of encouragement. Eight pairs of bumpers—including me—to fight it out pair by pair. Then a circle in the crowd, silence, boy with the bass drum and boy with the cornet standing there to beat and blow for each winner. And I who had always considered myself quite trim, heavy but rather handsome of form, holding up my trousers, perspiring now, I was called upon to make sport of myself, to join in the fleshly malice of this island game. Perverse. The death of modesty. But I could not refuse, could not explain that there was some mistake—rising to the catcalls in that human ring—could do nothing but accept the challenge and bump with the best of them and give them the full brunt of belly, if belly they wanted. I noticed that the old-timers were drinking down last minute pitchers of water so that they would rumble. But I was not intimidated. I would show them a thing or two with my stomach which all at once felt like a warhead. *Allons*. . . .

The fat began to fly. It was an obscene tournament. And if I had lost the night even before my abortive journey to the parking lot, or if I had begun to suffer the hour that would never pass when I first set foot in Jomo's car, or if I had tasted the thick endlessness of the night with my first hurried mouthful of chocolate cake, knowing that I was sealed more and more tightly into some sort of desperate honeycomb of dead time with every drink the bare-headed marine took from his bottle—drinking to my frustration, drinking me dry—and if I had already begun my endless sweat at the mere sight of dancers dancing, what then was my dismay among the belly-bumpers? What then my injury—pain of bouncing bags, cramp of belligerence low in the gut—what then my confusion and drugged determination as I stood there facing the glazed eye of time? Dimly I heard Doc's voice, "Hey there, no hands!" And slowly, slowly, I forced myself to learn the stance with body sagging to the front, back bowed, shoulders drawn tightly to the rear, elbows pulled close to the ribs and sharply bent, hands limp, fingers limp, barely holding up the trousers, forced myself to balance on the balls of my feet, to balance, pull in the chin, thrust, sail forward and bump, shudder, recover. Without moving my feet. Dead time. Spirited dismay.

Sweat in the eyes, breathless. Partners face to face, hands set and loose and dangling like little fins, bellies an inch apart, two mean idiotic smiles. Ready. And then the signal, crowd pressing in to see, and then the swaying start, the first bump, the grunt, the rhythm of collision, and in and out, up and down, forward and backward with shirt tails working loose in front and the bottom of the belly popping out and visible and pink and sore, bump and shudder and recover—tempo steady but blows rising in strength—until the look of surprise, the tottering step, the blush of defeat, and Skipper wins again. Another blast on the cornet, more blows on the drum. Some clapping, my weak smile. Then off again, off on another round.

I vanquished the local butcher, came up against Red's cousin, fought on until I nearly met my match in Uncle Billy. Because he was last year's champion and wanted to win. Because bare as the day he was born he weighed four hundred and eight pounds on the fish factory scales. Because he was sixty-three years old and prime. Because he wore no underwear on bumping days and bumped with his shirt unbuttoned, bumped with his blackened gray cotton workshirt pulled out of his pants and hanging loose and flowing wide from neck to somewhere below the navel. Because he also wore rubber-soled shoes and, tied in little finger-like knots at the four corners, a red bandanna on his big bald head

—nigger neckerchief to frighten opponents and keep the sweat out of his eyes—and from a heavy chain locked around his throat a big gold bouncing crucifix. And because he whispered in constant violation of the rules, and because he rumbled. Uncle Billy who knew all the tricks. King of the fat.

Old volcano belly. Worse than a horse, louder than a horse. Rumbling, sloshing, bearing down, steering his terrible tumescence with the mere sides of his wrists and for a moment I saw their faces in the crowd—Miranda, Jomo, Red, Bub, Cassandra, all in a row, all smiling—and I thought I saw Cassandra wave, and then I was laboring to keep my balance, to hold my stride, while with every painful encounter I could feel that Uncle Billy hadn't even begun to exert himself and was only biding his time, waiting me out.

And the catcalls: "Come on, Uncle Billy, bust him open!"

And close to me and through his little hard teeth the constant whispering: ". . .never been on a woman. Never had a woman on me. No sir. . . . Always saved myself. For supper, that's my big meal, and for bumping. . . . I eat a full loaf of bread whenever I sit down to table. And I make a habit of drinking one full gallon can of sweetened corn syrup every day. . . . So you know what you're up against. The picture of health," nodding the nigger neckerchief, tossing his cross, patches of short white whisker beginning to shine on his fat cheeks, "because the Good Lord gave me so much flesh that little things like piles or stones or a cardiac condition don't mean a thing. . . . Never know they're there. . . . Now wait a minute," going up on his toes, eyes bright, shadow of a jawline appearing above his jowls, "don't you try to trick me, now. . . . You look out for Uncle Billy because I measure eighty-nine inches around the middle and I'm just letting you get winded before I bust you right open as the fella wants me to. . . ."

Then: "Your mother," I whispered as we hit, "you bumped bellies with your mother, did you?"

Socko. Straight to the heart. *Touché*. And in that lapsed moment, single faltering moment when he tried to determine the exact nature of the insult—smile swallowed up in a gulp, jaw

91

unhinged, blinding light, pain in the muck of his morality—I shifted my weight and gave him everything I had and hooked him, hit him hard and at a fine unsettling angle, managed to work a little hipbone into the blow, man to man, final and fiercest of the thwacking sounds, and his flesh was surrendering against mine even before he sagged, gasped, staggered back from me in defeat, even before I heard the asinine cacophony of drum, cornet, and crowd. I shut my eyes and felt as if at last I had struck the high gong of the carnival.

"No hard feelings," I said, and wiped my face on my sleeve.

"You win, Mister. But here," fumbling with the chain, holding out his hand, "do me a favor and take this as a gift from me. I got it when I beat the Reverend Peafowl at belly-bumping. But now you deserve it more than me."

So with the chain and crucifix in my pocket and a five-pound chocolate cake in a box under my arm I set off calling through the crowd for Cassandra. And of course she was gone. All of them were gone. I was alone, abandoned, left behind. Outside I stood for a long while looking down into the violent ragged hole the fleeing hot rod had torn in the snow, stood watching all their scuffed and hurried footprints now filling slowly, gently, with the first snowfall which was still coming down. The gymnasium lights went off and the trees, the building, the sky behind the snow were all a deep dark blue. There was nothing to do but walk, so I shrugged, put my hands in my pockets, put my head down and started my journey home. Alone.

Trying to hurry, trying to keep out of the deepest drifts, trying to hurry along for Cassandra's sake. There were little black shining twigs encased in icicles, and fence posts and sudden gates opening through the snow. And my wintry road was littered with the bodies of dead birds—I could see their little black glistening feet sticking up like hairs through the crusty tops of the snow banks—and far off where the snow was falling thickest I could hear the sloshing and breaking of the black wintry sea. No lights. No cars. Not even the howl of a dog. It was a late winter night on the black island and I was alone and cold and plowing my slow way home. Digging my way home with my wet feet. Gloomy, anxious, hearing the ice castles shattering in the branches overhead and falling in tiny bright splinters around my ears.

Then the house, the kennel, the sword points of the picket fence, the chestnut tree under full white sail. At last. And thinking of the foot warmer with its brass pan of bright hot coals and seeing the hot rod black and squat and once more covered with new snow, seeing that car and so knowing I was in time after all, I began to clap the snow from my arms and to run the last few steps to the creaking cold veranda where wrapped in a quilt on the frozen glider and smoking a cigarette Miranda sat huddled and waiting for me in the dark. Miranda. Woman in the dark. Wet eyelashes.

"You," I said with my hand already on the old brass knob, "what do you want?"

"Skip," throwing off the quilt, stretching her legs, pitching the cigarette over the broken rail, "don't go in, Skip. They're young. Let's leave them alone."

"Where were you?" I said, and paused, pulled the door shut again softly, faced her. "Do you know what happened to me in that parking lot? Do you? As for running off without me at the end, a pretty cruel trick, Miranda."

"Never mind, for God's sake. They're only kids. But let's go out to the car, Skip, and leave them alone."

"Car? You mean Jomo's car? I wouldn't set foot in his car, Miranda. And besides, I want to go to bed."

"My car, for God's sake. Out back," and her breathing was clear and full and I could see the single gray streak thick and livid in her hair and already she was going down the steps and wading knee-deep in the untrampled snow and I was following her. Against my will. Against my better judgment. Shivering. Watching her closely. Because she had changed her clothes and was wearing the canary yellow slacks that had turned the color of moonlight in the snow and a turtle-neck sweater and a baby-blue cashmere scarf that hung below her knees and dragged in the snow. And the little wet flakes twinkled all over her.

"No snowballs," I said. "I'm warning you."

93

She muttered something without turning her head and I missed it, let it go by. The snow was falling in fine little stars but I was too cold and wet to enjoy it. Once I glanced back over my shoulder at the house and though there was not a single light in a window I thought I saw the dark head and torso of someone watching me in a downstairs window—Grandma? Jomo? Bub? —but I could not be sure. Apparently the night was full of snares and sentries and I hesitated, wiping the fresh snow out of my eyes, and then I heard Miranda rattling at the wrecked car and I hurried on.

Tall weeds matted deep in the snow. Crystals as big as saucers tucked in the eaves of the rotting shed. Outline of an old wheel-barrow. And canted up slightly on one side next to the shed the smashed and abandoned body of the wrecked hot rod—orange, white, blue in the soft cold light of the snow—and in that dark and gutted and somehow echoing interior Miranda with one white naked hand on the wheel. Dense shadow of woman. Queen of the Nile.

"Hop in," she said, and I heard her patting the mildewed seat, heard her ramming the clutch pedal in and out impatiently.

I tugged, stopped, stuck my head in, looked around—pockets of rust, flakes of rust, pockets of snow, broken glass on the floor —and slid onto the seat beside her. And the glass crackled sharply, the springs were steel traps in the seat, the gearshift lever—little white plastic skull for a knob—rose up like a whip from its socket, the dashboard was a nest of dead wires and smashed or dislocated dials. There was a cold rank acrid odor in that wrecked car as if the cut-down body had been burned out one night with a blowtorch, acrid pungent odor that only heightened the other smells of the night: rotting shed, faint sour smell of wood smoke, salt from the nearby sea, perfume— *Evening in Paris*—which Miranda had splashed on her wrists, her throat, her thick dark head of hair. A powdery snow was blowing against us—no glass in the windows, no windshield—and scratching on the roof of that dreadful little car, and I felt sick at last and wanted only to put my head between my knees, to cover my bare head with my arms and sleep. But I pushed the gearshift lever with the toe of my shoe instead, glanced at Miranda.

"Like it? Bub's going to fix it up for me in the spring. It only needs a couple of new tires."

"Your lipstick's crooked," I said, and sniffed, stared at her, ran my fingers along the clammy seat.

"Yours would be crooked too, for God's sake. But you can thank Red for that." She smiled, close to me, and the lines in her broad white face were drawn with a little sable brush and India ink and the mouth was a big black broken flower still smeared, still swollen, I knew, from the Captain's teeth. "Need I say more?" she said, and snapped out the clutch, picked up the fuzzy end of the baby-blue cashmere scarf and rubbed it against her cheek.

"That's all right, Miranda. I don't care anything about your private life. Shouldn't we be going back to the house?"

"We just got here, for God's sake. Relax. You're just like Don, never sit still a minute. But of course Don was love."

Silence. Hand pulling up and down aimlessly on the steering wheel. Snow falling. Snow singing on the roof. Then a movement in her corner, sudden rolling agitation in the springs, and her tight yellow statuesque leg was closer to mine and she was reaching out, pressing the cashmere scarf against my cheek.

And quickly: "What about Cassandra?" I said. "She won't do anything foolish?"

Another drag of the rump, leg another few inches closer, and she leaned over then—slowly, slowly—and with long moody deliberation removed the tip of the scarf from my cheek and wrapped it twice around my throat and fastened it in a single knot with one tight sudden jerk. Too vehement I thought. But tied together neck to neck. Hitched. And feeling the cashmere choking me, and seeing the head thrown back against the mildewed seat and the long leg bent at the knee and the angora sweater white and curdled all the way through—solid, not a bone to interrupt that mass, no garment to destroy the rise of the greater-than-life-size breasts—at last I felt like a sculptor in the presence of his nubile clay—to hold the twin mounts, Oh

95

God, to cast the thighs—and quickly I flung my right hand out of the wrecked car window, heard something rip.

"Cassandra? Cassandra?" she said, showing me the deep black formless mouth, the hair on the back of the seat: "Like mother, like daughter, isn't that about it? You and your poor little Candy Cane," she said, and she was laughing—low mellow mannish laugh, scorn and intimacy and self-confidence—and with one foot resting on the dashboard and the other hooked to the edge of the seat she rolled up the bottom of the sweater and took the heavy canary yellow cloth in both bony hands and, tensing all her muscles, pulled down the slacks and swung herself up and away on one cold and massive hip. Away from me. Face and hands and eyes away from me. Laughing.

Icebergs. Cold white monumental buttocks. Baffling cold exposure. Classical post card from an old museum. Treachery on the Nile. Desire and disaster. Pitiless. A soft breath of snow swirling in that white saddle, settling in the dark curves and planes and along the broad rings of the spine. And laughing, shaking the car, muffling her deep low voice in her empty arms she said: "Red's sleeping it off right now. So how about you?"

Drunk? Out of her mind with passion? Or spiteful? Who could tell? But in the rusty disreputable interior of that frozen junk heap she had mocked me with the beauty of her naked stern, had challenged, aroused, offended me with the blank wall of nudity, and I perceived a cruel motive somewhere. So I clawed at the scarf, tore loose the scarf, and supporting myself palm-down on her icy haunch for one insufferably glorious instant I gathered my weight, rammed my shoulder against the loud tinny metal of the rusted door—no handle, door stuck shut —and kicked myself free of her, kicked my way out of the car and fled. Burning. Blinded. But applauding myself for the escape.

When I reached the front of the house I realized that the snow had stopped and that the slick black hot rod under the chestnut tree was gone. When I reached Cassandra's room, puffing through the darkness, feeling my way, I knew immediately that she was not asleep, and without pausing I dropped to my knees beside her and took her cold hand—no rings—and confessed to her at long last that Fernandez was dead. That I had found him dead at the end of my final shore patrol on Second Avenue. That I thought she should know. Pixie stirred from time to time but did not wake. Then at the doorway I stopped and glanced back at the rumpled chunky four-poster bed, the black shadow of the cradle on the warped floor, the windowpane covered with snow.

And softly: "We were wrong about him, weren't we? Just a little? I think so, Cassandra."

In my own room I discovered Uncle Billy's crucifix in my pocket and pulled it out, held it in the palm of my hand and stared at it, then hung it around the neck of my white tunic on the dressmaker's dummy. Gold was my color. Another medal for Papa Cue Ball. Someone—Miranda? Red? Jomo? Bub? even Grandma was not above suspicion—had filled the foot warmer with water, and it was frozen solid. I frowned, set it carefully outside my door—blue tit—and inched myself into the cold comfort of that poor iron bed with bars.

Sleep with a gentle thought, I remembered, and did my best.

Vile, in the Sunshine Crawling

Yes, I have always believed in gentle thoughts. Despite everything, including the long-past calumnious efforts of a few cranks
in the Navy Department, I have always remained my mother's
son. And how satisfying it is that virtue—tender guardian, sweet
victor, white phantom of the boxing ring, which makes me
think of the days before the mutiny when Tremlow vainly attempted to give me boxing lessons every late afternoon in a
space cleared among the young bronze cheering sailors on the
fantail—how satisfying that virtue always wins. I have only to
consider Sonny and Catalina Kate and Sister Josie and myself to
know that virtue is everywhere and that we, at least, are four
particles of its golden dust.

Yes, everywhere. In getting down to business with one of
the cows, in blowing the conch that calls the cows across the
field to me, in noticing from time to time the remarkably rapid
growth of the child, another fleck of golden dust inside Catalina
Kate, in splitting a pawpaw with Sonny or spending an hour or
two over the year-old newspaper Catalina Kate had wrapped
the hot dogs in, or calling out "No beat the puppy!" to the small
black bowlegged boy who wallops the little pink squealing bitch

every afternoon between the overgrown water wheel and our collapsing barn, in all this, then, the virtue of life itself.

In the very act of living I see myself, picture myself, as if memory had already done its work and flowered, subjected even myself to the golden glass. Broad white window frame, white shutter with all but a few slanting lattices knocked out, long mahogany table, cane chairs, rusted hurricane lamp suspended by a chain from the ceiling that rises to a peak, pagoda style, and houses the bats; gray clay-colored wooden floor, hemp hammock filled with red petals, odor of slaves and curry and wine and hibiscus soft and luxurious on the dark air. Cup of the warm south. Beaded bubbles. And myself: drawn up to the table, studious, smiling at the thought of the little dark faces pressed into the enormous green and yellow leaves curling in at the window, frowning and smiling both with my upper body leaning on the table and my feet bare and my toes playing in the rich dust under the table, eyes and mouth burning slightly with the fever of our constant and deceptive temperature. Myself. Lunged quietly against my long table—bottle of French wine, bottle of local rum, handful of long thin unbanded black cigars stuck like pencils in a jam jar, swarms of little living fleas in the grooves of my note-taking paper—lunged at the table and seeing myself and smiling at the thought of yesterday, yesterday when I sat in the swamp with Sister Josie and Catalina Kate, and ruminating over the latest development of Kate's precious pregnancy—Kate has only about three more months to go, it occurs to me—and teasing the fleas.

And so I have already stepped once more from behind the scenes of my naked history and having come this far I expect that I will never really be able to conceal myself completely in all those scenes which are even now on the tip of my tongue and crowding my eye. The fact of the matter is that Miranda will have to wait while I turn to a still more distant past, turn back to a few of my long days at sea and to several other high lights of my more distant past. Mere victory over Miranda is nothing, while virtue is everything. So now for my past, for the virtue of my far-distant past.

But first my afternoon in the swamp.

God knows what time it was, but we had finished eating our noon meal of the sea creatures Big Bertha somehow digs out of the conchs, and Sonny was sleeping out in the barn and I was sitting at my table and toying with—yes, even after seven years I still wear it around my neck on its thin chain—toying with Uncle Billy's crucifix and thinking about certain problems of my profession. I was noticing that the insides of my hands were the color of golden straw, and was listening to the doves when suddenly a face appeared among the flat green and yellow leaves and spotted shadows outside my window, a tiny face as smooth as a wet kidney and the color of the black keys on a piano. Tiny little face without a line, with eyes like great timid pearls and a little nut-brown mouth and masses of artificial gold teeth—young as she was she had had all her teeth extracted and nice gold teeth installed for beauty's sake—and around the little black head the truly gigantic mauve headpiece of her official habit and the white thing that looked like a priest's collar shoved vertically over her tiny face. Serene, serious, silent.

"Sister Josie," I said, "is it really you? How nice. But Sister Josie, what do you want?"

Somber child. Dark wonderfully cowled little head in the corner of the window. Little black cheekbones. Pearls beginning to dissolve and more luminous and gentle than ever. Ready to open her mouth, this child, this black girl, thin devoted example of missionary madness. Sweating. Hot as the devil. Long time to answer. And then she smiled and in a murmur she asked me to come with her because Catalina Kate was asking for me and had sent her, Sister Josie, up to Plantation House to persuade me, if she could, to join her in a little walk down to the swamp.

"Well, of course, Josie," I said, and reached for my old yellowing cap and cocked it on my head, "I was wondering about Kate since you usually dog her tracks, don't you, Josie?"

Vigorous nodding in the corner of the window. Trembling of the little dark features. Master coming. Gift of God. Ecstasy. As usual I was pleased with her happiness and smiled and told her to wait for me by the water wheel. I extended my hand slowly, gently, and let it come to rest on the broad white sill so that it was directly in the path of a little black newborn lizard which I had noticed while listening to Sister Josie's soft interminable plea. And for a moment we watched the baby lizard together. It was black, fuzzy, about an inch and a half in length. It was covered with frills and tendrils, wore leggings, had absurdly large feet for its size and an absurdly large blind head. Ugly. And while we watched—did Josie make the sign of the cross? —the baby lizard crawled onto the back of my hand and stopped, little tail twitching at a wonderful rate, and stood still as I lifted him slowly into the warm sweet air that hovered between Sister Josie and myself. Lifted him up to my nose.

"Do you see, Josie? He hasn't any eyes. And look at that tail, will you? Excruciating!"

We laughed. Then I took a deep breath, puckered my lips and blew so that he sailed off in an orgy of somersaults and plopped onto a bright golden spot next to Josie's cheeks.

"I'll have to improve my aim, Josie," I said, and, laughing, shooed her off to the water wheel. No doubt the little lizard would turn into a dandy big fellow when he grew older. But I have always favored the birds, especially the hummingbirds, over the lizards and butterflies. Give me the mystery of birds or the strength and sweetness of honest-to-God animals like cows any time. What better than the little honeysuckers or the leather hides and masticated grass and purple eyes of my favorite cows? As for a blackbird sitting on a cow's rump, there surely is the perfect union, the meeting of the fabulous herald and the life source. And there are always the ground doves to give voice to my vision, soul to my love.

Since I was up and about I looked in on Big Bertha—mass of black fat, calico rags, old brazen face and dusty hands and fat breasts decorated with the fingerprints of the babies she had nursed, all of her crouched over the mortar and pestle and fast asleep—and I grinned at her, raised my finger to the visor of my cap in salute to her. I strolled around to feed a few fistfuls of green grass to the ducks, squatting, pulling up the grass, enjoying the greed of the ducks and the way they wagged their white tails. Then to my feet again and on through the shadows of the lime trees—perfect little pale yellow globules dangling amidst the riffling green leaves and shadows and nearly invisible thorns—until I came out into the sun and approached the barn.

I stood in the doorway, crossed my legs, leaned against the hot porous upright—remarkable labor of the wood ants—thrust my hands into my pockets and stared up at the star-shaped hole in the roof. Interesting star-shaped hole with a shaft of sunlight driven through it like a stake. Dry and sagging timbers, roof that would soon collapse and be no more. Sonny—my ingenious Sonny—wanted to remove some of the planks from the walls to repair the roof. But I preferred the barn as it was, or as it would be. We would just have to get along, I told Sonny, with a roofless barn, and I was pleased when he slapped his thigh and said, "Oh, you means a roofless barn. I understands you, Skipper. That's good!" I knew I could always count on Sonny.

I walked into the barn then and stood at the foot of Sonny's hammock and smiled down on him. Poor Sonny. Sleeping in the heat of the afternoon. Hands clasped behind his head, light streaming in the little rivers between his ribs, hammock swaying, one long black shrunken leg dangling out of the hammock, hanging down. He was naked except for a pair of combat boots—no laces, leather turned to white fungus—and a pair of my castoff white jockey shorts and a sailor hat with the brim reversed and airslits, diamonds, cut around the crown. And he had changed in seven years—thinner, a few white kinks in the hair, some of the rich oily luster gone from his black skin, incurable case of boils on one of his thighs—but was Sonny, still Sonny with every black bone showing and a smile sleeping on those living lips which looked as if they had been split open in a fight. The nearby shaft of sunlight cast a glow on the patched hemp of the hammock and sent little shadows dancing and shivering up and down this black length of Sonny in his stretched and swaying bed. I left him in peace, walked softly to the other end of the barn where Oscar the bull was watching us.

"What's the matter, Oscar," I said, "jealous of my attentions?"

Confusion and hatred in the crossed bloodshot eyes. Dust

swirling out of the shaggy white head of hair when I rumpled it. Flies in the ears. Mean old bull begrudging every invisible drop of his scattered seed. Flies, lice, mud. But marvelous shaggy machinery for my purposes.

"Don't be jealous, Oscar," I said softly, "your time will come." And I laughed and gave the brass ring in his nose a little tug and turned my back on him, walked out to the hot radiance beyond the doorway. I paused for a moment, squinted, fanned myself briefly with my cap, then made for the water wheel.

She was nearly invisible against the water wheel, my little blessed chameleon with bowed head and folded hands. But she was there and waiting. Patient and perspiring in the shade of the wheel. Each time I saw the water wheel, and I saw it a good many times each day, I stopped, always perplexed and startled to see its life-giving gloom. Because it was about twenty feet tall, this fusion of iron wheel and fragment of stone wall, and useless, absolutely useless, and inexplicable, statuary of unknown historic significance now drenched with green growth, robbed of its power. The wheel that could never turn, the wall that had ceased its crumbling. No water. And yet in every cracked iron cup, in every dark green furry ribbon of the climbing plants, in every black hanging leaf and every swaddling vine—there was even a little crooked gray tree growing out of the side of it—it appeared to be spongy and dense and saturated, seemed to drip with all the waters of the past and all the bright cold waters that would never flow. Monolith of forgotten industry, what on earth had it crushed? What sweetness extracted? The birds were singing and chirping among the red berries and in secret crevices in the moss. I listened until I could disregard no longer the little nun standing there meekly under the towering wheel.

"Well, Josie," I said, and stepped forward briskly, "Let's go and see what this is all about. OK, Josie?"

She told me that she was ready to go, though her little silk voice was so soft I could hardly hear it above the sound of the birds, and she told me that Miss Catalina Kate was hoping I would go to her. I smiled.

"Lead on, Sister Josie," I said, and sauntered along behind her as she picked her way down the hot path trying to avoid the thorns in the high grass. The wind was rolling about in that high grass—stretching out to sleep? getting ready to spring?—and there were trees growing out of trees, smooth gray trunks and bushy heads of hair, flowers like painted fingernails and occasionally underfoot a sudden webbing of little roots tied in knots. But Sister Josie had nimble feet and knew where she was going.

"Do I smell guavas, Josie?"

Vigorous nodding.

"Why don't you pick a load on our way back, Josie? I'm very fond of guavas."

More nodding, long soft statement of acquiescence.

When we passed the pile of dried conchs and stepped out onto the beach the bush was on our right and the sea on our left and the bush was impenetrable and the beach was a quarter-mile strip of snowy pink sand and the tide was sliding in, frothing, jumping up in little round waves. So there was much wetting of shoes and trouser bottoms and swaying skirts during that last quarter mile of our walk. Above us through the dead coconut leaves the sun was an old bloody bone low in the sky. I whistled, hummed, blinked, licked salt. Paused to help Sister Josie climb over the windfalls or crawl through the sea grape trees.

"Lovely spot, Josie," I said. "Good for the soul."

"Oh yes, sir." Furnace of gold teeth, habit soaked to the knees. "That why she here, sir."

"But surely she doesn't mean to have the child out here, Josie? Does she?"

"Oh, yes, sir. She want the baby in the swamp, sir."

"Well, there's courage for you, Josie."

"Yes, sir."

And then the bush fell away on our right and the beach swept wide into the sea on our left and rose, straight ahead, into a long white sandy shelf, and Sister Josie and I were in the open and pulling each other to the top of the broad sandy shelf. A fisherman's hut, a white stump, the green transparent tint of the endless sea on one side and on the other, where the shelf dipped down into a little rank stagnant crescent, the swamp. The beginning of the swamp. Dark green tepid sludge of silent waters drifting inland among the ferns and roots and fuzzy pockets and pools of the infested swamp. Harem of veiled orchids, cells of death.

"You see, Josie," smiling, raising my hand, gesturing, feeling the ocean breeze on my neck and smelling the lively activity of the fields of sunken offal in the swamp, breathing deeply and seeing how the pale blue-green light of the ocean met the dark greens and heavy yellows of the swamp, "you see, Josie, a true freak of nature. Wonderful, isn't it? And that fisherman's hut, who knows what's been going on in that fisherman's hut, eh, Josie? How about it now, a few small sacrifices to the gods?"

And head lowered, eyes lowered, voice soft and serious: "Sometimes she sleep there, sir."

The ants were racing through the holes in my tennis shoes and the tide was a rhythmic darkening of the sand and something was beating great frightened wings in the swamp. There were bright yellow turds hanging from a soft gray bough over the hut, and I began to scratch. But then I looked down and saw what I had somehow failed to see in my first sweeping glance at the warmer side of the sand shelf and beginning of the swamp. And I took slow incredulous footsteps down that sandy incline, leaned forward, held out my hands.

"Kate. Are you all right, Kate?"

She was lying there and watching me. Must have been watching me all the time. Lying there on her stomach. Chin in her hands. Naked. Legs immersed halfway up the calves in the warm yellowish pea soup of that disgusting water. And stuck to her back, spread eagle on her broad soft naked back, an iguana with his claws dug in.

"Kate, what is it, Kate. . . ."

But she only smiled. I stopped, hand thrust out, and kneeled on one knee in front of Catalina Kate who had the terrible reptile clinging to her back. His head reached her shoulders, his tail dropped over her buttocks, and he might have been twenty or thirty pounds of sprawling bright green putty. Boneless. Eyes like shots in the dark. Gorgeous bright green feathery ruff running down the whole length of him. Thick and limp and weak, except for the oversized claws which were grips of steel. Kate was looking at me and smiling and the iguana was looking at me, and I heard the noise of locust or cricket or giant swamp fly strangling behind a nearby bush.

"Hold on, Kate," I whispered, "don't move. Just leave him to me."

So then I rose carefully from my position on one knee and tried to think of what to do, of how to go about it. There at my feet was Kate, and she was stretched out flat on the sand, had dug a nice deep oval hole for her belly, and her naked skin was soft and broad, mauve and tan, and the shadows all over her arms and calves and flanks were like innumerable little bright pointed leaves. At one end of her the scum from the swamp water lay in fluffy white piles against her calves; at the other her black hair was heaped up in a crown, shaped in oil, and the long thick braid hung down over one shoulder into the sand. A child with real pink sea shells for ears, child with a disappointing nose but with lips as thin as my own and bowed, moist, faintly violet and smiling. A dark mole—beauty mole—on one cheek. Body as big as Big Bertha's. A garden, but shaped by her youth. There at my feet. Kate.

And on her back the monster.

So I straddled her—colossus over the reptile, colossus above the shores of woman—and hearing the lap and shifting of the sea, and wiping my palms on my thighs and leaning forward, I prepared to grapple with the monster. My eyes were already shut and my hands already feeling downwards, groping, when Josie, little Sister Josie, took courage—for her it must have been courage—and called out to me.

"Oh, no, sir. No, sir. Don't touch iguana, sir. Him stuck for so!"

She had risen from her seat on the stump in front of the fisherman's hut, wringing her hands, squeezing her ankles together beneath her skirts, doll in the sunshine, straight and small, but sat down again quickly as soon as I glanced at her. Little black face, pained eyes, ankles and knees and hands all rigid and pinched together, unbearable hot weight of cowl and little buttoned shoes and God knows how many skirts. I was in no mood to take advice from Sister Josie and told her so.

"That's all right, Josie," I said. "I'll handle this."

From inside the rich brown layers of drapery or from one of her sleeves she produced a tiny Bible and licked a finger, began to read. She looked like a little black beetle hunched up and reading the Bible in the sunlight. The forked tongues were crying out in the swamp. I shook my head. And lunged down for the iguana.

I got him with the first grab. Held him. Waited. And with my feet buried deep in the sand, my legs spread wide and locked, my rump in the air, tattered shirt stuck to my skin like a plaster, nostrils stoppered up with the scum of the swamp, heart thumping, I made myself hold on to him—in either hand I gripped one of the forelegs—and fought to subdue the repellent touch of him, fought not to tear away my hands and run. Cool rubber ready to sting. Feeling of being glued to the iguana, of skin growing fast to reptilian skin.

"Now," I said through clenched teeth, and opened my eyes, "now we'll see if you're any match for Papa Cue Ball." And slowly I pulled up on him, gently began to wrestle with him. He yielded his putty, stretched himself, displayed a terrible elasticity, and everything rose up to my grasp except the claws.

"It's just like being in the dentist's chair, Kate," I muttered, and grinned through my own agony, "it'll be over soon." But Catalina Kate gave no sign of pain, though now her head was resting on her folded arms and her eyes were closed. So I kept pulling up on the iguana, tugged at him with irritation now. With every tug I seemed to dig the claws in deeper, to drag them down deeper into the flesh of poor Kate's back in some terrible inverse proportion to all the upward force I exerted on the flaccid wrinkled substance of the jointless legs or whatever it was I hung on to so desperately. And he wouldn't budge. Because of those claws I was unable to pull him loose, unable to

107

move him an inch, was only standing there bent double and sweating, pulling, muttering to myself, drawing blood.

"Well, Kate," I said, and let go, stood up, wiped my brow, "it looks as if he's there for good. Got us licked, hasn't he, Kate? Licked from the start. He means to stay right where he is until he changes his mind and crawls off under his own power. So the round goes to the dragon, Kate. I'm sorry."

I climbed off, dipped my hands in the scummy water—even scummy water was preferable to the iguana—rubbed them, wiped them on my trousers, mounted the slope, flung myself down in the sand beside Sister Josie. And grimacing, pulling the visor down fiercely over my eyes, "There's nothing to do but wait," I said. "We'll have to be patient."

"She plenty patient already, sir. She already waiting."

"That's right, Josie," I said, "you young ladies better stick together."

Sister Josie read her Bible, I twirled Uncle Billy's crucifix on its gold chain until the sun came down. And we waited. Coconuts knocking together, sun drenching the sand, dry bones scraping in the middle of the swamp, peacock tails of ugly plants fanning and blazing around the edge of the swamp, a little pall of late afternoon heat settling over us. Like Sonny and Big Bertha and the rest of them I must have dozed. Because suddenly I was leaning forward to the stillness of the warm south and trembling, giving the nun a signal on her little knee.

"Do you see, Josie? Do you see? The iguana moved!"

It was true. He had unhooked his claws and slid down onto Kate's right hand and deep rosy shoulder and upper arm, and now his ruff was humming, his tongue flexing in swordplay, swishing in all the tiny hues of the rainbow, and the eyes were dashing together like little sparks.

"He's hungry! Do you see that, Josie? He's hungry now, he's going off to hunt flies! Thank God for Kate. . . ."

So he plopped from her shoulder and waddled down to the scum, this bright aged thing livid in the last thick rays of the sun, and inch by steady inch pushed himself under the lip of a broad low-hanging yellow leaf and into the scum, and lashing his tail, kicking suddenly with his stubby rear legs, he disappeared. Succubus. I would have gone after him with a stone had it not been for the failing light and for Catalina Kate who had raised herself up on her arms and was smiling and beckoning and opening to me like some downy swamp orchid.

I ran to her and sank down next to her, panting, brushing the sand from her breasts.

"Well done, Kate!" I whispered, "well done, my brown Joan of Arc. You know about Joan of Arc, don't you, Kate? The lady burned up in the fire?"

Smiling. But a gentle smile and only faintly visible. A color in the face. Touch of serenity about the eyes and at the corners of the mouth. Nothing but the radiance of the fifteen or sixteen years of her life on this our distant shore, our wandering island.

I took her hand. I covered her back with the remnants of my own dissolving shirt and I reached down into the enormous egg-shaped hole in the sand and helped Kate to feel with her soft young fingers what I could feel with mine: the warmth of the recent flesh and the little humped hieroglyphic in the warm sand.

"Feel the baby, Kate? Unborn baby down there in the sand, eh, Kate? But no more iguanas, you must promise me that. We don't want to let the iguana get the baby, you know."

She nodded. Kate understood. And that's all there was to it. I helped her to her feet and arm in arm we climbed the little velvet slope of sand together and walked up to Sister Josie—another sign of the cross, big gold flash of teeth—who rose, held out her arms and embraced my own nude Catalina Kate. That's all there was to it. Except walking back alone to Plantation House in our moment of darkness, brushing aside the leaves and thorns and stumbling knee-deep in the salty foam, I saw the few lights and long black silhouette of a ship at sea and smiled to myself since apparently our wandering island has become quite invisible. Only a mirage of shimmering water to all the ships at sea, only the thick black spice of night and the irregular whispering of an invisible shore.

So now I sit staring at the long black cigars and at the bottle of French wine. Perhaps I will open the French wine when the child is born, drink off the French wine when the child is born on the Night of All Saints. And now I goad myself with the distant past.

So hold your horses, Miranda! Father and Gertrude and Fernandez, sleep! Now take warning, Tremlow!

Wax in the Lilies

"We can sell the tires along the way if we have to, Papa Cue Ball," said Fernandez, as in pairs we rolled them—white walls, retreads, dusty black tires as smooth as balloons—from his little improvised garage to his old disreputable forest green sedan. "Besides, I couldn't leave them behind. They might be stolen. Nobody's honest these days, Papa Cue Ball. The war makes everybody steal."

"You know best, Fernandez," I said. "But there isn't room for all these tires. And what will your bride think of setting off on her honeymoon in a car loaded up to the hilt with black market tires? Not very *sympathique*, Fernandez?"

"Look, Papa Cue Ball, look here," letting two fat ones roll to a stop against a fender, and then leaping into the car, leaping back into the dust again, "I throw out the seat—so—I throw out all this ugly stuff from the trunk compartment—what would anyone be doing with all these rags—and we have plenty of room for the tires. As to your second objection," stooping to the nearest tire, glaring up at me darkly—I hastened to give him a hand—and speaking slowly and in the most severe of his Peruvian accents, "it will be a very short honeymoon, Papa Cue Ball, I assure you. A very short honeymoon."

I smiled. In the long summer twilight of the trailer camp—soft magenta light through temporary telephone poles and brittle trees, distant sound of schoolboys counting off like soldiers, sound of tropical birds caged up behind a neighbor's salmon-colored mobile home—and with his little shoulders square and hard under the white shirt, and his trousers, little tight pleated trousers, hitched as high as the second or third rib, and wearing the white linen shirt and crimson braces and the rattlesnake belt and tiny black pointed boots, surely Fernandez looked like a miniature Rudolph Valentino—eyes of the lonely lover, moistened lips—and I could only admire him and smile.

"Short but passionate, Fernandez?" I said then, and laughed.

"Don't try to be indelicate with me, Papa Cue Ball. Please."

"You misunderstand me, Fernandez," I said, and paused, frowned, extended my hand. "Since you have married my daughter I thought I could speak to you—well—frankly, and also joyously."

"OK, OK, good Papa Cue Ball. Let's forget it."

"Just as you say, Fernandez," I said, and reached out, took his small cool hand in mine, shook hands with him. "I share your happiness, Fernandez, I want you to know that," I said, and for a moment I leaned against the old waiting automobile and my head was light and my mouth was dry and tart and bubbling with the lingering dry aroma and lingering taste of the warm champagne. Because I had considered champagne indispensable. And I had supplied the champagne, carried it to the City Hall in a paper bag, and after the service and in the dim institutional corridor between the City Clerk's office and a Navy recruiting office we three had sipped our warm champagne straight from the bottle. I had counted on paper cups, but as luck would have it, the water cooler was dry and filled with dust and there was not one paper cup to be found in the holder. Toward the end of the bottle, when there were only a few drops of our celebrative wine remaining, I kissed the bride, there in the dark corridor of the City Hall. And now I remembered the kiss, the champagne, the City Clerk with dirty fingernails, and I wanted only to please Fernandez, to please Cassandra, to make the day end well.

So I did my share of the work and together we rolled the last of the unruly bouncing tires out to the waiting Packard and stowed them aboard. The chickens, little red bantams, and little white frightened hens, were cackling in the makeshift garage and squawking in sudden alarm, and I was tempted to toss them my remaining left-hand pocketful of confetti—yes, I had thrown my fiery flakes of confetti at Cassandra on the hot sidewalk in front of the red brick City Hall—but Fernandez had told me that the chickens were good layers and I thought better of it, left the confetti in the pocket where it was. Instead I stooped and clucked at the chickens, tried to nuzzle a little white stately hen under my arm. But it was a suspicious bedraggled bird and much too quick for me.

"The car needs some water, good Papa Cue Ball," Fernandez called from the steps of his stubby one-man aluminum trailer—it sat on blocks like a little bright bullet in the fading sunlight—so while Fernandez gathered together his guitar and cardboard suitcase and extra pair of shoes and drew down the shades and locked the trailer, I managed to attach the hose to the outdoor spigot, pried open the enormous and battered hood, braced myself against the smashed-in grille and filled up the great black leaking radiator. Then I flung down the hose—nozzle lashing about in a perverse and frenzied circle, lashing and taking aim and soaking the lower half of my fresh white uniform—and dropped the hood and wiped my hands on an oily rag, straightened my cap, smoothed down the pure white breast of my tunic and gently shooed away the chickens and patted the old battered-up green hood of the car. The sun was going down, the champagne was tingling and Cassandra, I knew, was waiting where I had left her with Gertrude at the U-Drive-Inn.

"Ready, Fernandez?" I called. "Bride's waiting, Fernandez."

Then Fernandez must have felt the champagne also because suddenly the three broken car doors were tied shut with twine and I was behind the wheel and the sun was turning to gold the tall white plastic Madonna screwed to the dashboard and Fernandez was sitting up straight beside me with a bunch of crimson flowers in one hand and a large unlabeled bottle of clear liquor in the other. I waved to a fat red bantam hen, and the two of us, Fernandez and I, called good-by forever to his life in the splendors of Tenochtitlan Trailer Village. As we drove out between the rows of mobile homes—wingless airplanes, land yachts, or little metal hovels with flat tires and sagging aerials—suddenly I had the impulse to pat Fernandez on the knee, and did so and smiled at him through the sunlight which was full in my face.

"Courage, Fernandez," I said softly. "She's a charming girl."

"Don't worry about me, Papa Cue Ball," cradling the bottle, clutching the flowers in his tiny bright mahogany fist, "Fernandez is no innocent."

Sand flats, mountains of gravel, abandoned road-working machines, conveyer belts, fields of marsh and silver oil tanks, hitchhiking soldier, a pony ring, and the aged dark green Packard swaying and knocking and overheating on that black highway south.

"Faster, Papa Cue Ball, the hour is very late."

Nonetheless I thought we had better eat—hamburgers in toasted golden buns at the side of the road, butter and pickle juice running through our fingers, two cold bottles of Orange Crush for the dark-faced groom and perspiring good-natured naval officer who gave the bride away—and my better sense told me that someone must attend to the Packard—unpardonable delay in lonely service station, gallons of gasoline, buckets of water, long minutes in the rest room where we, Fernandez and I, took our first drink of the colorless liquor which burned away the Orange Crush and killed the champagne—so that the sky was dark and the moon was a lemon curd by the time we reached the little suburban oasis called El Chico Rio and honked the horn in a prearranged enthusiastic signal—so many longs, so many shorts, so many trills—and parked in front of Gertrude's accommodations in the U-Drive-Inn.

"Where are the flowers, Fernandez?" I whispered, and set the hand brake. "Quickly, hold the flowers up where she can see them."

"The flowers were foolish, Papa Cue Ball." Glum. Somber. Squaring his shoulders at the Madonna. "I dropped them in the big wire basket in the toilet back there at the Texaco station. A good place for them."

But I pushed him out of the car then, straightened his linen jacket, squeezed his hand, and turned, smiled, removed my stiff white cap—civilian habit I was never able to overcome—because Gertrude's door had opened and there was a light on the path and Cassandra was walking toward us carefully in high heels, and Cassandra was composed, calm, silvery and womanly and serene as she came walking toward Fernandez and myself and the old hot smashed-up Packard in these her first moonlit moments of matrimony. I caught my breath, held out my arms to her. And glancing down, I whispered, "Kiss her, for God's sake, Fernandez. Look how she's dressed up for us. You must do something!"

And it was true. Her hair was down, yet drawn back slightly so that we could see the little diamond pendants she had clipped to the lobes of her tiny ears; her waist was small and tight and her little silver breasts were round; she was cool, her dress was crocheted and white; and in honor of Fernandez, in honor of his Peruvian background, she wore draped across her narrow shoulders a long white Indian shawl with a fringe made of soft white hair that hung down below her knees. She carried a black patent leather purse, new, and also new a small black patent leather traveling bag monogrammed, I discovered once she got into the car, with a large golden initial C. We could smell the perfume and breath of talcum powder and sharp odor of nail polish—pink as the color of a peach near the stem, still wet— even before she reached the car, and I felt myself choking and gave Fernandez a shove, and dropped my cap and reached out and caught up the purse, caught up the traveling bag. Pride. Embarrassment. My daughter's porter.

But he did not kiss her. He merely secured the bottle of liquor under one arm and put his little heels together and bowed, bent low over Cassandra's soft white hand. The fingers of her other hand—two silver bracelets, a silver fertility charm—were curled at the edge of the high tight collar and her eyes were bright. Then I saw her breasts heaving again and knew that everything was up to me.

"Well, Cassandra," I said, "my little bride at last!"

"My bride, Papa Cue Ball," ruffled, holding the bottle by the neck, "you misunderstand, Papa Cue Ball."

"Naturally, Fernandez," I said, and smiled and felt Cassandra touch my arm and wished that I hadn't already kissed the bride in the City Hall. "But are we ready to go? And shall I drive, Fernandez? I'd be happy to drive. If only you two could sit in back. . . ."

"The three of us will sit in the front seat, Papa Cue Ball. Naturally. And remember, please, this is my honeymoon, the honeymoon of Fernandez. I am the new husband and on my honeymoon my wife will do the driving. So that's settled. The wife drives on the honeymoon. And you will sit in the middle if you please, Papa Cue Ball. So let's go."

I helped Cassandra into the car and managed to jam her traveling bag among the tires and slid in beside her, sighed, settled down with Cassandra's purse in my lap and her smooth white ceremonial shawl just touching my knee. It was the first time Fernandez had cracked the whip, so to speak, and she took it well, Cassandra took it well. I glanced at her—mere doll behind the wheel, line of firmness in her jaw, little soft hands tight and delicate on the wheel—and her eyes were glistening with a new light of pride, joy, humility. Obedient but still untamed. Shocked. Secretly pleased. Mere helpless woman but summoning her determination, pushing back her hair, suddenly and with little precise white fingers turning the key in the ignition and, with the other hand, taking hold of the gearshift lever which in Cassandra's tiny soft hand was like a switchman's tall black iron lever beside an abandoned track.

"Got your license with you, Cassandra?" I asked. "But of course you do," I murmured in answer to my own question and smiled, caressed the little black patent leather purse in my lap, then balanced the purse on my two raised knees, played a little game of catch with it. How carefully, slowly, Fernandez climbed back into the old Packard which he himself was unable to drive, and then took hold of the broken door handle and pulled, pulled with all his might so that the door slammed shut and the car shook under the crashing of that loose heavy steel. Another side of Fernandez? A new mood? I thought so and suddenly realized that the enormous outdated Packard with all its terrible capacity for noise and metallic disintegration was somehow a desperate equivalent of my little old-world Catholic son-in-law in his hand-decorated necktie and crumpled white linen suit.

"OK, Chicken," he said, another vagary of temper, another cut of the lash, and without a word to me he thrust the bottle in my direction, "we want to head for the hideaway. And please step on the gas."

"I'm with you," I wanted to say to Cassandra as I took the bottle, held the purse in one hand and the tall clear bottle in the other, "don't be afraid." But instead, "Away we go!" I cried, and rolled my head, glanced at Cassandra, put the clear round mouth of the bottle into my own aching mouth and shut my eyes and burned again as I had first burned when I leaned against the tin partition in the Texaco filling station and sampled the rare white liquor of the Andes.

"My wife drives well. Don't you think so, Papa Cue Ball?"

"Like Thor in his chariot," I said. "But a toast, Fernandez, to love, to love and fidelity, eh, Cassandra?"

Moonlight, cold dizzying smell of raw gasoline, dry smell of worn upholstery, sensation of devilish coiled springs and lumps of cotton in the old grease-stained front seat of the Packard, wind singing through Cassandra's door and the hot knocking sound of the engine and a constellation of little curious lights winking behind the dashboard, and I was snug between Cassandra and my son-in-law of several hours now, and the Madonna was standing over me and holding out her moon-struck plastic arms in benediction. She was the Blessed Virgin Mary, I knew, and I smiled back happily at her in the moonlight.

"Skipper?" Cassandra was staring ahead, whispering, driving with her bright new wedding ring high on the wheel, "Light me a cigarette. Please." So I opened the purse—how long now had I been waiting for an excuse to open that purse? for a chance to get a peek inside that purse even in the smelly darkness of the speeding car?—and found the cigarettes and a little glossy unused booklet of paper matches and put one of her cigarettes between my lips and struck one of the matches—puff of orange light, sweet taste of sulphur—and smelled the blue smoke, and placed the white cigarette between the fingers which she held out to me in the V-for-victory sign. And during all the long miles we chalked up that night—tunnels of love through the trees, black Pacific deep and hungry and defiant down there below the highway, which was always honeymoon highway to me when that night had passed—and until we reached the hotel far up in the mountains, that was all Cassandra said to me, but it was enough. She had changed. There is a difference between a young bride with crimson flowers and a young woman driving a dirty old forest green Packard with her white pointed toe just reaching the accelerator and a cigarette burning in her pretty mouth. What bride wants to keep her eyes on the road? So she had changed. She would never lose the invisible encyclopedia balanced on the crown of her head and would always be identified for me with the BVM. But behind her anticipation— why else the new purse? why else the patent leather traveling bag? or why the monogram?—and behind whatever vision she may have had of matrimony, there was a change. Still hopeful, still feeling joy, but smoking an unaccustomed cigarette and tasting fate. In the darkness I noticed that one of her pendant earrings had disappeared, and I was sorry and irritated at the same time, wanted to tell her to remove its mate or to let me take it off myself. But I held my peace.

And Fernandez? Fernandez, I knew, was drunk. At least he was a jealous custodian of the bottle, or inconsiderate groom, a testy son-in-law. And forty or fifty miles beyond El Chico Rio the black sprawling ominous interior of the Packard was filled suddenly with the elated piercing sounds of a wolfish whistle, and I saw that Fernandez was sitting on the edge of the seat with the bottle gripped between his knees and two fingers stuck between his teeth, grinning, staring at Cassandra, whistling those two loud terrible notes of his crude appreciation, and I knew that Fernandez was drunk or at least that he had given way, at last, to the psychic tensions of his mysterious past.

"Control yourself, Fernandez," I said, trying at any cost to preserve the humor of our journey, "we have a long night ahead of us."

"The heart cries out," he said, dully, morosely, "the heart demands satisfaction, nothing less. But my wife will know what I mean," nodding, wiping his brow. "Know what I mean, Chicken?"

The mere expression on her white face appeased him, though not for long because all at once we could see the moon shattering on the black chaos of the Pacific far below us and the first cigarette package was empty and Fernandez was hunched in the furthest dark corner of the car.

"Fernandez?" Softly, cheerfully, touching him lightly on the shoulder: "Are you all right? Shall we stop for a minute?"

"Drive on, good Papa Cue Ball, drive on," he said, and I saw that he had removed his shoes, removed his green socks, rolled the white linen trousers up to his knees. What next? His legs were perfect white shapely bowling pins, and he was arching one foot, wriggling the toes, flexing one calf.

"Hey, Chicken! You like cheesecake? You like cheesecake, Chicken?"

The Packard swerved once—headlights chopping through the trees—but Cassandra applied the brakes, steadied her hands on the wheel, and we recovered again, accelerated, sped around a curve with the moon going great guns again and Fernandez quickly repeating the marriage service to himself in Spanish. And then my heart was floating in a dark sea, in my stomach the waves were commencing their dark action. And yet for two more hours I was aware of everything, the climbing Packard, sudden feeling of elevation, hairpin turns in the road, small rocks in the road, Cassandra's white skirt riding above her knee, moon flitting behind stark silhouetted peaks, the white plastic Madonna fixed and comforting on the dashboard, clearly aware of Fernandez sitting upright and all at once talking happily at my side.

"It's silver mining country, Chicken. You see? Mountains of the great silver deposits. Think of the lost cities, the riches, thousands of little sure-footed burros laden with silver. Do you understand my feeling, Chicken? Silver is the precious metal of the church, the metal of devotion, ceremony, candlelight. The treasure of the heart, the blessed metal of my ancestors and of my somber boyhood. Out of these mountains they dug silver for old coins, Chicken, silver for the heavy girdles of young brides. Think of it. . . ."

And slumped between them I listened, held my peace, drifted higher and higher into those black gutted mountains. There were ravines and cliffs and falling boulders all waiting to finish off the Packard, and we left our tire tracks in patches of fresh snow. Yet I merely grinned to myself, tried to imagine what our exact altitude might be.

. . . stumbling forward with the monogrammed traveling case in my hand, in the beam of the headlights stumbling, trying to breathe, feeling exhilarated despite the dizziness and pain in my eyes. "Is this it, Fernandez?" I called over my shoulder, hatless and suddenly hot and cold at the same time. "Pretty high up, Fernandez!"

"This is it, Papa Cue Ball," he called back to me. "Honeymoon Hide-Away, which is the best place in all Southern Cal for the young men and women who have just taken the vows of marriage!"

Narrow rock-strewn deserted place, beginning of a steep gorge ringed with peaks, and I stumbled, paused, struggled for breath, looked up at the cold diminishing stars and birdless peaks. We were trapped, I knew. And yet I was unaccountably pleased to see that at the end of the headlights' dull beam there was a shattered stone wall of a demolished building and leaning against it, fat and sullen and holding a little hairless dog in her arms, a Mexican woman who remained alone now with her little dog in all this rubble. I wondered how long she had been leaning there waiting to meet us.

"*Señorita*," I called, "*buenas noches!*" And I waved—she was a match for me, the fat brown unsmiling mother of that wrecked mining town—and hurried after her with the blood draining from my eyes and my heart pounding. Around the corner I found only a single sharply inclined street of the abandoned mining town, only a barred window, a row of doorless openings, a chimney fallen intact across the street like the skeleton of some enormous snake, a few streaks of moonlit mortar and a few jagged heaps of dislocated stone still lodged there in the bottom of the sheer gorge. Ruin. Slow collapse. The rank odor of dead enterprise.

But there was light in the hotel and the heavy long empty bar was ornamented with the plump naked bodies of young Victorian women carved in bas-relief and lying prone on their rounded sides down all the length of that dark dusty wood. A light in the Hide-Away, and I rushed inside, dropped Cassandra's traveling case beside the bar.

"Three beers, *Señorita*," I said—she was standing in the shadows next to an old nickel-plated cash register that looked like a cranky medieval machine of death—"and the rooms are ready? You've got the rooms ready for us, I hope?"

She waited. Her small eyes were bright and glittering in the shadow, she could have been afraid or sullen but there was beauty still in the dark reticence of her enormous size. Then she moved, stood the little silver hairless dog on the bar—obedient, trembling, scared to death—and turned her back on me, groaned and stooped out of sight. It was a slow intimate process, the procuring of that first beer, headless, tepid, drawn in a small Coca-Cola glass and from what spigot or rancid keg I was unable to see, but at last she set the glass in front of me and braced herself against the bar, moved the dog out of my arm's reach. Then she turned again and in the same way produced the second glass, and the third, until the three glasses stood in a bitter row and the dog tipped its sharp trembling ears at me from the far side of the cash register. I thought the woman's eyes were warmer when she slid the last beer in line, at least her breath—rich, flaring, full of provocative hot seasoning and rotten teeth—was closer to my face and stronger.

"Now the rooms," I said. "You've got the two rooms? OK?" She nodded.

"Excellent," I said, "excellent. You're a real old queen of the Pampas." She watched me, resting her breasts on the bar, and there was still beauty in the lines of her greasy face, still a strange promise of strength and gentleness in her short blackened fingers. I smiled, picked up the glasses, and was just arranging them on a dusty table when I noticed the soldier, a lone soldier near the jukebox with his dark head on his arms and khaki shirt wet and clinging to his thin ribs, and heard Fernandez calling out in the darkness beyond the fallen wall.

"In here, Fernandez! In here, Cassandra! Can you see the light?"

I waited, paced up and down. There was the odor of mildewed cardboard, odor of pack rats under the sagging floor, the Mexican woman had tacked an out-of-date girlie calendar above the jukebox. Then they appeared—I knew at once that they had been holding hands—and I embraced Fernandez, embraced Cassandra, seated them at our private table and sighed, smiled at both of them, winking at Fernandez, winking happily at Cassandra, and took a quick sip of my flat tepid beer.

"So, good Papa Cue Ball, you have seen to everything and all is in order?"

"All in order, Fernandez. Except for our unfortunate friend over there," and I nodded in the direction of the soldier, tried to catch Cassandra's eye over the rim of my glass. Fernandez turned, glanced at the sleeping figure, shrugged.

"It's nothing, Papa Cue Ball. Merely a drunk GI. The GI's are all over the place these days. Don't give it a thought. But look, a woman of my own color! A very good omen, Papa Cue Ball, a very good omen."

"I thought you'd be pleased, Fernandez."

"Fernandez is very pleased. And Chicken," looking now at Cassandra, putting his little brown hand on her wrist, "do you see that she's a woman who has borne many children? Do you see from her size that she's a woman of many glowing and painless births? Take heart from her, Chicken. Put a little flesh on the bones. . . ."

And interrupting him quickly: "Well, what do you think of having the wedding supper now, Fernandez? Pretty good idea?"

"Magnificent, good Papa Cue Ball. You think of everything!"

Tortillas. Soft brick-colored beans. Bitter nuts, half-moons of garlic, fish sweated into a paste with hard silver slices of raw onion. Ground meal, green peppers the shape of a finger and the texture of warm mucilage and filled with tiny black explosive seeds, and chicken, oh the tortured chicken skewered and brown and lacerated, running with pink blood and some kind of thick peppered sauce, chicken that fell away from the bone and in the mouth yielded first the delicate flavor of tender white meat and then the unexpected pain of its unleashed fire, chicken and murky soup and bits of preserved vegetable poisoned in such a way as to bring a sudden film to the eyes and pinched dry shriveling sensations to the nose and throat. So Fernandez kept calling out in Spanish to the Mexican woman, and the Mexican woman—now there was a new glazed color in her cheeks, a new odor of hot charcoal amongst the other smells of her enormous and unrevealed self—kept coming to us with still another clay pot steaming in one brown hand and always the little dog shaking helplessly in the other. And Fernandez ate, cocking his head, holding the food appreciatively on his tongue, then nodding, chewing, demanding more, and of course I ate right along with him, cooling myself, saving myself with innumerable glasses of the beer which was suddenly sparkling and as cold as ice.

"You know about the *cojones*, Papa Cue Ball? This is a feast for the *cojones*, let me tell you. . . ."

So that's what our old mother of the mesquite was up to, and I blushed then, glanced at Cassandra—poor Cassandra, soft and unsmiling in the light of the half-candle which the fat woman had brought with the first brusque Spanish command—and bit down as hard as I could on a little tough root that was filled with devils. I was always afraid that Cassandra would marry a marine like so many of the girls she knew at school, but what would those marine wives think if they could see her now, waiting out this wedding night in the dark dining room of an empty hotel which was once the call house of our little abandoned and evil-smelling and still collapsing silver town? For that matter, what was I to think? No doubt I was too full, too excited, but eager, strangely eager nonetheless, to think.

In the end there was candy—what secret cache expended loyally for the sake of Fernandez? what dirty old shoe box or earthen pot lovingly exhumed and made to yield up this cracked plate of thick dark sticky chunks of sugared fruit?—and two twisted black Mexican cigars and a tiny glass filled to the brim —rare cordial? primitive aphrodisiac?—for Cassandra. I ate, I smoked, I looked the other way when I saw her slender white fingers reach for the glass.

"Well, Fernandez," I said, and pushed back my chair, stood up, blew the ash off my black cigar—sickening cigar, heavy pungent odor of bad dreams—and for a moment held myself where the food lay, "how about a little music, Fernandez? Shall we try a song?" The sallow wizened face looked up at me and he was unable to smile, unable to speak, unable even to nod, but the eyes told me that he wanted me to try a song. Cassandra was still holding the full glass, Cassandra still untouched by these disreputable ghosts or the chorus of the pack rats below the floor. The candlelight was flowing in her hair and on her ring finger there was a little bright chip of fire. I wanted to suggest that I call out the titles of the numbers and that she, my poor Cassandra, select our song. But clutching the back of the chair I looked down at her and the phrasing of this well-intentioned thought never came to my lips.

I left them together, left the two of them sitting together in the midst of the debris of the feast of the *cojones*, as my son-in-law had said, and somehow turning abruptly toward the dusty colors of the obsolete jukebox, I knew that once I walked away from the table, away from the wreckage of the indelicate wedding supper, I would be walking away from them forever. It was a difficult moment, an awkward pause. But I stepped out, telling myself I always enjoyed the mystery of push buttons and the flamboyance of bright undulating colors.

Unsteady steps across the rotten floor. A good look at the white neck of the sleeping soldier. And then the old machine, the colored water moving through the tubes, the rows of bright square buttons and, inside the dusty glass, the rows of printed song titles each one of which was a further notch in my knowledge of romance. I leaned down, hands on knees, never looking back at the table, and very carefully and slowly read each one of those little romantic titles twice. Then I made my choice, fumbled around in my pocket for a coin, pushed the bright button down. A click, a scratching sound, then music, and I started to wag my head to the rhythm of that awful tune.

Listening, swaying, smiling, hands still on knees, I did my best to dream up a little reverie of my own, a little romance of my own, and I did my very best, stood it as long as I could, then simply had to turn around and did so, humming along with the record, snapping my fingers, putting another nickel in the slot, turning slowly—oh I wasn't going to miss a trick that night—until I stood facing them once more, but in shadow and with the colored lights revolving and dissolving across my poor wrinkled uniform. They had gotten up from the table—Fernandez, Cassandra—and I was just about to call good night to them, thinking that they wouldn't leave the room until I called good night to them, when I saw the Mexican woman taking charge of them, watched with a curious shrinking sensation on my lips, my smile, as she took Cassandra's submissive white face between her greasy hands and kissed her in the middle of that mere ghost of a white brow and then let go of Cassandra and quickly gave Fernandez a couple of coaxing pats on his white linen rump, and then pushed them out the door.

"Good night, you two," I called anyway, and was alone with my music, the drunk GI, the woman who began clearing away the debris. Alone with the miniature silver dog. But not for long. Because before I could sit down with the drunk GI Fernandez retuned, breathless, guarded, already smelling of Cassandra's scent, and held out to me the Edgeworth tobacco tin in which he kept his spiv, that terrible little weapon made of a broken razor blade.

"For you, Papa Cue Ball," he said. "Take it. In case that one there," jerking his elbow at the soldier, "in case that one tries to cause you any trouble when he wakes up. It's better to be ready for him, just in case. . . ."

"Thanks, Fernandez. But wait," trying to detain him, watching him slip off not toward the shrouded staircase but toward the littered street outside, "where are you going?"

"For the guitar, Papa Cue Ball. There would be no romance without my green guitar."

But I was alone. Alone in this mining town of rusted iron pipe and settling rock and corrugated paper turned to mold. Alone with my heavy stomach, my heartburn, the dizziness I still suffered from the altitude. I paced up and down the dark room, I tried unsuccessfully to make friends with the wretched little silver dog. Apparently the woman expected me to climb to my own room upstairs and sleep, but I told her that I had spent so many months at sea that I found it difficult to sleep in a bed ashore. Why didn't she bring me a beer, I asked her, and also one for the soldier and, if she liked, a beer for herself as well? She nodded, and then she put her fat brown hand on my arm and gave it a squeeze.

I told her I would sit down and keep the soldier company. So I pulled out a chair and took a seat. The head of black curly hair was buried in the crossed arms, the khaki shirt was disheveled, the cuffs were unbuttoned and drawn back from the thin gray wrists, and I noticed the outline of a shoulder patch which had been removed and no doubt destroyed.

"Hey, Joe," I said. "Wake up, Joe. How about joining me for a beer?" No answer. No sound of breathing, not even the faint exhalation of a low moan. I leaned close to the hidden head to listen but there was nothing. I touched his elbow, I shook him by the arm. "Joe," I said, "two lone servicemen ought to join forces, don't you think?" But there was nothing. Only the rats, a little wind through the timbers, the first wailing chords struck on the guitar upstairs.

Then, on a tray this time, she brought out three beers and also a tin basin of warm water and a scrap of rag. And slowly she put down the glasses, arranged the rag and basin next to the GI and sat close beside him. We drank to each other—dark eye on mine, little silver dog huddled between her breasts—and still holding her glass and without taking her eyes from mine she reached out her free hand, took a chubby fistful of black curly hair and pulled the GI upright, let his head loll over the back of the chair.

"Is he OK?" I whispered, "is he alive?"

She nodded, drank another sip of beer. Then she showed me the back of her small shapeless hand, held her hand up like a club.

"You did it?" I whispered and pushed aside my beer, leaned away from the two of them. "You mean you did that to him yourself?"

More nodding, more sipping, a soft shadow of pride passing over the greasy brown contours of her round face, more searching looks at me. And then suddenly she finished off her beer and, softly talking all the while to the dog and now and then glancing at me, she cradled the GI's head and dipped the rag and went to work on him. With age-old tenderness she ran the rag over the lips, under the eyes, around the nose, again and again dipping the rag, squeezing, returning with heavy breath to the gentleness of her occupation. The white face began to emerge and already the water, I could see, was a soft rich color, deep and dark.

When the dog tipped its tiny nose over the edge of the basin I stood up. And quickly, without commotion, I left them there, the preoccupied fat woman bent over her task and the soldier moaning in the crook of her arm—he had begun to moan at last—and I groped my way outside and knelt at the nearest pile of rubble and upchucked into the rubble to my heart's content, let go with the tortillas, the hot tamales, the champagne, nameless liquor and beer, knelt and clung to a chunk of mortar and gooseneck of rusted pipe and threw open the bilge, had a good deep rumble for myself.

Anyone who has gotten down on his knees to vomit has discovered, if only by accident, the position of prayer. So that terrible noise I was making must have been the noise of prayer, and the effect, as the spasms faded and the stomach went dry, was no doubt similar to the peace that follows prayer. In my own way I was contrite enough, certainly, had worked hard enough there in the rubble to deserve well the few moments when a little peace hung over me in the wake of the storm that had passed.

I breathed, I smeared my face in my handkerchief, I climbed to my feet. It was a job done, and now the night, I knew, was going to fly away fast. Too bad for them, I thought, too bad for me. It hadn't ended well but it had ended.

And now I was wandering and the opera house was like a decapitated turret or the remains of a tiny and monstrous replica of a Rhine castle. A few curtain wires flapping loose in the wind, a couple of sandbags and a little gilt chair upside down in the entrance hall, a pile of handbills. Another house of pleasure for the men in the drifts. And how many performances did my Mexican love attend? How many with some other little hairless rat-shaped dog tucked under her arm? How many with a mouthful of *pepitas* and a heavy hand on her rolling thigh and bright candles lit all the way across the little stage? I would never know. But there was life yet in that miniature lopsided castle of bygone scratching orchestras and flouncing chorus girls and brawling applause. So I began to feel my way up the narrow stairs. I climbed as high as the first balcony, climbed up into the fading night and could go no further, for the second balcony, the roof, the stage, all of it was gone and there was only a scattering of broken glass, the wind in my face, the feeling of blackness and a good view of the pitiless gorge and hapless town. I could make out the squat deeper shadow of the far-off Packard, I could hear the guitar. The dawn was rising up to my nostrils.

And then I saw those two enormous soft rolls of faded tickets which—by what devilish prank? what trick of time?—had been printed up for a movie that had starred Rita Hayworth, I remembered, as the unfaithful mistress of a jealous killer who escaped from prison midway through the first reel of the film. Shotguns, touring cars, acid in the face, long hair soaking wet in the rain—it was a real find, that memory, those rolls of tickets, and I scooped them up and tore them into ten-foot lengths and tied them to the broken railing, to upright twists of iron, to the arms of ravaged chairs, and watched all those paper strips snapped out onto the wind and listened to the distant sounds of my little son-in-law shouting at my poor daughter and beating on the neck of the guitar, and emptied my pockets, threw my remaining handfuls of confetti out onto the wind. It was a fete of mildewed paper and wild sentiment, a fete for three.

And in that flapping dawn—sky filled with rose, silver, royal blue—I opened the Edgeworth tobacco tin, for a long while stared at the razor blade inside. Then slowly, can and all, I tossed it over the edge of the first balcony. And seven and a half months after that flapping dawn in the mountains Pixie poked her little nose into the world—premature, an incubator baby— and sixteen months after that same rose and silver and royal blue dawn they were putting Gertrude's poor body into the ground. Thank God for the old PBY's and for a captain who did not interfere when I left the ship to be on hand back home as needed in City Hall or maternity ward or cemetery. Thank God for the boys who flew those old PBY's straight to the mark.

"That's all you are, Papa Cue Ball. The father of a woman who produces a premature child. The husband of a woman who kills herself. I renounce it, Papa Cue Ball. I renounce this family, I renounce this kind of a man. Can you explain? Can you defend? Can you speak to me with honor of your own Papa? No. So I renounce, Papa Cue Ball, I will escape one of these days. You may take my word. . . ."

"If you don't wish to come, Fernandez, then you may stay behind."

"That's what I wish. I do wish it, Papa Cue Ball, now that you put the words in my mouth! And believe me, I will follow my heart. . . ."

In front of the mirror in the little room stacked knee-high with the cardboard cartons which I had half-filled with poor Gertrude's clothing, I was having trouble with the sword. Our limousine was waiting, scheduled to depart from the U-Drive-Inn, while the hearse was scheduled to depart, of course, from the mortuary. Or rather our limousine was scheduled to rendezvous with the hearse at the mortuary, the two black vehicles to proceed on from there together. And we were late and I was having trouble with my sword. Poor Gertrude. In the mirror I saw the smart dark blue uniform—it was Christmas, after all, the Christmas of '44 and time for blues—saw the polished brass buttons, the white shirt still open at the neck since the baby was playing with my black tie, saw my bald head, freshly shaven cheeks, furrows over the bridge of my nose, and the unhooked and unwieldy sword. It was not my sword, it was the old man's sword, and I had borrowed it late on that last night on the *Starfish*. I had thought a sword necessary for Gertrude's funeral and now a couple of hooks were giving me trouble and the black scabbard was growing heavy in my hands.

"Cassandra," I said into the mirror, "I wish you'd cry. And Sonny," leaning forward, looking around for him in the mirror, "can't you give me a little help with the captain's sword?" Sonny was beginning to mourn, grief was beginning to overtake him in this ransacked room in the U-Drive-Inn, and he was scowling at Fernandez and holding Pixie on his lap. It was Sonny who had given the baby my black tie.

"All's you got to do is speak up, Skipper. You knows that. I've helped the old man with his sword, and I can help you with it. You knows that."

Sleeve of her camel's-hair coat dangling from one of the boxes. Odor of gin. A scattering of small change, cuticle sticks, keys, all gleaming in the far corner of the room where I had been going over them, sorting things out. And on a fluffy beribboned hanger hooked to the top slat of the Venetian blinds her negligee, her pink negligee—I had rinsed it in the bathroom sink the night before, hung it to dry—now doing its long empty undulating dance in the cool currents of the air freshener that was humming low on the west wall. Poor Gertrude. I could never hold a grudge against Gertrude. No matter the motorcycle orgies with members of my own crew, half a season on a nearby burlesque stage, the strange disappearances, insinuating notes to Washington, and bills, bruises, infidelity here at the U-Drive-Inn, and even a play for faithful Sonny, no matter how she had tried to injure me or shame Cassandra, still I could never despise the early wrinkles, the lost look in the eyes, the terror I so often saw on the thin wide mouth, the drunken floundering. She was a helpless unpretty woman with dyed hair. She got a rash from eating sea food. She gave a terrible ammunition to those young members of my crew with whom she managed to have her little whirlwind affairs. And her early V-letters were always the same: "I hope they sink you, Edward. I really do." She said she was going to drink up my insurance money when I was gone. Poor Gertrude. "You are going to hate me, Edward," she wrote, "at least you won't deny me hate, will you?" But she was wrong. Because the further she went downhill the more I cared. And Gertrude was no match for my increasing tolerance.

"Now give me my tie, Sonny," I said, and there was the empty camel's-hair sleeve, the sword at my side, my own uneasy look of consternation in the mirror. "The baby will have to play with something else. On the double, Sonny, we're late already."

"What about the child, Papa Cue Ball? You don't intend to leave the child with me?"

"Yes, Fernandez. That's the plan. Exactly."

Then Sonny helped me with the knot and gave me his arm and Cassandra found my hat in the bathroom. Gertrude's fingerprints were everywhere, her smell was everywhere—sweet lemon and a light haze of alcohol—and in the wastebasket a crumpled tissue still bore the lipstick impression of her poor thin lips stretched wide in the unhappiness of her last night alive.

And Sonny: "Look at that baby there, Skipper. She sure misses her Grandma!"

I nodded.

So I leaned on Sonny and Cassandra preceded us—bright sun, black limousine, bright shadows in the empty driveway—and so at last, and only twenty-five minutes late, we pulled away from the U-Drive-Inn and headed east in fairly heavy traffic to keep our rendezvous with Gertrude's hearse. I could tell they had vacuum-cleaned the inside of our limousine. The upholstery was like gray skin and the sun was hard, brilliant, silent through the clear glass.

"Them swords are the devil to sit down with, Skipper. Ain't they?"

I agreed with him. And then: "If we used the jump-up seats we could be carrying six instead of three. Did you notice that, Sonny? Wonderful room in these limousines. But I wonder why there aren't any flowers?"

The traffic was heavy and all the other cars were filled with children. I could see them through the sealed glass, the smooth bright silence of our slow ride. Faint brand-new automobile smell, hard light, subtle sensation of new black tires humming gently through the perfect seat—gray skin, foam rubber, a bed of springs—and rising like a thin intimate voice into the receptive spine. And of course the driver. Something familiar about the driver—charcoal chauffeur's jacket, white collar, charcoal chauffeur's cap, dark glasses—a curiously muffled and familiar look about the driver. But I couldn't place him and went back to stroking the warm handstrap and staring at the tints that were beginning to appear in the curves and along the edges of our shatterproof glass.

"Ask him if he has his lights on, Sonny. Funeral cars always have their lights on, don't they, Sonny? We'd make better time with lights, I'm sure."

We were only forty-eight minutes late, exactly, when we drifted to a marvelous stop beneath the bright green caterpillar awning and waited while the driver climbed the smooth white marble steps to report inside. The place looked empty. No sign of the hearse. No attendants in black swallowtails. Nothing. Then Sonny went in after the driver—grief riding his shoulders, dreading the interior of this establishment which was like home to me—and in close conversation, stooping, black shoes making startled noises on the marble, they returned together. Sonny opened the car door, stuck his head in, and Cassandra and I— Cassandra in her trim black dress, hair drawn tightly under the little hat—leaned forward as one. The black face was wet and the long black cheeks were more hollowed out than ever. His panther hand was trembling.

"Been some mistake, Skipper," shaking his head, fanning himself with his black chief's cap, "hearse gone on ahead without us. The man inside couldn't tell us a thing. Anyways, we got to get a move on now."

"Well, hop in, Sonny," I said. "Let's go." Then leaning forward, touching the stiff driver's charcoal arm and wishing I could see his face, "Listen," I said, "it's a matter of life and death. Do you understand?"

"Got his lights on now, Skipper," nudging me, peering down into my face, staring at me with those hard-boiled eggs of his, "and them lights ought to help for sure."

"That's good, Sonny," I said. "I'm glad."

Then suddenly the highway was wide open, clear, a long rising six-lane concrete boomerang with its tip driven into the horizon and all for us. Soft gray seats and chrome and the sunlight standing still on the ebony dashboard, and only the highway itself took my attention away from the chrome, the felt padding under our feet, so that for a moment I saw the lemon trees, the olive groves, the brown sculpted contours of the low hills.

There was a shadow in the front seat next to the driver, a dark amorphous shadow that swelled and tried to change its position and vague shape according to the curves in the road, black shadow that seemed to be held in its seat by the now terrible speed of the Caddy. The driver had both hands on the wheel and now the speed was whispering inside my spine. I noticed that the tints of the window and windshield glass had slid, suddenly, onto Cassandra's black dress, were shining there in the black planes of her body, and that she was looking at me. The black shadow was snuggling up to the driver.

"Hurry up," I said as loud as I could, leaning forward and fighting against the sword at my side, "hurry up, will you? We haven't got all day."

And then the turn-off, the gentle incline over gravel, a long sweeping glimpse of the lemon sky, the archway flanked by two potted palms—there was an angel floating between the palms—the still sunlit aspect of the cemetery at the end of the day. And a little sign which I saw immediately—*Speed six miles per hour*—and far off, at the top of a dun-colored hill, a little activity which I tried not to see. Sonny was suffering now, moaning to himself, and doing a poor job of controlling his fear of graveyards.

"Look, Sonny," I said, "isn't that the hearse?"

"Appears to be the hearse, Skipper. Sure enough."

We crawled toward the hill and toward the green speck—it proved to be a tent for mourners—and toward the other elongated speck, black and radiant, which was the hearse. The sky was a pure lemon color, quite serene.

"But, Sonny," clutching his arm, reaching up quickly for a fierce grip on the handstrap, "it's moving, isn't it? It wasn't moving before, but it's moving now."

"Appears like you're right, Skipper. That hearse just don't want our company, I guess."

And then the stillness of the limousine, the grease and steel sound of the door opening—we left the car door open behind us, large and empty and catching the sun—and Sonny holding one of my arms and Cassandra the other, and we were walking across the carpet of thick green imitation turf in the gentle light on top of the dun-colored hill, and no one was there.

"All right," I said, "they can begin. Let's get it over with."

But I knew better. There was no one there, the place was empty. The remains of flowers were scattered around underfoot, red roses, white carnations, the debris of real activity, I could see that. But I rushed to the tent, for a long while stood looking into the darkness of that warm tent. There was a shovel lying on the ground and the smell of earth. Nothing else.

The flowers were heaviest where the digging had been going on. Piled up, kicked out of the way, crushed. And there were a few strips of the thick green turf lying more or less around the edges of what had been the hole, and the three of us, standing there together, gently touched the green turf with the toes of our shoes. They must have thought they were burying a piano, and judging by the width and depth of the new earth the hole must have gone down a hundred feet. There was the deep print of a workman's boot right in the center and I squatted, kneeled, brushed it away.

And kneeling, weighing a handful of the new earth in my cold hand: "So they went ahead without us," I said. "They put poor Gertrude into the ground without us. You know," looking up at the two black figures rising into the soft lemon sky, "I told them I wanted Gertrude to have a white casket. A white casket with just a touch of silver. But they might have put her into mahogany and gold for all we'll ever know. How can we tell?"

I stood up, raised my palm, straightened out my fingers: "Pretty sandy stuff, isn't it, Sonny?" I said, and tossed it away, wiped my hand on the back of my pants. I turned to go.

And then the whisper, the quick soft whisper full of love and fear: "Ain't you got something for the grave, Skipper? Got to leave something for the grave, Skipper. Bad luck if you don't."

I nodded, thought a moment, pointed. He understood. Sonny understood and unhooked the hooks and raked out a little trough about three inches deep in the loose skin-colored soil. He buried the sword about three inches deep in the loose soil, tamped it down. Perhaps he was right. Perhaps we would have had worse luck had we not left it there. At least it was no great loss.

The driver took us the long way around the cemetery on our way out, drove us at six miles per hour along the gentle road that was like a bridle path through a hovering bad dream. At the far end of the cemetery there was a line of eucalyptus trees, and leaning forward, staring out of the tinted glass and between the trees, I saw a mountain of naked earth heaped high with flowers —dead flowers, fresh flowers, an acre-long dump of bright tears for the dead—and I knew that poor Gertrude's flowers would soon land on the pile.

"When we get home, Cassandra," I said, and leaned back against the perfect cushion and shut my eyes, "I want you to try on that camel's-hair coat. I think her camel's-hair coat might fit you, Cassandra."

The Brutal Act

White lifeboat. I heard something, steel, ratchet, a noise I must have known was descending cable, and there was an eclipse of the porthole, a perfect circle of blackness flush against the side of the ship at the spot where the great ring of brass and glass was hooked up with a little chain. The porthole was always open as it was now because I liked to catch the first pink edges of the tropical dawn, first breath of day, first patter of bare feet on the deck above. But it had never gone black before, that porthole of mine, and for a moment—squall? tidal wave? another ship between ourselves and the sun?—I felt what it was like to be faintly smothered in some new problem of seamanship. Slowly I put on my cap, set aside my torn gray copy of the serviceman's a-bridged edition of the New Testament. Then carefully I thrust my head through the porthole and attempted to twist myself about and look topside. No luck at all. So I looked down. Suspended a long way below me, yet out of reach of the waves, motionless, a white lifeboat was empty and absolutely still down there. For some reason I lowered the port, spent precious minutes screwing tight the brass lugs, even though I was swept immediately by my usual swift fear of ocean nausea. Then I looked at my wrist, 0500 hours, and then I locked the cabin door, climbed topside. For three days, in a sudden effort to keep abreast of Mac the Catholic chaplain, I had been reading the New Testament each dawn. The lifeboat destroyed all that.

I came out with a light in my eyes and the brisk wind catching my cap by the visor, and dead ahead was an enormous field of shoal water emerald green in the dawn. East, I thought and smiled, blotted a little fine spray with the back of my hand. I had to shade my eyes. But the lifeboat was there all right, though swung up as she should have been on giant fishhooks of steel and not suspended above the waves where I had first seen her, and she was motionless up there, hauled now a good distance above my head, and she was as large as someone's private cruiser and, in her own shade, a solemn white. I wondered whether or not it was the same boat. But the fishhooks were canted slightly, the blocks were pulled from under her, the giant tarpaulin lay heaped on the deck, and after a moment I knew that it must be the same boat. I stood there, shaded my raised eyes, waited.

Because someone was standing on her bow. He was nearly a silhouette to me, and yet I took him all in, the long spread legs, the fist on the cable, the faded denim jeans, the flapping sky-blue shirt, the long black hair whipped in the wind, the white hat rolled up and stuck halfway down the front of the jeans. I watched him in the shelter of the white lifeboat and in the bright warmth of the sun. But he was a man of the wind, a tall bony man of this sudden topside wind, and he was bracing himself on the enormous soft white prow of the lifeboat and grinning down at me.

I cupped a hand, tried to see into the sun, called up to him: "Tremlow? Started painting the shack yet, Tremlow? How about knocking off early for a little boxing?"

It was the windward side of the ship, the eastern side, and even in the shelter of the boat the air was loud so that I could hear nothing but whistling overhead and far forward a heavy singing in the anchor chains. But I could see him and he had moved one foot so that it rested now against his rigid knee, and he was shaking his head at me, still grinning.

"By the way, Tremlow," squinting, cupping my hand again,

"who told you to take the tarp off the lifeboat? The tarp's supposed to be on the lifeboat at all times. See to it, will you?"

I gave him a half-salute then—mere boy only a third my age and six feet five inches tall and a perfect Triton—and turned on my heel. The lifeboat remained a white impression in my mind, a floating thick-sided craft with a wide beam, deep draft, brass propeller, an enormous white sea rover with something amiss. But at least I had been too quick for Tremlow, once again had managed to avoid his deliberate signs of insubordination.

I took my bearings and made my way aft in time to help Mac into his vestments. We were in the sick-bay which was the most suitable spot on the ship for holding Mass, as I had insisted to the old man, and a few of the men leaned up on their elbows to watch.

"How goes it, Mac?" I said.

"Late as usual," he said.

"No rush, Mac," I said, "no rush," and slipped the purple stole around his damp shoulders. "Did you notice the coral shoals off our starboard side around 0600 hours, Mac? Like a field of underwater corn or something. Or perhaps it was a couple of acres of broken bottle-green glass, eh, Mac?"

But I could see that he wasn't listening, so I opened the white locker where he kept the cross and took it out, unwrapped it, gave it a few licks with the chamois.

"OK, Mac," I said, "all yours."

I was in the middle of my four-year stint on the U.S.S. *Starfish* and it was a bright pink and green dawn in early June and I was helping Mac, seeing how I could give him a hand. Helping Mac serve Mass though in the background, just hovering in the background, just doing what I could to help Mac start his day. I wanted to tell him about the lifeboat but kept quiet, busied myself with the various odd chores of Mac's silent hour. But the bell was tinkling and I was trying to make myself look small. From far forward near the anchor chains the mushy rapid-fire sounds of a machine gun died away. I nodded, glanced significantly at Mac, because they knew better than to have machine gun practice when Mac was holding services in the afterpart of the ship. I walked over to a porthole—sea the color of honey now, sky full of light—then turned at a nearly inaudible little SOS from Mac and put a towel on my arm, stationed myself in the background. But not before I had seen that one of the black pelicans was flying high off our starboard quarter with his broken neck thrust forward and homely wings wide to the wind. The bird was good medicine for the lingering vision of the white lifeboat though not good enough as I discovered. Even the hours I had devoted to helping the chaplain failed to save me.

The sick and wounded were first and we made quick work of them, Mac and I, passing from bed to bed with the speed of a well-oiled team, giving to each man his short ration of mysterious life, freely moving among the congregation, so to speak, and stooping, pausing, wiping the lips—it was my job to wipe the lips—then disengaging the hands that clasped our wrists and hurrying on. I leaned over, felt the impression of parted lips through the linen, shut my eyes and smiled down at the unshaven face. "Feeling a little better today?" I whispered softly because Mac was already murmuring to the man ahead, and I daubed once more at the lips with the linen towel. "We'll get you off to a good start anyway." And I carefully found a clean spot on the towel.

And then the medicos were kneeling and it was 0730—time was passing, that much I knew—and Mac was straightening up and signaling to me to throw open the infirmary doors. So I threw them open, nodded to a couple of familiar faces, hurried back to Mac. Blond hair faded almost to white, wet blue eyes, enormous unhappy face like the tortured white root of a dead tree, tall brawny heavyweight wearing vestments and purple stole and khaki shirt and pants, poor Mac, and I watched the watering eyes, the dimples that were really little twitching scars in his great pale cheeks, watched Mac and everything he did as if I knew already what I owed him and as if all those days were upon me when Mac would be gone.

"Cheer up, Mac," I whispered, "there's a pelican following us. That's a good sign, isn't it?"

But still he was not listening, so I looked around, asked one of the medicos to bring me a fresh towel. Mac was standing in front of the cross with his chest caved in and his clasped hands trembling and his walleyes large and yellow and fixed on the silent faces of the men. I stood beside him, nudged him, and in a louder whisper tried again.

"The men are pretty devout, Mac, at least they aren't taking any chances. They're waiting for you. Let's go."

More tinkling of the bell. Infirmary jammed with men. Faces looking in at every porthole. Silent faces watching until they could have their turns inside. And inside all the heads were bare—gray pebbly helmets carried by chin straps or stuffed under perspiring arms—and tan or black or blond or red almost all of them were shaved, packed together like so many living bones, and in the silence and looking over Mac's white shoulder I thought that all those young vulnerable skulls must have been cast from the same mold. The men were breathing—I could see the movement of their chests—they were waiting to return to battle stations, to return to work. Somebody coughed.

And then Mac shuddered and began. They pressed forward at 0800 hours, pressed toward the cross, all of them, with the blank vaguely apprehensive faces of young sailors who never know what's coming—ocean, destruction, living dream—on their way toward the unknown. Blue denim, white canvas, wind-burned skin, here and there a thin-lipped smile, a jaw hanging down. I saw Sonny in the crowd, saw him trying to elbow his way to the makeshift altar and sneaking a couple of extra steps whenever he could. I smiled.

"Let me get up there," I heard him whisper, "me next," and then he too was in the front row and on his knees and when we passed, Mac and I, passed with cup, plate and towel, I felt the tug on my sleeve and knew suddenly that Sonny's reverence was not all for God. "Got to speak to you, Skipper," he whispered as I touched the corner of the towel to the shapeless swelling of those trembling lips, "got to have a word with you right away. . . ."

I nodded.

So at 0940 hours the last stragglers crossed themselves and we were done. Mac went below for a shower while I wrapped the cross in the chamois, stowed it again in the white cabinet. The sea was still a honey-colored syrup streaked with green, the blue of the sky had faded nearly to white, I thought I could smell the spices of a distant land on the smooth clear moving air. If only I could have heard a few birds; I always missed the song of the birds when we were at sea. At least the pelican, sweet deformed lonely creature, was still high off the barrels of our sternmost guns.

I stooped under number three turret then and began to whistle, forgetting as usual that it was bad luck to whistle on a ship. Sonny slid out from behind a funnel, we fell in step.

"Well," he said, "we got troubles. Oh my, we surely got troubles now. Ain't you noticed anything peculiar yet today? You ain't seen a thing to make you suspicion the ship ain't exactly right? Well, let me tell you. Somebody is fiddling with the boats. How's that? Sure as I know you is you I know somebody is fooling around with them lifeboats. That's bad. But that ain't all. Somebody else has broke into the small arms locker. Yes sir, somebody has busted into that locker and swiped every last small arms on the ship. Ain't that just the devil? But you want to know what I think? Here's what: I think they means to kill all the officers and dump the bodies in the lifeboats! Some kind of devilish thing like that, you wait and see. . . ."

I returned to my cabin and unlocked it, opened the porthole, hung my head out of the porthole where there was nothing to see except the golden water, the paste of foam, the passing schools of bright fish, the shadow of the ship sliding down to the deep. And all the while overhead there was a stealthy clamor around the white lifeboat—I remembered that *33 persons* was stenciled on the bow—and I nodded to myself, closed up the port again, because poor faithful Sonny was never wrong. But at least the ocean was calm and I wasn't sick.

So I spent the day in my damp bunk reading, still trying to catch up with Mac, spent the day in hard meditation and drinking warm clear water from the regulation black Bakelite pitcher which I filled at the tap. Around 1600 hours I went topside briefly to assure myself that Tremlow had not abandoned his interest in the lifeboat. He had not. I saw him stow a wooden box —sea biscuits? ammunition? medical supplies?—under the tarp and then with heavy grace and fierce agility drop down beneath the tarp himself and begin to laugh with someone already secreted in that hot white arc. Standing flat against steel, beautifully hidden, I looked skyward then—the poor pelican was gone —and then I skimmed down below again and poured myself another glass of water.

When I felt the sunset imminent I simply spread open the New Testament over my eyes and fell asleep. . . .

I woke even before Sonny kicked with his old black blucher on my cabin door, woke in time to hear him muttering, grunting under the weight of an axe, flapping and sweating down the companionway toward my cabin door. But the cabin was filled with moonlight and there was no hurry. I ran my fingers over the books in the little shadowy bookcase screwed to the steel plate at the head of my bunk until I found the slot for the New Testament and shoved it home. Then I emptied the remains of the water pitcher into my right hand and rinsed my face, snorted, wiped my face on the rumpled sheet. The moon filled the cabin with its pale nighttime color; my palms and the backs of my hands, I saw, were green. I was covered with green perspiration. But I knew I wasn't going to be sick this time, had nothing to fear from my ocean nausea now.

And opening the door: "Topside, Sonny," I said, "the first thing to secure is the pilothouse."

"Now I want to tell you," panting, chugging along with the bright fire axe, leading me through the darkness and into the sudden green pools, "now you want to watch yourself. They's got a ringleader."

"Ah, yes," I said, "a ringleader."

"A ringleader, just like I says. And they been having a party. That's right! They been having a party on the fantail ever since the dark come down. And they're full of beans! Hear? You hear it?"

A shot, a tinkle, a scream from somewhere aft, the far-off massed clatter of running men. Hand on iron, foot on a rung, I paused and gave the ship my craning and hasty inspection: a black ship in a bright lunar field, and high above us little steel cups were whirling on the mast and there was smoke in the smokestack. The bow dipped, then recovered itself.

"Now about this party," pulling me around, pointing upward with the luminous head of the axe, for a moment thrusting his enraged face close to mine, "that devil been the whole show, that's the devil got them stirred up this way."

"Tremlow?"

"You got the name on your lips. You ought to know. That's him. Now this devil thought up a party and worked the whole thing out hisself and I was down there on the fantail too—old nigger spy, that's Sonny—and I want to tell you I never seen a party like that before. It sure stirred them up. You know how? Hula-hula, that's how. I tell you, when he done the hula-hula, he had them men in the palm of his hand."

"Tremlow?" I said, "Tremlow doing some kind of Hawaiian dance?"

"That's right," but whispering, drawing me back into the protection of a funnel and pointing firmly, contemptuously, out to a white stretch of the deck where half a dozen of them suddenly raced by dragging burden, victim, spoils of some sort through the green glow of that southern night. "Yes, hula-hula. That's what I mean and with all the trimmings. He danced that dance hisself. And you know what? He got them full of intoxication, that's it, downright intoxication, with all that hula-hula stuff, got them cheering and bumping around and dancing themselves, the way he beat around there in the middle of that moonlit fantail with two fellows playing those little tinny stringed instruments and two more beating on galvanized iron pots for drums. He even had a real grass skirt that swooped all the way down to his ankles and a shirt fixed over his head so you couldn't tell whether he was a chief or one of them hula-hula girls. It did

143

the trick, so I guess it didn't matter which he was. That devil. . . ."

Another shot, another brief turbulent huddle, the arc and soar of something pushed, tossed, heaved and then sailing overboard. And the deep green velvet night was in my face, the whole ship glistened under its coating of salty moisture, and now there was the moon itself adrift in its own mirrored ocean and the ship was in the sway of the moon, and Tremlow, so Sonny said, had done his dance.

"It must have been amusing, Sonny," I said, and I was hanging on tightly to the moonlit ship though she was still, flat in the water like a melting iceberg. "But I hope they don't bother Mac. He's discouraged enough already, eh, Sonny?"

"That chaplain? That chaplain's on the skids. We coming to each man for hisself now, you wait and see. . . ."

"Yes. But wait a minute," I stopped short, caught hold of his sleeve, leaned out over the rail, "there, do you feel it, Sonny? Quick, what's happening?"

Rigid. Black wet nose in the air. Long black paw held up for silence. And then: "Turning." And moving his head then until his white hallelujah eyes were again fixed on mine, and looking at me and sighing with the hopelessness of all nigger warnings and prognostications, he repeated the word: "Turning."

"Changing course, Sonny? Are we? Out with it, is she changing course to starboard?"

"Turning," he repeated, "turning to port. Now you're the one wants to secure the pilothouse, now here's your chance."

"On the double," I said, and the axehead lunged, the ship was straining, moving into the tension of a giant curve, leading us into some forbidden circle. And then the PA was coughing, whistling, piping the madness of its call to Battle Stations and suddenly and dead ahead of us, the green moonlight and black shadows assumed a more solid and dangerous shape: lifeboat, bridge wing, pilothouse, it was all there, each piece in its proper place and rising in tiers and frosted together like the sections of some giant wedding cake. Then hand over hand and up the last green frosted rungs and feeling the whole of that starboard bridge wing heeling down slightly under the centrifugal force, strain, of that tight turn, and bringing each other to a standstill at the open door of the pilothouse where he, Tremlow, was clutching the spokes and even yet trying to get another degree out of the locked wheel.

Moonlight. Green brass binnacle. Green brass barometer. Madness on the decks below, clatter of falling helmets, bodies stumbling, falling, diving into gun mounts, and up here in the wheelhouse our near-naked wireless operator, Tremlow, at the helm of the ship. Sonny began to swing high the axe, but I stayed his arm, for a long moment could only stand there waiting, holding my breath, surveying that ludicrous scene of Tremlow's plan. Because there was Tremlow in the moonlit pilothouse, alone on the bridge, and he was wearing only the long grass skirt and the sweat of the dance was still bright and slick and heavy on his arms, his shoulders, his long muscle-banded back.

"Let go, Skipper," whispering, shuffling, "let me chop him down!"

And then there was the flash of the head, the toss of the long black hair, and Tremlow leapt from the wheel and assumed a crouch. The grass skirt was matted into a smooth bulky fibrous round over the terrible bones of his hips, fell long and sharp and undulating to his bare ankles. Even when he crouched it swished. The wheel was abandoned and the brass speaking tube was calling us, fiercely, shrilly, and moonlight was all about Tremlow and suddenly was also falling flat on a long dark flank that had come out of the grass like a tiger.

"No, no, Sonny," I whispered, holding the arm, turning away the axe, keeping my eyes on the muscles bunching up to spring, "when I hit him, you take the wheel. We must think of the ship. . . ."

So the bright axe fell under our feet. And Sonny sprang out of the way and I threw up my guard. The moon, I noticed, made luminous scar-shaped blotches on the slick brown of that violent breast and flashed and swam and was scattered in all the sharp folds and blended spaces of that now hissing and roaring grass skirt which was coming at me and barely covered him, swinging, swaying in his headlong strides. He was still grinning.

"Tremlow," I tried to say when he socked me. He knocked down my guard with a tap of his bright fist, and vaguely I thought that it wasn't fair, that he was supposed to respect my age, respect my rank, that he was supposed to be down in the shack communicating with the rest of the fleet. Knocked down my guard and socked me in the mouth, and I should have ducked at least because the line of that blow was as clear as hate in the steady eyes, though I still missed the idea, the plan, which was surely riding far forward by then in Tremlow's eye.

"Wait," I said, and my mouth was bleeding, "wait a minute. . . you don't know what you're doing. . . you'll be sorry, Tremlow."

But he hit me in the mouth again. Same fist, same mouth, more bloody mud, more pain. Why not the nose, I thought, or the naked eye, or the stomach, why this furious interest in my loose and soft-spoken mouth?

"Tremlow," I said, tried to say, "you're on duty. . .and Battle Stations. . .the shack. . .please."

We went over the rail, off that wing of the bridge and down, down, with his fist wedged among my bloody teeth and the grass skirt flying, and together, locked together in his hate we burst through something—canvas, I thought, the tarp!—and landed together in a black embrace. Faint odor of dried-out bilge. Faint odor of new hemp. And of cork and lead and paint. And feeling another kind of pain, suddenly I knew that we had fallen together into the bottom of the white lifeboat—*33 persons*—and that we were not alone. For a moment, hearing laughter, listening to Tremlow swear, for a moment my eyes in darkness found the star-shaped hole in the tarpaulin overhead, and for that single moment I watched the gentle moon pulsing to all the limits of the great canted star cut in the canvas. I must have moaned.

Because the star fled and suddenly the fight went on and the tangle of arms, legs, hands, began to twist again in the sloping darkness inside the boat which all the while I never forgot was white, and my whole poor self told me that the others, whoever they were, were piling on. There seemed to be a purpose in that struggle, but still it escaped me. And then hands, the crook of a naked arm, everyone pulling in a different direction in the darkness until all at once they seemed to work together, those hands, that vicious elbow, and I heard the ripping of cloth and felt myself floundering, flopping helplessly, because they had gotten a little rough water cask under my stomach and were rolling me in some odd fashion on that little rough barrel. And in the darkness. Forever in the darkness and crippled, bleeding away my good blood in my poor battered mouth. There was no laughter now.

"What the hell!" I said, or at least thought deep in my heart, and over the barrel then I began to fight like a fish. Oh, I grunted at them, gagging on blood, grinding the top of my bald head into the invisible deck, and I flexed every possible muscle and bucked, did my best to buck, thrashed around good and plenty in the darkness with someone breathing his hot breath into my ear and the cloth ripping away from my flesh as if they were running the tip of a hot wire down the length of my thigh.

And then: "Dear God," I said, but this too was merely a quick sensation deep in the heart because the grass skirt—wet rough matting of cruel grass—was rammed against me and there was only darkness and a low steady fatigued scuffling sound in the bottom of the white lifeboat along with my last spent cry of pain.

But they must have had an accomplice stationed on the deck because the darkness bolted then, myself and water keg and kneeling men all knocked together, smashed, set whirling in the very darkness that had been tipped, freed, cut loose, was now falling. Surely there was an accomplice who pushed her out and cut the cables, because one moment I was tumbling in the darkness and the next I was standing straight out of the star-shaped hole with my hands raised up and my eyes thrust up into the moonlight. The lifeboat was falling but I was standing inside the star with my head in the air and my eyes fixed on one tiny figure far above who was leaning out over the deck, throwing down a rope. It was Mac. Mac with his vestments flying and his tiny face white with fear, Mac who flung down the rope and, hand over burning hand—I was free on the end of that rope when the lifeboat struck—pulled me back aboard.

Struck, yes, and the splash reached up and soaked my legs even while I clung to the rope and twirled slowly around and around on the end of it.

"Pull her up, Mac," I whispered, "for God's sake. . . ."

There were three lifeboats, as it turned out—Tremlow was in the lead—and on the cold deck I lay half-naked and propped on my side and watched the three of them turn away from us in the moonlight and sail away. Three white sitting ducks in the moonlight. And perhaps I should have unlimbered one of the three-inch guns and ordered them picked off. It would have been easy. And they deserved it. But I lay on the deck half-naked and wet and shivering and thought I saw Tremlow small and dark and confident at the tiller of that first white gently rolling boat. So I let them go. Merely watched and wondered what the sun would do to Tremlow in that grass skirt, wondered what he would say when he was picked up. Claim to be a survivor of a torpedoed ship? God knows. Or perhaps, I thought, perhaps they would never be picked up.

"Let him go on dancing," I said to Mac and tried to smile.

They disappeared like three drops of milk dissolving in a creamy soup, those three boats. And wiping my nose, rubbing myself gently, lying at Mac's feet on our wet and unyielding deck I watched them, watched those three little white boats until they were gone. Follow the leader, I thought. And later, much later, I reported the group of them to be missing in action and told the old man we lost the boats in a storm.

The floating paradise, the brutal act, a few memories on a distant shore. . . .

. . .dropped to my knees beside her and took her cold hand—no rings—and confessed to her at long last that Fernandez was dead. That I had found him dead at the end of my final shore patrol on Second Avenue. That I thought she should know.

Yes, I thought she should know. And yes, I told her the truth, made my confession, got it off my chest that night the snow fell into the trembling arms of the larch trees on our black and ragged island rooted fast in the cold and choppy waters of the Atlantic. Yes, I told her, my own daughter. For her own good. For her own good and mine, for our mutual relief. And yes, yes, I thought she might spare herself if she knew the truth, might spare her own life somehow. But I was wrong, of course.

The truth. Yet wasn't I deceiving her even then? Wasn't I sparing her certain details, withholding others, failing somehow to convey the true tonality of the thing? Well, I should hope to God! Because how could I or anyone else convey the true tonality of Second Avenue, kneeling as I was by Cassandra's little lumpy four-poster—little nightcaps secreted for years under that embroidered pillow—in the cold dark room in that prim rotting house with fresh white snow on the sagging eaves and those dark trenches—Puritan graves—awake and listening in the cellar? No. Second Avenue could not survive that moment in a winter's night. Then why did I wait, why bother to talk to her at all? Because I should have acted then and there, should have done something on the spot, so to speak, in the middle of the flickering darkness of Second Avenue. Yes, I should have left the body, bodies to be true to fact, exactly where I found them in the flickering chaos of the cheap room in that Second Avenue hotel, flophouse, whatever it was, and posted a guard and driven the gray Navy pickup truck back to that other cheap hotel myself, and waked her and bundled her into a blanket and driven her, still half-asleep, back down those twenty or so wet blocks and carried her up the broken tiles of those stairs and into the room of blood where she could have taken a good look at him with her own eyes. Yes. That's what I should have done. I know it now. But I waited.

Yes, I waited those two or three months, and they made all the difference, they tipped the scale, shadings of the true tonality were lost, and certain details were kept to myself. Cassandra never knew, for instance, that I took care that she should not be alone that night. Small matter, yet it might have helped. And I never told her how my stomach felt as if it were going to boil over like a car radiator. These and a few other small points omitted, gone. And I shall never forgive myself the loss. A hair's breadth might have kept Cassandra from killing herself, merely a hair's breadth. Now I shall never really forgive myself the loss.

But if I missed those many years ago I won't miss again. So now for everything, for what I told her as well as what I didn't tell her in the upstairs bedroom of the cold island house, everything I can think of now to restore a little of the tonality, to set to rights my passion. A small recognition, a brief scene of blood, some light on our lost affections.

There was the regulation .45 caliber Navy automatic, for instance, stuck like a four-pound T-bone steak point down on my hip. And a web belt—too small, they were always too small for me—buckled around the girth of my white tunic and squeezing me, puckering the skirt of the tunic with deep awkward pleats. And the dark bright blue brassard on my arm—white letters SP a mile high—and then the gaiters. Little canvas things with laces and hooks and eyes and canvas straps to go under the instep, little canvas sleeves to bind the ends of the white trousers to the fat ankles, and it must have been two o'clock in the morning, Eastern War Time, when I sat on the floor in our shabby room in the cheap hotel trying to fasten on the gaiters, puffing, struggling, moving my lips in silence because Cassandra and Pixie too were both sleeping in the single bed. And finally the cap, my old white garrison cap—eagle going to seed on the front, golden threads of the eagle turning black—the old cap pulled square on my head to simulate, if possible, the policeman's style, the policeman's look of authority. My rig, my poor rig. Thank God she never saw me in that rig.

It was raining. Once more we were across the street from a Greyhound terminal, though it was an eastern rather than a Pacific terminal and though we were in a hotel instead of a Chinese restaurant, and it was raining. A vaguely familiar terminal, the return to a hardly altered darkness, the city-wide relentless song of the rain, and in a wet envelope in my pocket, my orders. A final shore patrol for Skipper. More shore patrol, more drunks in a dream, more faces inside the cage. Didn't they know I had had enough, that I was done with the sea? At least I withheld this information from Cassandra, kept her from knowing that she would be alone that night while I, her father, was off exposing himself to God knows what harm. So we crossed the street in the rain at half-past one in the morning—no more 0130 hours for me, no more—and ran for the nearest doorway and in the red-eyed pain of interrupted uneasy slumber we shook ourselves like dogs in front of the desk clerk and piled into the dingy, self-service elevator.

Even from across the street and through the rain I spotted that hotel for what it was: a place for suicide.

"Where are we, Skipper?" she asked once, but I shook my head. I needed time, I needed silence, I had to think. The elevator had a tic in its ratchets and one of the push buttons had fallen out, it banged from side to side in its dismal shaft and smelled like the flooded lavatory of the bus we had just escaped from. There was a crumpled six-inch black headline in the corner. We groaned and banged our way up the shaft.

A place for suicide obviously, and my orders were in my pocket and Sonny was three or four thousand miles away that moment in Southern Cal. Surely I couldn't seek help from the clerk who had sent us up with malice, oh, with what obvious malice to the fourteenth floor which was really the thirteenth floor, I knew. Never have I been taken in by the number fourteen in a cheap water front hotel but have always known beforehand that other number it concealed. The light went out when we reached the fourteenth—thirteenth—floor and, knowing I could not trust Cassandra alone, I gasped, fumbled for the door lever in the darkness, caught my fingers in a joint that was packed with grease.

So we disembarked quickly into the bare corridor, and as I was turning the key in the lock I saw the figure down on its knees with scrubbing brush and pail at the far end of the corridor and I knew that for the moment at least Cassandra was safe. A lucky break on our unlucky floor.

The single bed, the broken radio, the cigarette burns on the chiffonier, the stains on the toilet seat, the broken window shade which came down in my arms. A room in the wartime metropolis of the world for Cassandra, a cut above a flophouse for Cassandra, just the place for her, with its hairs on the pillows and old disreputable impressions on the gray sheets. How little I knew.

"Are you trying to look like Mussolini, Skipper? You look like Mussolini, Skipper, you really do when you hold your chin out that way."

I smiled. "You're tired, Cassandra," I said, "you better hop right on in. Big day coming up, Cassandra."

So it was 2 A.M. and mother and infant were sleeping together in the narrow bed with the loose springs which on many another night gave quick unconcealed clamor to the hidden desires of young servicemen, and I was lacing my gaiters in the middle of the floor and staring at the rain-refracted puddle of neon light that my feet were in. It always rained hardest between midnight and early dawn, I thought.

And then hat, gun, gaiters and envelope of orders and I was ready, paused for a last look at the two of them in the lonely bed. "Grandpa's going on shore patrol," I whispered, "be a good girl." I carried a straight-backed chair with me and left the door ajar when I stepped into the hall.

I set down the chair, cleared my throat, beckoned slowly with my finger. From far down the hall she peered at me, dropped the brush into the pail. She swept away the wings of hair with her wet hands and gasped, rolled her eyes at me, climbed to her feet and bundled up the rags of her skirt and came to me as if I were pulling her in steadily on a golden string. She was plucking herself into a vague new shape, her eyes were white and fixed on mine, to those young eyes I must have looked like General Douglas MacArthur in the bare corridor of that disreputable hotel.

Sixteen years old and haggard, dismayed by the faint lingering sensation of her missing youth, confused by her age, already a sallow and lonely legend of the late-night elevated trains. Scrub woman and still a child. And staring at the phantom officer high in that vulgar building while the rain fell.

"Late for you, Sissy," I said. "Pretty late for you, isn't it?"

Something crossed her face then and she wiped her nose and tried to conceal what must have been a pain in her side. I drew her close to me—fragile jaw, transparent flesh, a certain color in the hair, human being despite the rags, the tin pail, endless vigil on the fourteenth floor. I glanced at the crack in the door, the chair, and back to the girl with her eyes, bright nose, lame spirit, carfare rolled up in the top of her stocking.

"Now, Sissy," I said, "can you sit in the chair? Do you think you can do that?"

She looked inward for some obscure source of moral vision, then measured the distance to the chair, then looked long and hard at me, then, "That's it, that's it," I said, and then she sat down.

"Now, Sissy, listen to me. I must go down in the elevator now, and I will be gone until the light comes through the window over your bucket and brush. You see it, Sissy? Now you must stay in the chair until I return. Don't let anyone go into the room, don't let the lady come out. And if you hear the lady moving about in the room, you go to her and stay with her. Do you understand me, Sissy? You must keep awake and take care of the lady. Take good care of the lady."

And stinking elevator, empty desk, rain in the street. And at the curb and occupied, I knew, there was the small gray windowless pickup truck with its official number and spotlight on the driver's side. It had the unmistakable look of all penal vans, the rain was a thin film over its dents and bruises. Each dent, each chip in the official gray paint meant a thrown brick or a struggle in the street, a punchy body smashed against the side of the gray truck and beaten up, carried away. I sighed, craned up for a final sight of the fourteenth floor and straightened the big blue brassard on my arm and climbed into the truck. The engine kicked over and we pulled out into the deserted thoroughfare of glistening worn trolley track and black girders of the elevated overhead, began to cruise, to weave rhythmically between the girders.

Twenty blocks of girders, fruit carts shrouded for the night, occasional strip-tease theaters—light bulbs, ticket booth, bright naked posters in the rain—while armed merchant ships waited on both the rivers and GI's drank their late glasses of beer or Nedick's orange juice. Cruising down Second Avenue through the rain, killing a last official night toward the end of the war, fat and uncomfortable and fatigued—gaiters too tight, poor circulation— until, as luck would have it, we saw the crowd and the chief who was driving popped on the light, the little spotlight, and speared the crowd.

"Got your hackles up, Chief?" I asked, "the boys ought to be able to do a little bloodsucking right here, don't you think?"

So we hit the curb, drove over the curb, cut a swath through the rain, and just in time I braced myself against the battered tin dashboard and saved my head.

"Why, look," I said, "they're mostly women," and all the gray tin doors flew open at once and we were accosting the women on Second Avenue and looking for trouble.

"Blew your buttons already, Chief?" I said, but he didn't hear me.

And from deep in the crowd and choking herself with the bathrobe collar and shaking the bright rain in her long blonde hair and pulling the robe tight in the middle: "Hey, girls, the Navy's here!" she said. But the bare throats were still—no laughter—and the robes and negligees were wet, the lips were wet, the eyes were full of something they had seen upstairs. No love. Mere sheep huddling away from death. Though the blonde pushed forward then and gave a tug on her bathrobe cord.

"What about you, Happiness?" she said. "What about you, Honey?" But her eyes were full of another face, not mine, and something, I could tell, was wrong.

"All right," I said. "Now tell me. Any sailors in trouble around here?"

And watching me, letting the rain run down her cheeks: "Upstairs," she said.

"Thought so," I said. "Well, Chief, lead the way."

The entrance hall was dark and crooked and full of rotten vegetables, stray cats, one of the dark doorways off lower Second Avenue and lean, improvident, brushed here and there with scum. And there were five flights of stairs. Five long flights. Already the chief and the other gray members of our shore patrol—three more pairs of gaiters, three hickory sticks—and even the women had passed me on the second landing when I stopped for breath. Already the chief and armed sailors and women sounded like dark dray horses in an abandoned warehouse overhead, and I was puffing up the stairs with my hand ready on the T-bone steak and my full heart beating slow time to the climb.

The top. Rain on a little window, rain among broken aerials, another dark corridor in one more house of crumbling skin and I waited—a foot on the last step, foot on the landing, forearm across the upraised thigh—and took a few slow breaths to quiet everything.

"What is it, Chief?" I called, and tried to loosen my tight gaiters.

Then I walked down the corridor, pushed through the women, and looked for myself. I pushed through, blood or no blood, and fell to my knees beside his body while my face began to tingle and my stomach started to boil up like the radiator of an overheated car. I looked at the body and I swayed, glanced once about the room. And at least Fernandez had found his hideaway, his true hideaway, at last. Peruvian face mask, a pair of black castanets, long white tasseled shawl like the one he had once given to his bride, these he had hung at interesting artistic angles on that sagging wall of skeletal white lath and flaking plaster. Another rain-refracted neon light flicked on and off through the window, lit up a portion of the wall and fell across me where I was kneeling close enough to touch him and to memorize forever each shattered line of that little corpse. There was a woven straw chair with an enormous high rounded back and gently curving arms and a solid basket bottom, and the assailants, murderers, whoever they were, had knocked it over, hacked away at it with some kind of sacrificial hatchet. And they had found his collection of old silver coins, had flung the old bright coins all about the room where they glowed like blood money, old silver coins of honor, in the flickering cheap neon light. But no matter how destroyed, it was still his hideaway, I could see that: here on the top floor of the building of condemned lives, here he had gathered together his bric-a-brac —earthen jugs, horsehair switch, dried poppies in a little Chinese vase—here feathered the poor wrecked nest which I had found, stumbled into, invaded with my gaping shore patrol.

He was naked. Covered with blood. Yes, Fernandez lay on his back on the floor and his neck was fastened to the iron leg of the day bed with one of the strings of the smashed guitar. The murderers had jumped on the belly of his new guitar and smashed it. There was a white mountain-goat rug flung across the day bed but they had killed Fernandez on the hard bare floor. Stabbed, beaten, poked and prodded, but he was finally choked to death with the guitar string.

And the fingers. Yes, all five fingers of the left hand. All five. The clasp knife, the wine-dark pool, the fingers themselves, it was clear, too clear, what they had done and that the severed fingers were responsible for the spidery red lines scattered over everything. The wild tracings, the scene of blood—I touched him on the shoulder once and then I managed to reach the corridor and, while the blonde held me under the arm and cupped her wet hand on my forehead, I doubled over and let everything in my hot stomach boil up and out.

When I returned to the room I pried open the window and let the rain beat in. I remained standing on my feet and staring at the second body until the job was done. The other belonged to a sailor and was fully clothed in white bell-bottomed pants, crumpled white middy blouse. A big man face down. Hands buried beneath the face. Legs kicked far apart. Killed by the single driving blow of another clasp knife which they had left in his back.

"His name's Harry," the blonde said.

"Harry," I said. "Poor Harry."

And then all of her weight was on my arm, her voice suddenly tremulous, she was crying. She said she knew what had happened and wanted to tell me. So I righted the hatcheted straw chair and made her sit down, held her cold hard hand and looked at Harry while the hand squeezed and the elbow shook and the voice talked on. She said that she had heard the noise upstairs and that there was nothing unusual about the noise, but that when the man came down and banged on her door, another sailor, she said, and as big as Harry, very much like Harry in fact, she told him she didn't want to with anyone who had just been fighting, that she wasn't going to give herself to anybody with a swelling eye and the blood still on his knuckles and running out of his nose. But she couldn't help herself, she said, and it wasn't bad, all things considered. So he waited until it was over and then while she was trying to do something with her hair and he, the sailor, was still breathing hard on her bed, why then he caught her eye and kept looking at her and told her all about it. He and a couple of others had killed a little fairy spic upstairs, that it was a game they had to let some fairy pick them up and then, when they were in the flophouse room, to pull out the knives. . . .

"He waited, you see? Waited until he was done to tell me. So now for ten bucks the blood's on my hands too, and all over I'm dying, I can feel it. That guy there, that Harry," pointing down, drawing the robe tight between her knees, "he came in too soon, you see, and tried to save his buddy, so they killed him. . . . I wish it was me."

I let go of her hand, I helped to turn up the bathrobe collar, I wrapped the white mountain-goat rug around her lap. Her head was down. I touched the thin blonde hair on the back of that small ageless skull and spoke to the chief, made it clear to him that I didn't want to see the sailor's face.

And then the chief gave orders: "Get the basket stretcher out of the truck. You two, wrap him in the sheet. But leave the little one alone, he's not ours. . . ."

Was Tremlow's first name Harry? Was it Tremlow lying now at the bare feet of the streetwalker sitting in the shiny partially chopped-up straw chair? Tremlow killed at last while defending my little lost son-in-law? Or was it Tremlow who had swung the sacrificial hatchet, destroyed the hideaway, lopped off the fingers? This, I thought, was more like Tremlow, but I could not be sure and was careful that I would never know.

I looked again and saw the little white calfskin book lying near the left hand of Fernandez. It was a book from the past, a soft white unread book just out of reach where I left it.

"Don't worry," I called softly to the bowed figure on the straw chair, "there's no blood on your hands."

And web belt, meaty automatic and gaiters, these I dropped into the back of the pickup truck with Harry's body, stared at the sheeted form bound into the mesh of the basket, and stepped away, flagged down a taxi, returned as quickly as I could to the predawn silhouette of my own cheap hotel.

She was sitting in the straight-backed chair, poor Sissy, and wide awake, clear providential eyes fixed on the elevator. I held the door so it wouldn't bang and took off my cap and smiled. Then wrinkled and bloodstained and more haggard than Sissy herself, I approached her slowly and helped her out of the chair and took her into my arms and kissed her. Her mouth tasted like old wax paper but it was the kiss of my life.

And we were wrong about him, Cassandra, weren't we? Just a little wrong, Cassandra?

"Papa," I cried, "no, Papa. Please. . . ."

"I shall do it, Edward, I tell you. See if I don't. . . ."

"But please, please, what about Mamma, Papa? What about me?"

"Some things, Edward, can't be helped. . . ."

And crouching at the keyhole of the lavatory door, soft little hands cupped on soft fat knees and hot, desperate, hopeful, suddenly inspired: "Wait, Papa, wait, I will play for you, poor Papa."

"No, no, Edward, never mind. . .it will do no good. . . ."

But I raised one of my hands then, clapped it over my lips, waited. And when I failed to answer him there was only silence behind the lavatory door. Was he caught off guard? Uncertain? Or stricken even more deeply with despair, sitting on the old brown wooden toilet seat with vacant eyes and pure white boneless mortician's hands clasped vacantly between his knees? I knew by the peculiar intensity of that prolonged silence that I was safe for awhile, that he could do nothing at least until I had played him my Brahms. It was the dripping faucet that gave the silence its peculiar tight suspended ring, the dripping faucet that convinced me: it would hold his attention until I could play my Brahms.

"Are you there, Edward?"

But as small and fat and ungainly as I was, and as much as I wanted to talk with him, plead with him, I had just been inspired and knew enough, suddenly, not to answer. One sound, I understood, and he might well blow his head off then and there.

"Edward?"

But his voice was weaker while the monstrous dripping was louder, more dominant, more demanding. And my cheeks were fatter than ever with my held breath, my ears throbbed, my eyes throbbed, I stole away into the bright noon sun of that hapless Friday in midsummer. I flew to my room, as much as any inspired and terrified fat boy can fly, and for those few moments—mere sunlit suspended moments saved by a rotten washer in the right-hand faucet in the lavatory sink—for those extra moments of life he was none the wiser.

I ran to my room though I was not a quick child, ran with my short plump bare arms flung out in front of me and not a sob in my throat, not a snuffle in my little pink naked rosebud of a nose, so bent was I on staying his hand with my cello. And the sunlight, bright sunlight coming through every window in planes as broad as each sill and filled with motes and little stationary rainbows that warmed leg, knee, pudgy arm, home full of light and silence and suspended warmth. And only the two of us to share my Brahms.

The cello was under my bed and without thinking I flopped to my hands and knees and hauled it out, and then tumbled it onto my bed, turned back the corners of the old worn-out patchwork quilt in which my mother always wrapped that precious instrument. Cello in the sunlight, tiny shadows beneath the strings, wood that was only a shell, a thin wooden skin, but dark

159

and brown and burnished. The sunlight brought out the sheen of my cello—tiny concentric circles of crimson moons—brought out the glow of the thick cat strings. I stood there, put my palm on its thin hard belly, and already it was warm and rich and filled with my slow awkward song.

So I tightened the strings, tightened the bow and hugged the now upright cello and held my breath, trotted back silently— bulging sway-backed child, bouncing cello—to my lonely sun-lit post by the locked door. And then—no noise, no noise—the terror of touching the cello's middle leg to the floor and of rest-ing the waxen neck in my shoulder and pressing down a string and raising the bow, flinging up the bow and staring at the key-hole and waiting, watching the keyhole, smiling, in silence hold-ing everything ready for the song.

"Now, Papa," I said suddenly, and there was a startled jump-ing sound behind the door, "now I am going to play!" And my arm fell and the bow dragged, sawed, swayed to and fro—hair on gut, fat fingertips on gut—and the cello and I rolled from side to side together. I kept my eyes on the little black hole in the door, with every ecstatic rhythmic roll crossed and recrossed my legs.

So I played for him, played Brahms while my father must have been loading the pistol, played while he swept an impatient and frightened hand through the gray thinning hair and made fierce eyes to himself behind the door. I played with no thought of him, really, but he must have gagged a little to himself in there, choked like a man coughing up blood for the first time as he tried to decide how best to use the nickel-plated weapon, forced his fingers inside the trigger guard. I suppose the first sounds of the cello must have destroyed the spell of the faucet. So I played on, phantom accomplice to his brutal act, and all the while hoping, I think, for success and pleased with the song.

And then: "Edward!"

Bow in mid-air. Silence, catch in my throat, legs locked. Be-cause his voice was loud. He had gotten down on his knees and had put his mouth to the keyhole: "Edward," he said firmly, "stop it!"

And then cello, legs, bow, myself, heart, Brahms, all locked together for a moment of immobile frenzy because I heard the lock turn in the lavatory door and thought he was coming out to me.

"Edward! I have opened the door. There is no point in making someone break down the door to get me. . . ."

So the bow swung free and again I was squatting, leaning close to the door: "But, Papa, may I come in then?"

The shot. The tiny acid stink at the keyhole. And the door opened slightly of its own accord, hung ajar so that I saw one twisted foot, trouser cuff jerked above the ankle, and my own release, my cry, my grief, the long shocked moment when I clung to the cello and heard the terrible noise and wondered when it would ever end. He may have spoken to me one last time—"Good-by, Edward"—but I couldn't be sure. The shot, after all, killed everything.

Everything, that is, except my love. But if my own poor father was Death himself, as I think he was, then certainly I was right to tell Cassandra how familiar I was with the seeds of death. Wasn't I myself, as a matter of fact, simply that? Simply one of those little black seeds of death? And what else can I say to Father, Mother, Gertrude, Fernandez, Cassandra, except sleep, sleep, sleep?

Land of Spices

High lights of helplessness? Mere trivial record of collapse? Say, rather, that it is the chronicle of recovery, the history of courage, the dead reckoning of my romance, the act of memory, the dance of shadows. And all the earmarks of pageantry, if you will, the glow of Skipper's serpentine tale.

Cinnamon, I discovered when I was tossed up spent and half-naked on the invisible shore of our wandering island—old Ariel in sneakers, sprite surviving in bald-headed man of fair complexion—cinnamon, I found, comes to the hand like little thin brown pancakes or the small crisp leaves of a midget tobacco plant. And like Big Bertha who calls to me out of the black forest of her great ugly face I too am partial to cinnamon, am always crumpling a few of the brittle dusty leaves in my pockets, rubbing it gently onto the noses of my favorite cows. And what better than cinnamon for my simmering dreams?

Yesterday, if I can trust such calculations in my time of no time, yesterday marked the end of Catalina Kate's eighth month. Four weeks to go and right on time, and Kate has stretched and swelled and grown magnificently. My Kate with a breadbasket as big as a house, tight as a drum, and the color of old brick and shiny, smooth and shiny, under the gaudy calico of that tattered dress. And wasn't Sister Josie pleased? "Baby coming in four weeks, Josie," I told her. And weren't we all? But yesterday was also the day I knocked up Sweet Phyllis in the shade of the calabash tree. A big day, as I told Sonny, a big day all around.

"Cow's calling, Skipper. Just hear if she ain't!"

Dawn. The first moment of windy dawn, and the bright limes were dancing, the naked flesh hung down from the little cocoa trees, and already the ants were swarming. Red-eyed Sonny stood there—metamorphosed, waiting forever—among the broad leaves and shadows framed in my large white rotting casement. Sonny was waiting, yawning, rubbing his eyes in my view of the world.

"Cow's calling for sure. And ain't that Sweet Phyllis, Skipper? Sounds like Phyllis to me!"

"All right, Sonny," leaning forward, scratching myself, smearing the ants, watching the shifting torso in my window, listening, "it's all right, Sonny. She'll wait." I could hear the faint far-off appeal, the dumb strained trumpeting of Sweet Phyllis in heat. She sounded ecstatic, was making a brassy sustained noise of grief. Sonny had a good ear.

"Tell Big Bertha to fix us a lunch, Sonny. We might as well make a day of it. And tell Bertha that she and Kate and Josie may come along if they'd like to. Fair enough?"

"Oh, they'll want to come along, Skipper," grinning, shifting softly and erratically in the window with his arms pressed tight to the long thin torso and somehow active, up to something, though in no way suggesting his intention to be off, to be gone about my business, "them girls wouldn't miss a hot fete for Phyllis if you allows them the privilege and lets them get off from work, Skipper, you knows that!"

The old smashed petty officer's cap this time, the indecent angle of the cap, the long shrunken torso like a paste of hickory ash and soot, the fixed grin, the unshaved black jaw working. "Well, Sonny," I said, "how about it? Are you going to tell Big

Bertha what I told you?" And then, listening, watching, returning his grin: "Sonny," I said softly, "Sonny, are you relieving yourself against Plantation House? Under my very window, Sonny? You have no scruples. You have no scruples at all."

And shaking his head in pretended pain, showing me that long wry black face and contorting his brows, blinking: "That's right, Skipper," he said, "I don't have none of that scruples stuff. No, sir!"

So that's how yesterday began, with the live sounds of the calling cow and Sonny's water. It ended after dark with a bath, one of the prolonged infrequent sandy sea-splashing baths for Sonny and myself. And in between, only our little idyl down with the cow. Only the five of us in the shade of the calabash tree with Phyllis. And the girls, as Sonny called them, added their charms to the cows' and enjoyed our little slow pastoral down in the overgrown field with Phyllis and Alma and Edward and Freddy and Beatrice and Gloria. More water, of course, and a little song and so many soothing hands and a nap on a pile of green calabashes and the taste of guava jam, it couldn't have been a better time for Phyllis, a better time for us.

"All right," I said, "everyone here? Now let's not have a lot of noise. I don't want you making a lot of noise and frightening that cow. You hear? I don't want to get kicked." And then I started off, leading the way. And Sonny in the old chief's cap and ragged white undershorts followed, and then Big Bertha with our lunch on her head in an iron pot, and then beautiful sway-backed Kate and Sister Josie, who in her mauve hood and cowl, long mauve skirts hiding her little black shoes, loved all the wild cows and mockingbirds and indecent flowers. In a long single file and in that colorful order they followed me through the bush, and I was the Artificial Inseminator of course, and in one hand I carried the little black tattered satchel and in the other hand swung Uncle Billy's crucifix. A slow languid single-file progress through the bush with the women jabbering and the orchids hanging down from the naked Indian trees and Sonny slapping flies and the sun, the high sun, piercing my old white Navy cap with its invisible rays. And I swayed, I swung myself from side to side, opened up our way along that all-but-ob-literated cow path on the saw-toothed ridge among the soft hibiscus and poisoned thorns and, yes, the hummingbirds, the little quick jewels of my destiny. From the frozen and crunchy cow paths of the Atlantic island—my mythic rock in a cold sea —to this soft pageant through leaf, tendril, sun, wind, how far I had come.

"Got to go a little faster now," I said, and raised the dripping satchel so they could see it, "must hurry it up a little, Sonny and young ladies, or the ice will melt."

And from the other side of the ridge and on the floating air she was calling us, Sweet Phyllis, was holding her quarters rigid and sticking her nose through the calabash leaves and blaring at us, blaring forth the message of her poor baffled fertility. It was a signal of distress, a low-register fire horn, and I recognized more than Sweet Phyllis's voice drifting over the ridge.

"You hear it, Big Bertha?" I said, "hear it, Kate? And you, Sister Josie, do you hear it too? They're all calling now. Alma and Beatrice and Gloria and Edward and Freddy—hear them calling? They've gotten the idea from Phyllis, eh? All of them think it is time for a hot fete, even the steers. Isn't that so, Josie?"

Little black Josie, old Bertha with the pot on her head, my dusty rouge-colored pregnant Kate with her club of dark hair hanging down to her breast and her belly slung down and for-ward near the end of her time—they giggled, each one of them, and pointed at the wet shirt clinging to my enormous back, pointed at the dripping satchel. I smelled them—little nun, old cook, mother-to-be—and knew that they were in a processional, after all, and that each one of them was capable of love in her own way.

"The way things is going, Skipper, old Sonny's about to start a little calling of his own any minute now. I just feels a big call catching right here in this skinny throat of mine. Got to bellow it out any minute, Skipper, damn if I don't."

"You want to call too, Sonny," I said. "Why not? A little call-ing wouldn't hurt you. It's the hammock that's bad for you, Sonny. Too much time in the hammock is bad."

And I laughed, glanced over my shoulder—Sonny flopping along in his unbuckled combat boots, Sonny pulling up his drawers—and the three dark women were watching us and listening. Love at last, I thought, and I thrashed out onto a small golden promontory above the field. Blue sky, bright pale blue of a baby's eye, our golden vantage point, the field below; and in the center of the field the dark low sprawling shape of our deep green tree, and under the tree the cows—two steers, four heifers, six young beauties in all—and in the branches of the tree, which were tied together, knotted together like tangled ribbons in a careless head of hair, the birds, a screeching and wandering tribe of birds that were drawn to Phyllis's song like ourselves and now swarmed in the tree. Love at last. I smiled over my shoulder and we started down.

To the last we held our single file. To the last we maintained our evenly spaced formation, our gentle steps, delicate order, significant line. Tennis shoes filled with burrs, white trousers torn, old rakish and rotting white cap, shreds of once-white shirt plastered to my mahogany breast and back, and except for these I was naked. Sniffing the sweet air and keeping my chin lifted, and swaying, riding slowly forward at a heavy contented angle I, Skipper, led the way. I knew the way, was the man in charge—the AI—and there was no mistaking me for anything but the leader now, and they were faithful followers, my entourage. Down we went, and the tennis shoes and combat boots and little black pointed shoes from the missionary's museum and two other lovely pairs of naked feet hardly touched the earth, hardly made a sound, surely left no prints in the soft wild surface of the empty field. It was a long slow day with the cows, a picnic under the calabash tree, a gentle moment, a pastoral in my time of no time.

We maintained our places in line up to the very tree itself, and then one by one and without breaking file we stopped and folded aside the tender branches, one by one entered the shade, joined the loud animals in the din of the birds. The spot I chose for entering was not an arm's length from Sweet Phyllis's dripping nose which was thrust through the leaves and sniffing us, giving the sound of desire to our approach. But she was not frightened. And as soon as I entered that grove of shade I rested my hand on her shoulder, thrust my own nose through the leaves, was just in time to watch Kate take the last twenty or thirty steps of our amorous way.

She was like a child, like a young girl, because despite her weight and swayed back, despite sore muscles and the rank sweat on her exotic brow, she was taking those last steps with her hands held behind her back—backs of her hands nesting in the small of her back—and with her elbows held out like wings, and she was waggling her elbows, tossing her head, taking light happy strides on her naked toes. It was a sinuous slow-motion seductive cantering, the heavy oblivious dance of my young Kate. Despite the water under her skin. Despite the big precious baby inside the sac.

"Come along, Catalina Kate," I cried, "I'm watching you!"

And then we were all together and the bellowing stopped, the birds simmered down, Bertha wedged the iron pot into the above-ground roots of the tree, and I—humming, musing, stripping off the rags of my shirt—I squatted and opened my official black satchel and removed the little sad chunk of ice, deposited the little smooth half-melted piece of ice in the lip of the spring that was a black puddle among the lesser roots at the far edge of the tree. And carefully—down on my knees, smiling—I took the little glass bottle from the satchel and weighed it in my hand—a mere nothing in the hand, but life, the seeds of life—and stood it carefully on the chunk of ice. Safe now. No worry now. I could take my time.

"See there, Kate? That's Oscar. Oscar in the little bottle, Kate! For Sweet Phyllis, do you understand?"

And smiling, glancing at the bottle, glancing at me, fixing the shiny black club of plaited hair between her young breasts and indifferent to the sweat that trickled down her bare throat and down her arms, down the sides of her young face and even into the corners of her dark eyes, she said softly: "Oh, yes, sir, Kate know what you mean."

"Good girl," I said, "I'm glad." And then: "Well, what about it, Bertha, time to eat? Poor Sonny looks pretty hungry to me!"

So while the spring kept Oscar cool, the five of us sprawled close together and held out our hands to the fat black arm that disappeared inside the pot and came up dripping. Calypso herself couldn't have done better. Sweet guavas and fat meat that slid into the fingers, made the fingers breathe, and crushed leaves of cinnamon on the tongue and sweet shreds of coconut. We ate together under the dark speckled covering of the tree, sprawled together, composed, with no need for wine, and the cows stood about and nosed us and a blackbird flew down and sat on Sonny's cap. We ate together among the smooth green oval calabashes that were as large as footballs, and lay among the calabashes and licked our fingers. I told Josie to take off her shoes—"Take them off, Josie," I said, "you have my permission." And while she was trying to unfasten the little knotted strings Edward took it into his head to jump up on Sweet Phyllis and the bird hopped wildly about on Sonny's cap. And my namesake—reluctantly I say that name, reluctantly admit that name—left bright thick gouts of mud on each of Sweet Phyllis's soft yellow flanks.

And Sister Josie spoke. Holding the tiny broken-heeled shoes in her lap and poking a little naked foot from under the madness of the mauve skirts, at last she felt the need to speak, to speak to me: "Edward trying to walk down the road on Phyllis, sir?"

"Of course he is, Josie," I said softly, "of course he is."

"Walk down the road for babies?"

"Yes, Josie. That's what he wants."

So we ate out of Bertha's pot, watched Edward jumping up, watched Freddy using his nose for life—"See how he goes at it, Kate," I said, "no holding him back"—Freddy ramming his head straight out and nuzzling, drawing back his lips, that famished steer, and snuffling and waving marvelous long streamers from his glazed bubbling nose. And in our lazy heap we noticed idly that Alma and Beatrice and Gloria were playing tricks with their tails or trying to mount each other or one of the steers.

"Poor Alma," I said. "She looks like Pagliacci, don't you think so, Sonny? But look there, Sonny, when Beatrice tops Gloria and then Gloria tops Beatrice you really have something, don't you, Sonny? Divine confidence, isn't that it? Blessed purpose anyway, eh? And who's to say nothing will come of it?"

They planted their hoofs among our legs—sticky hoofs, out-stretched legs—and they lowered their brown eyes on us, and Gloria licked my cheek and Beatrice even lay down next to little Josie, cow's head next to cowled head, breaths mingling.

"Now, what about this poor little Sweet Phyllis, Skipper? You going to make her wait all day?"

"In good time, Sonny," I murmured. "She'll wait, she'll keep, don't worry."

The blackbird danced, the cows switched flies or picked off torn little leaves with their big teeth or tried to get everything started up again, the black spring continued to steep the roots of the tree and keep Oscar cool. We dozed. And Sonny sighed for Bertha, put his long skinny panther paw on Kate. "Hugging is all right, Kate," I thought to say, "but nothing more, Kate, do you understand? You mustn't hurt the baby." Then I pulled little Sister Josie's swaddled head down to rest on my broad steaming mahogany chest, gave her Uncle Billy's crucifix to hold.

"No lady of the cloth ever had it this good, Josie," I whispered—shoe-button eyes unmoving, mouth big with gold—and in my half-sleep I heard the animals and through a warm speckled film saw Kate kneeling and rinsing out Sonny's drawers in the spring, then standing in shadow and turning, reaching, as I seemed to see the very shape of the earth-bound child, and hanging Sonny's white drawers on a dead limb to dry. Shades beneath the calabash tree, soft sounds, leaf-eating dreams, grove of perpetuation. Silence. The tree was suddenly still, perfectly still, down to a bird. Love at last.

But we awoke together, and like Josie, Catalina Kate must have felt the need to speak, must have thought that it was her turn to speak to me, because she was leaning over Sonny and looking down at me, and I could see the shoulder, arm, small face, naked hair, and I heard what she was saying: "God snapping him fingers," she said, and that sudden moment of waking was just what she said, "God snapping him fingers," though it was probably Edward breaking a twig or one of the birds bouncing a bright seed off the smooth green back of a resounding calabash.

And on my elbow, suddenly, and wide-awake in my old time out of time: "Yes, Kate," I said. "Snapping for you!" She giggled. And had the hours passed? Days, years? I put down the thought because I was wide-awake and the sharp harmony was like a spear in the ribs.

"Now, Sonny," I said, and already I was crouching at the lip of the spring, "let's take care of Phyllis. What do you say?"

Black spring, black ferns, last remnant of ice the size of a dime, bright little glass bottle upright, gleaming, cool. The genie had wreaked havoc on Oscar, I thought, and I picked up the bottle—the bull in the bottle—and weighed its fragile cool weight in my palm.

"Come, now, Sonny," I said briskly, "let's be done with her. Where's the tube?"

He whipped it out of the satchel then, that resilient tube, long amorous pipette, and I snapped the neck of the bottle, stuck an end in the bottle and caught the other end between my teeth and quickly sucked the few pure drops of Oscar into the pipette and dropped the empty bottle down the spring and popped my finger over the end of the tube to keep Oscar where I wanted him.

"Battle stations, everyone," I said softly, but they were already moving, dancing, and the somehow suspicious cows were already composing themselves into a single group-attitude of affection, and the arms were raised, curved, quick and languid at the same time. Apparently some brief intelligence was stirred in Alma, Freddy, Edward, Beatrice, Gloria, because suddenly they had sense enough to keep out of our way, and drew back and hung their heads and watched us with big round glowing sylvan eyes.

Late afternoon under the calabash tree. Closing in on Phyllis. Speckled shadows. Trembling, smiling, soothing. A cow and her sisters. And it was a simple job for me, and nothing for her, merely a long hair rolled up lengthwise and lost in a hot muscular blanket of questing tenderness, but nonetheless we smiled, closed in carefully and in our own sweet timeless time, expectant, bemused, considerate, with fingers and arms and in soft dalliance transplanting the bull and stopping the tide of the heifer.

Late afternoon and only faint sounds of breathing, brief shifting activity in the shadows, and Sonny was embracing the smooth alerted head while Catalina Kate and Josie were posted on her starboard side, were rubbing and soothing and curving against her starboard side and Bertha, Big Bertha, was tending the port. And I was opposite from Sonny and knew just what to do, just how to do it—reaching gently into the blind looking glass with my eye on the blackbird on Sonny's cap—and at the very moment that the loaded pipette might have disappeared inside, might have slipped from sight forever, I leaned forward quickly and gave a little puff into the tube—it broke the spell, in a breath lodged Oscar firmly in the center of the windless unsuspecting cave that would grow to his presence like a new world and void him, one day, onto the underground waters of the mysterious grove—and pulled back quickly, slapped her rump, tossed the flexible spent pipette in the direction of the satchel and grinned as the whole tree burst into the melodious racket of the dense tribe of blackbirds cheering for our accomplished cow.

And wasn't she an accomplished cow? And wasn't it, this moment of conception, this instant of the long voyage, a time for bird song and smiling and applause? So she gave a sprightly kick then—one pretty kick from Sweet Phyllis but too late, much too late, because I had seen that pretty kick coming even before I took Oscar's little bottle off the ice and was standing back well out of her way and smiling when she let fly so prettily in the face of her fate—and then, and only two years old, she gathered herself in sulky modesty and pushed through the screen of leaves and without much hurry but with clear purpose trotted off alone across the empty field. I waved, I watched her diminishing and rising and falling brown body until it turned into the heavy bush and was gone.

"Well, too bad, Phyllis," I said to myself, "you won't quite catch up with Kate," and I smiled and shook my head.

And then Sonny was pulling on his sun-bleached under-drawers and Bertha was hoisting up her pot and Josie was putting on her shoes and Kate was plaiting her long dark hair again and trying to arouse my heart, I thought, with sight of the child. Any time now, I knew, and the sun would die.

"Good-by to the dark-eyed cow," I said. "And now Big Bertha and Catalina Kate and Sister Josie, I want the three of you to return to Plantation House together while Sonny and I go down to the south beach and have our bath. You lead the way, Bertha; be careful, Kate; remember what you do at sundown, Sister Josie."

So I retrieved Uncle Billy's crucifix from Sister Josie, and they started off.

And in darkness and in silence Sonny and I made our way to the south beach and naked except for our official caps sat together in the sand on the south beach, ground ourselves back and forth, back and forth in the abrasive white sand and scrubbed our calves, thighs, even fleshy Malay archipelagos with handfuls of the fine sand that set up a quick burning sensation in tender skin. By the time we waded out to our shoulders the moon was on the water and the little silver fish were sailing in to nibble at the archipelagos. My arms floated out straight on the warm dark tide, I rinsed my mouth with sea water and spit it back to the sea, I tasted the smooth taste of salt. When we rose up out of the slow-motion surf the conchs were glistening at us in the moonlight.

"I tell you what, Sonny," I said, and dried the crucifix, pulled up my tattered white pants, "why don't you look in on Josie or see what Bertha's fixing us for chow? I just want to stop off a moment at the water wheel. OK?"

So I left him at the corner of the barn and whistled my way to the water wheel and found her waiting. I stood beside her, mere heavy shadow leaning back against dark broken stone and moonlit flowers, and I smelled the leaves of cinnamon. I put my arm around her and touched her then, and part of the dress—sweat-rotted dissolving fragment of faded calico—came off in

172

my hand. But it was no matter and I simply squeezed the cloth into a powder and dropped it and put out my hand again.

Her eyes were soft, luxurious, steady, in the darkness she reached out and tore off a flower—leaf, flower, taste of green vine—and looking at me put it between her teeth, began to chew.

"Saucy young Catalina Kate," I whispered, "eight months pregnant and still saucy, Kate? Iguana going to get you again if you keep this up."

She giggled. I felt the shadow then, the firm shadow of tiny head and neck, little upswept protecting arms. Felt, explored, caressed, and by the position of the moon and direction of the scent of spices I knew that the island was wandering again, floating on.

"Now tell me, Kate," mouth close to her ear, hand holding her tight, "what's it going to be? Little nigger boy, Kate, or little nigger girl?"

And spitting out the leaf and smiling, putting her hand on mine: "Whatever you say, sir," she said, "please God. . . ."

Yesterday our pastoral, tomorrow the spawn. A mere four weeks and I will hold the child in my own two hands and break out the French wine, and after our visit to the cemetery, will come to my flourishing end at last. Four weeks for final memories, for a chance to return, so to speak, to the cold fading Atlantic island which is Cassandra's resting place. And then no more, nothing, free, only a closed heart in this time of no time.

So on to the dead reckoning of my romance. . . .

Drag Race on the Beach

Red sun in the morning, sailor's warning. I knew that much. And hadn't I sworn off the sea? After my one thousand days and nights on the *Starfish* hadn't I sworn off the sea forever? There was my mistrust of the nautical life, the suspicion of my tendency toward seasickness, the uneasiness I had come to feel in the presence of small boats whether in or out of the water. My sympathy for all the young sun-tanned and shrapnel-shredded sailors in deep southern seas would never die, but I was done with the water, the uncomfortable drift of a destructive ocean, done trying to make myself acceptable to the Old Man of the Sea. So what drew me to the *Peter Poor?* How to explain that dawn in March which was an eastern blood bath, in the first place, and full of wind? Why did I interrupt our Mah Jongg games or my friendly fights with the black Labradors? Having recovered from the indignities of that crippling December dance, and having spent three frozen months in the calm inside the gale—trying a little of the Old Grand-Dad myself now, not much, but just a little, and building the fires, drying the dishes, dragging Pixie down the cow paths on a miniature creaky sled with turned-up wooden runners—why, having watched the snow at the window and having kept my mouth shut during all those Sunday dinners and having learned to sleep at last on those hard cold nights, why, suddenly, did I trot right down to the dock with Cassandra and submit myself to the *Peter Poor* which was a fishing boat and didn't even have a head?

"Go on, Skip, don't spoil the fun. It's a good way to see the island. And Skip," clicking the needles, giving the log in the fireplace a shove with her bare toes, "it's just what Candy needs. My God, Skip, how could you refuse?"

And toying with the East Wind, watching her: "What about you, Miranda?" I said, "it's not like you to miss a good time?"

And throwing back her head and twinkling the light in her glass and laughing, "No, no, I've already been out sailing with the boys. Besides, every girl deserves to be the only woman on the *Peter Poor* just once in her life."

But Cassandra only looked at me and took my hand.

So it was on a red dawn in the month of March that I succumbed to the idea of Crooked Finger Rock and sunken ships and a nice rough ghostly cruise around the black island, succumbed and gave Cassandra the one chance in her life to be the only woman on the *Peter Poor*. And it was in the month of May that I raced down the beach for my life in Miranda's hot rod, in May, the month of my daughter's death. And in June that we got out of there, Pixie and I, June when I packed our flight bag and hurried out of that old white clapboard house and carried poor Pixie off to Gertrude's cousin in New Jersey. Four months. Four short months. A brimming spring. And of course I know now that there was a chance for Cassandra up to the very moment she swung her foot gaily over the rail of the *Peter Poor* and stood with her hair blowing and her skirt blowing on the cluttered deck of that water-logged tub of Red's. But there was no chance really for Cassandra after that. No chance at all. The second of the four seasons sucked her under, the sea was cruel. March, then May, then June, and the last fragments, the last high lights, last thoughts, the time of my life.

Red sun in morning, sailor's warning. That's it. And the dawn was lying out there on its side and bleeding to death while I fidgeted outside Cassandra's door—accomplice, father, friend, traveling companion, yes, old chaperon, but lover and destroyer too—and while Miranda waltzed around the dark kitchen in her kimono and tried to fix an early breakfast for Pixie. Dawn bleeding from half a dozen wounds in its side and the wind blowing and my old bird fighting its slow way across the sky.

"Hurry, up, Cassandra," I called through the closed door, blowing on cold fingers, stuffing a fat brown paper sack—lunch for two—under my arm and watching the bird, "you'll have to hurry a little, Cassandra, if the Captain is going to make the dawn tide." Even upstairs in the cold dark house I could feel the tide rising, feel the flood tide reaching its time and turning, brimming, waiting to sweep everything away. But there was no need to hurry. I should have known. I should have known that Red had been waiting seven months already for this tide, this dawn, this day at sea, and that he would have waited forever as long as he had any hopes at all of hearing her heels clicking on the deck of the *Peter Poor*, that he would have let the *Peter Poor* list forever in the green mud for the mere sight of Cassandra coming down his weedy path at six o'clock in the morning, would have sailed the *Peter Poor* onto rocks, shoals, reefs, ledges, anywhere at all and under any conditions if he could once persuade Cassandra to climb aboard. No hurry. And yet perhaps I was aware of his bald-headed, wind-burned, down-East, inarticulate seagoing licentious patience after all, and fidgeted, marked the stages of the dawn out of the intuitive resources of my destructive sympathy. God knows. But she appeared to me then, unsmiling—unsmiling since the blustery high school dance when I had done my best to tell her everything, make her understand—and wearing a little pale blue silk kerchief tied under her chin.

"I thought you were going to wear slacks, Cassandra," I said. "Slacks are more appropriate to a boat, you know. Much more appropriate than a full skirt, Cassandra. But of course it's too late now anyway."

We went downstairs together—shadows and little playful drafts on the stairs, and if it wasn't a big prize bow for a high school dance then it was a big billowing rust-colored skirt for a windy day—and in the kitchen she hugged Miranda and kissed Pixie's forehead. Then hot coffee, standing up, and then another hug, another kiss, and then good-by.

"While we're gone, Miranda," I said, "don't fool around with the nipples or do anything harmful to the child. OK, Miranda?"

"My God, Skip, you've got a sore memory, haven't you? But everything's forgiven, Skip. Don't worry."

The wind, the red sun, and I tried to take her arm under the chestnut tree, but she walked on ahead of me with the kerchief tilted back and her two small white hands pressed down flat against the tiny round abdomen of the orange skirt which lunged and kicked and whirled in woolen fury. The hard thin mature white legs were bare, I could see that, and I tried to come abreast of her again on the empty road.

"That skirt's going to give you trouble, Cassandra," I said, just as all at once she turned off the road and began to run lightly down the weedy path with the skirt whipping and fumbling about her legs and the tight kerchief changing color in the dawn light.

"Wait, Cassandra, wait for me," I called. I wondered what figure of unhappiness it was that I could see plainly enough in the stiffness of the slender shoulders and forlorn abandonment of the little swathed head. Her feet were describing those sad uncomfortable circles of the young female who runs off with wet eyes or uncommunicative smile or tiny cry clutched, held, in the naked throat, and I wanted to stop her, wanted to walk awhile with my arm about her shoulder and her hand in my hand. But it was no use.

"Jomo, good morning," I heard her say in her best voice, and I saw it all, Cassandra still lightly running and Jomo looking at her from where he was crouched at the gasoline pump and Red watching her from the bow of the *Peter Poor* and Bub buttoning his pants near the overturned skiff and grinning into the wind and watching her. So I put on the steam then and caught up with her.

And leaning over the tin can with the hose in the hole and peering up at me from under the bill of the baseball cap and shielding his mouth with his hand: "How's Papa?" Jomo said, and spit through his teeth.

"OK, Jomo," I said, "I'm OK, thanks." And softly and under my breath, "Viva la Salerno, Jomo," I said to myself.

"A little winded, ain't you?"

"Well, yes, Jomo, I've been running."

But he was returning the nozzle to the pump, spitting between his teeth again, catching the wire handle of the tin can in his hook and lifting it, holding the tin can out to Bub: "Here, Bub, take this fuel to the Captain. On the double. Tide's full."

I thought of offering Bub a hand and then thought better of it. So I stood on the end of Red's jetty—mere crumbling slatted catwalk covered with mollusks and broken pots and splashes of old flaking paint—and watched Cassandra balance herself down the plank to the *Peter Poor*, watched Red take her hand, her elbow, brace one massive palm in the curve of the little sloping rib cage until she had swung her foot, boarded the boat, and I watched Bub lug the gasoline down the plank black with oil and tar and the dawn tide, and wished that he would slip, that he would take a plunge, tin and all. But Bub was steady that morning with chicken feathers sticking to the seat of his pants and the wind in his hair.

And helping her around the anchor and leading her aft: "Sea's rough," I heard Red say, "hope you like a rough sea."

And Cassandra: "I'm a good sailor, Red—Captain Red—really."

March wind, gulls putting the dawn curse on us, cold harsh shadows breaking apart and scattering and the jetty swaying and shaking and the *Peter Poor* yanking at the hawsers and now and again smashing into the side of the jetty and spray and chunks of black water and field mice cowering in the white-haired crab grass—it was a malevolent unpromising scene and it was all I could do to keep my feet. The strongest smell was of gasoline; the next strongest smell was of dead fish.

"You're coming, ain't you?" Jomo said. "We're shoving off," and he indicated with his hook that I was to start down the plank.

"You go first," I said.

"Can't," Jomo said, "the lines."

"Well," I said, "no pushing," and felt the plank bending under me and the black sea beginning to move and just as I found the gunwale with my toe and caught one of the rusted stays in my right hand, I heard the first hawser thundering past my ear and knew the plank was gone. Beneath the floor boards and somewhere toward the stern the engine sounded like an old Model-A with pitted cylinders and water in the exhaust. Rolling, pitching, moody little fishing boat, cold fiery dawn, we left the jetty with a puff of acrid smoke tangled up in the shrouds and the other hawser floating, dragging out behind us on the choppy sea.

"Say, Red," I called, "is there a place for me to sit down back there?"

And from the black and oily cockpit, and holding a full fifth of whiskey in his right hand, easily, lightly, gesturing with it, and smiling at Cassandra and saying something to her under cover of the wind: "Why, sure," he called, "we can make room for you. Sure we can."

"Thanks," I shouted, and managed to reach the cockpit hand over hand.

Lowering sun, wind that socked us counter to the black waves, cockpit full of salt spray, and Bub at the little iron wheel and Jomo crouching on the stern with the bill of his baseball cap level, unruffled, and his hook in the air, and Red, tall, heavy-set, bald, early morning reddish whiskers wet on his face, and his pale blue eyes hard and bright in the furnace of his desire, Red knee-deep in yellow oilskins in the unsteady dirty cockpit that revealed the old rotten ribs of the *Peter Poor*.

"Going to be wet when we get out of the cove," Red said. "Wet and rough."

I hung on. I had burned my palm once already on a tin chimney, so I hung on to a convenient but slimy cleat and to a thin inexplicable rusted wire that came down from somewhere overhead. "See all the signs, do you," I said, and let go for a brief moment to wipe my face.

"Yup," he said. "I see the signs all right."

The eye that looked at me then was like a pale translucent

grape in a wine-dark sea. Kind. Intelligent. Contemptuous. Then he looked away and the arms and fingers and hands kept moving.

Red among the oilskins. Red getting ready. He pulled on thick loose yellow pants, worked himself slowly into a thick loose shiny yellow coat, fastened a jet-black mountainous sou'wester on his sun-colored head. The captain, the tall stately bulk of the sea-wet man. And then he turned and helped Cassandra into one of the yellow coats—too big, charm of sleeves that covered the hands, all the charm of the perfect small woman's body in the slick ocean-going coat too large—and on her small head and over the kerchief he tied another crinkled black sou'wester, so that she looked like a child, a smiling child, in a captain's rig. She had a little face that should have been on a box of pilot biscuits. Great black protective helmet and soft wet cheeks and shiny eyes. No hands, no breasts, but wet white skin and plaintive eyes.

And then: "Here's yours," he said, and glanced to the wobbling top of the mast and tossed me a bundle, frowned.

"My second skin," I said, because I had gone out once before in oilskins, and I laughed, ducked, took the flying crest of a wave full in the face. "Which way is up?" I laughed, wiped my eyes, held the thick yellow bundle of empty arms and legs in my own fat arms. "How about it, Red?"

"Oilskins," he said clearly, patiently through the wind, the spray, the now billowing sun, "better put them on. . .going to be plenty rough out there."

So I struggled with the monstrous crackling togs, turned them over, turned them around, lost my footing—shoulder smack up against the ironwood edge of the top of the dirty cabin, sudden quick pain in the shoulder—burned my fingers, finally, on the hard wet skins, felt my cheeks puffing out under the ear flaps of the little tight preposterous sou'wester, felt the chin strap digging in.

"It's much too small," I said, but Red was talking.

"That's Crooked Finger Rock over to leeward," he was saying, gripping Cassandra's little shoulder where it was hidden inside the yellow oilskin, gripping her and pointing away with one long red bony finger that was as steady and sure as the big needle of an enormous compass, "and that's the Dog Head Light —she's abandoned—over there to windward. . . ."

"I see," I heard Cassandra say softly in her most interested voice, "I see," as if they were studying an atlas together in Miranda's parlor, and her eyes, I saw, were fixed on the stately wet red features of Captain Red's squinting seagoing face.

"What's that about Crooked Finger Rock?" I said, but Red was telling her about the draft and sailing qualities of the *Peter Poor*, telling her that the *Peter Poor*, fish-smothered little filthy scow, was really a racing craft, a little Bermudian racer which he had only converted to a fishing boat a few years ago for his own amusement. And then he gave an analysis of Bermudian racers and then a discussion of nautical miles and speed at sea and the medal the Coast Guard had given him for heroism on the high seas. Steady deep wind-whipped voice. Rapt attention. Bub doubled over in stitches at the little wheel.

But I, at least, made an effort to see the landmarks he thought worthy of our attention, and twisted to leeward and saw a chip of black rock rising and falling in those black crests and hair-raising plumes of spray, and I twisted to windward and a couple of miles away made out the tiny white spire of the lighthouse.

Waves, bright sun, the bow falling, and suddenly I knew what was on my mind, had been on my mind from the first moment I had seen the *Peter Poor*. "Red," I interrupted him, cupping my hands, insisting, until the big red face swung in my direction and Cassandra stared down at her feet, "Red, there's no dinghy. Is there, Red?"

"Nope."

"But, Red, we've got to have a dinghy. Don't you care about our safety?"

Face sniffing the salt, eyes clear, big legs spread wide in the cockpit: "Dinghy couldn't last in this water. Too rough. Man can't last either. Too cold. Might's well go down the first time when the boat goes down."

"Good God," I said, "what a way to talk in front of Cassandra."

"Candy don't mind. No, sir. She's a sailor. Told me herself."

Tiny face composed under the sou'wester. Water on the eyelashes, flush in the cheeks, eyes down. Modest. No objections. Not a glance for father. Not a smile. So I nodded, felt myself thrown off balance again as Bub laughed and swung the little iron wheel that was clotted now with lengths of bright dark green seaweed. How was it, I wondered, that the others were in league with the helmsman, what signals were they passing back and forth while only I heaved about moment by moment in the hard rotten embrace of that little tub?

"Cassandra gets her sea legs from her mother," I said, but the sea was against me, the Old Man of the Sea was against me, and the waves smelled like salted fish and the engine smelled of raw gasoline and Jomo was still crouching high on the stern and watching me. And all at once I was unable to take my eyes off him: Jomo going up, Jomo going down, up and down, Jomo swaying off to starboard, Jomo swinging back to port, and holding his hook on high where I could see it and aiming the bill of the baseball cap in my direction and fingering his sideburns now and then but keeping his little black eyes on mine and sitting still but sailing all over the place. Without moving his head he spit between his teeth and the long curve of the spittle, as it reached out on the wind, was superimposed against Jomo's unpredictable motion and dark anxious face. And then I heard him.

"You don't look too good," he said. "Don't feel good, do you? Why don't you go below? Always go below if you don't feel good. Here, let me help you down. . . ."

Even as the *Peter Poor* pitched out from under me, Jomo spit one more time and then hopped off the stern, carefully, without effort, and approached me, came my way with his quick black eyes and on his forehead a sympathetic frown. Jomo with his hot advice, his hot concern for my comfort.

"You want to try sleeping," he said. "Try can you get to sleep and see if I'm not right."

It sounded good. I was bruised, hot, wet, sleepy, and my mouth was full of salt. Salt and a little floating bile. My face and fingers were wrinkled, puckered, as if I had spent the morning in a tepid bath. And the red sun had turned to gold and was hot in my eyes.

"Jomo," I murmured, "there's no dinghy, what do you think of that? But the life jackets, Jomo, point them out to me, will you?"

And roughly, stuffing me into the little wooden companion-way: "You ain't going to need no dinghy nor no lifejackets neither. . . . Now put your feet on the rungs."

So I went down. I went down heavily, a man of oilskins and battered joints, while Jomo stayed kneeling in the open companionway with his arms folded and his chin on his arms—"I got to see this," I heard him say over his shoulder—watching until my feet touched something solid and I fell around facing the cabin and managed to hold myself upright with one hand still on the ladder.

Pots and pans and beer bottles were rolling around on the floor. Two narrow bunks were heaped high with rough tumbled blankets and a pair of long black rubber hip boots. Little portholes were screwed tightly shut, the exhaust of the gasoline engine was seeping furiously through a leaking bulkhead, and in front of me, directly in front of me and hanging down from a hook and swaying left and right, a large black lace brassiere with enormous cups and broad elasticized band and thin black straps was swaying right and left from a hook screwed into the cabin ceiling.

"Jomo," I said, "what's that?"

"Never you mind what it is. Just leave it alone."

Water on the portholes, stink of the engine, rattle of tin and glass going up and down the floor, long comfortable endless pendulum swinging of her black brassiere and: "But, Jomo, what about the owner?"

"Don't you worry about the owner. She's coming back to get that thing. Don't worry."

And then: "Jomo. I'm going to be sick. . . ."

"Well, hot damn, just hike yourself up here on deck," laughing over his shoulder, gesturing, then scowling down at me again through the dodging companionway, "just drag ass, now, I can't let you puke all over my cabin."

I got my head and shoulders up through the hole and into the open air in time to see Captain Red and Cassandra sitting side by side on the thwart and opening our brown paper bag of sandwiches, got there in time to see the wax paper flying off on the wind and one white sandwich entering the big red mouth and the other white sandwich entering Cassandra's mouth. Then they were smiling and chewing and I was hanging my head into darkness that was like the ocean itself and trying to keep the vomit off the fresh yellow bulging breast of my borrowed oilskin coat.

Third occasion of my adult life when my own pampered stomach tried to cast me out. Third time I threw up the very flux of the man, and for a moment, only a moment in the darkness of a cold ocean, I couldn't help remembering the blonde prostitute on Second Avenue who held my forehead in the middle of the night and shared my spasms, because now I was stuffed into oilskins and slung up in a tight companionway and retching, vomiting, gasping between contractions, and there was no one to hold my forehead now. But it was the sea that had done this to me, only the wide sea, and in the drowsy and then electrified intervals of my seasickness I knew there would be no relief until they carried me ashore at last.

Red was standing in front of Cassandra now, my head was rolling, for some reason Jomo was at the wheel and the sea, the wide dark sea, was covered with little sharp bright pieces of tin and I saw them flashing, heard them clattering, clashing on all sides of the *Peter Poor*. The drops on my chin were tickling me and I couldn't move; I felt as if I had been whacked on the stomach with a rolled-up newspaper soaked in brine.

Then blackness. Clap of pain in the head and blackness. Mishap with the boom? Victim of a falling block? One of the running lights shaken loose or a length of chain? But I knew full well that it was Bub because my eyes returned suddenly to tears and sight returned, settled again into bright images of the yellow oilskin, the hook at the wheel, the stern half-buried and shipping water, and somehow I accounted for them and knew suddenly what had become of Bub, could feel him where he crouched above me on the cabin roof and held upraised the old tire iron which they used as a lever to start the engine with.

But no sooner had I worked it out, that Bub had struck me on the head with the tire iron, than I saw the rock. Red, Cassandra, and then behind them the long low shelf of rock covered with a crust of barnacles and submerged every second or two in the sea, and we were wallowing and drifting and slowly coming abeam of the rock which looked like the overturned black petrified hull of some ocean-going vessel that would never sink.

Had it not been for Crooked Finger Rock I might have done something, might have reached around somehow and caught Bub by the throat and snatched away the tire iron and flung it at Red. Somehow I might have knocked Red down and taken over the *Peter Poor* and sailed us back to safety before the squall could threaten us from another quarter. But I saw the rock and heard the bell and Captain Red and Cassandra were posed against the rock itself, in my eye were already on the rock together, were all that remained of the *Peter Poor* and the rest of us. So I could only measure the rock and measure Red and wait for the end, wait for the worst.

I didn't want to drown with Bub, I didn't want Cassandra to survive with Red, and so I watched the hard black surface of the rock and swarthy bright yellow skin of the man, could only stare at the approach of the rock and at what the old man was doing. Jomo had let go the wheel and was watching too.

Because Cassandra was sitting on the edge of the thwart with her head thrown back and her hands spread wide inside the puffy tight yellow sleeves, and because the rust-colored skirt was billowing and I could see the knees and the whiteness above the knees which until now had never been exposed to sun, spray, or the head-on stance of a Captain Red, and because Red had thrown open the stiff crumpling mass of his yellow skins and was smiling and taking his hands away.

"There 'tis," he said.

And that's when I should have had the tire iron to throw, because there it was and I saw it all while Cassandra, poor Cassandra, saw only Red.

Because she looked at Red, stared at him, and then pulled the string yet gave no sign that she knew the black sou'wester was gone or that she cared—but I did, I watched it sail up, roll over, shudder, actually land for a moment on the rock, slide across the rock, drop from sight—and then she pulled at the knot of the pale blue kerchief and held the idle tip of it between two fingers for a moment and then let it go. Drop of blue already a quarter mile astern and the hair a little patch of gold in the wind, the sun, the spray, and the white face exposed to view.

"No, no," I said thickly, because she had reached out her hand—bobbing, swaying, undisturbed—and had drawn it back and was extending it again and Red was waiting for her.

"Cassandra," I mumbled, "Cassandra," but the buoy began to toll and Bub hit me again with the tire iron. So I went down and took her with me, pulled her down into my own small corner of the dark locker that lies under the sea, dragged her to rest in the ruptured center of my own broken head of a dream. Waxed sandwich wrappings, empty brown paper bag, black sou'wester, kerchief—all these whistled above her, and then I was a fat sea dolphin suspended in the painful silence of my green underseas cavern where there was nothing to see except Cassandra's small slick wide-eyed white face lit up with the light of Red's enormous candle against the black bottom, the black tideless root, of Crooked Finger Rock.

The squall came down, I know, because once I opened my eyes and found that I was lying flat on my back in my oilskins on the floor of the cabin, was wedged into the narrow space between the bunks and was staring up at the open companionway which was dark and filled with rain. The rain beat down into the cabin, fell full on my face, and I could hear it spattering on the pots and pans, driving into the piles of blankets thrown into the bunks. The black brassiere was circling above my head and lashing its tail.

We were offshore, three or four miles offshore in a driving squall. We pitched, reeled, rolled in darkness, one of the rubber

186

hip boots fell out of the starboard bunk and down onto my stomach and lay there wet and flapping and undulating on my stomach. At least something, I thought, had saved us from a broadside collision against Crooked Finger Rock.

And later, much later, I awoke and found that they had hoisted me into the port bunk, dumped me into the bunk on top of the uncomfortable wet mass of blankets. I felt the toe of the other rubber boot in the small of my back, the tight sou'-wester was still strapped to my head. And awake I saw the low and fading sun on the lip of the wet companionway, felt the tiny hand on my arm and managed to raise my eyes.

"Skipper? Feeling a little better, Skipper? We're coming into port now, aren't you glad?"

Wet, bright. Uncovered. The small white face that had been cupped in the determined hand of unruly nature. Little beads of sea violence in the eyelashes. Wet bright nose. Wet lips. Bareheaded, smooth, drenched, yellow skins open at the little throat, hair still smacking wet with the open sea and sticking tight and revealing the curve of her little sweet pointed skull. And smiling, Cassandra was smiling down at me. But she was not alone.

"Red—Captain Red—has been teaching me how to sail, Skipper."

And moaning and licking my sour lips: "Yes, yes, I'm sure he has, Cassandra. That's fine."

The Old Man of the Sea, timeless hero of the Atlantic fishing fleet, was standing beside her with his pipe sizzling comfortably and the blood running back into the old channels, and I knew that I could not bear to look at him and knew, suddenly, why everything felt so different to me where I lay on the tumbled uncharitable blankets in the wet alien bunk. The sea. The sea was flat, smooth, calm, the wind had died, the engine was chugging so slowly, steadily, that I began to count the strokes.

"Ahoy, *Peter Poor!*" came the far-off sound of Miranda's voice, and I knew that Cassandra was right and that we were heading into port, heading in toward our berth at the rotten jetty. Peace at last.

But then: "Skipper? Are you well enough to show Red what you have on your chest? I'd like him to see it if you don't mind."

Resisting, mumbling, begging off, trying to push her little hand away, but it was no use of course and she peeled away the layers and smoothed out the hairs with her own white fingers until the two of them leaned down together—two heads close together—and looked at me. Their ears were touching.

"That's the name of my husband, Red. Isn't it beautiful?"

He agreed that it was.

"Where's the Salerno kid?" I asked, and it was a thick green whispered question. "Don't you want to show him too?"

But Red was already helping her up the ladder and we were coming in.

And then Miranda was waving from the end of the jetty: "Ahoy, *Peter Poor*, welcome home!" And half a dozen stray young kinky-faced sheep were huddled in front of her on the end of the jetty and calling for mother.

"Boy, oh boy, are you a sight!" Miranda said. And then they kissed, and from where I sat propped on the jetty I looked and saw our skins piled high amidships on the *Peter Poor*. Our wretched skins. And above the pile with the black strap looped over his steel hook and the rest of it hanging down, Jomo was standing there and holding out his arm and grinning.

"Got something of yours, Miranda," he called. "You want it?"

And laughing, and arm in arm with Cassandra: "You bet your life," she cried, "bring it along!"

Silence. Shadows. A moonlit constellation of little hard new blueberries against the picket fence. An early spring. The glider was jerking back and forth beneath me and grinding, squeaking, arguing with itself like a wounded crow. And the bottle of Old Grand-Dad lay at my foot and I sat with glass in hand.

"Now go to bed, will you, Skip? My God. She's probably gone to the show with Bub. That's all. What's wrong with that?"

The Labradors came out of their kennel, one head above the other, and looked at us—at me in the painful shadows of the glider and at Miranda sitting on the porch rail with her head against the post and one big knee beneath her chin—and sat down on their black bottoms and began to howl. The Labradors, Miranda's blunt-nosed ugly dogs, were howling for my own vigil and for Miranda's silhouette, because Miranda was wearing her black turtle-neck sweater and a Spanish dancer's short white ruffled skirt which the raised knee had slipped into her solid lap like a pile of fresh white roses.

"Even the dogs know she's not with Bub," I said, cracking the neck of the bottle quickly and gently on the lip of the glass, "nobody can fool those dogs, Miranda. Nobody. They're not howling for the fun of it."

Wasn't she looking at her fingernails in the moonlight? Wasn't she studying the tiny inverted moonlit shields, one hand curved and fluted and turning at arm's length in front of her face, and then the other, peering at her enormous hands and yawning? Of course she was. Because it was May and time for Miranda to appraise her big waxen fingernails by light of the moon. And even in the chill of the late May night I knew there would be no goose flesh on her big waxen silhouetted leg, no hair on the smooth dark calf.

"You're an old maid, Skip. Honest to God."

And staring out at the chestnut tree that was trying to pull itself into leaf once more, I lifted my chin and smiled and drooped the corners of my mouth: "I'm afraid I can't say the same for you. Far from it. But I tell you, Miranda," tasting the iodine taste of the Old Grand-Dad on my heavy tongue, sitting on the head of a spring and holding it under, "I'll give her five more minutes, just five, Miranda, and then I'm going to Red's shack and pray to the BVM. that I'm still in time."

She laughed.

But I meant it. Yes, I meant still in time, because there had been the rest of March and April with no more mishaps, nothing but Cassandra suddenly light on her feet and fresh and helpful around the house, Cassandra spending all our last days of winter walking from room to room in the old clapboard house with Pixie held tight in her arms and some kind of song just audible in her severe little nose. Now it was May and Cassandra had changed again and as I must have felt and was soon to know, it was the last of my poor daughter's months. So still in time. I needed to be still in time. Because of March and then May and then June and the last thoughts, fragments, high lights of the time that swept us all away.

"Laugh if you want to, Miranda," I said. "You have nothing to lose."

"For God's sake, Skip," looking my way, plucking the ruffles, resting a long dark hand on the angle of the silhouetted thigh, "and what about you, Skip? What about you?"

She must have known what I had to lose since she destroyed it for me. She must have known since she arranged for the destruction, nursed it, brought it about, tormented both herself and myself with its imminence, with the shape of the flesh, the lay of the soul, the curving brawn that was always gliding behind her plan. And what a vision she must have had of the final weeks in May, since the abortive outcome had already been determined, as only she could have known, on a windy day in March.

So I was about to tell her what I had to lose, was sitting forward on the edge of a broken-down glider and collecting myself against the loud irritating pattern of her asthmatic wheeze—she was still propped on the veranda rail with her long heavy legs exposed, but she was wheezing now, staring at me out of her big dark invisible eyes and wheezing—when the black hot rod shot around the corner by the abandoned Poor House and roared toward us down the straightaway of the dark narrow dirt road, honked at us—triple blaring of the musical horn— and disappeared among the fuzzy black trunks of the larches which were tall and young and mysterious in our brimming spring. And I jumped from the glider and reached the rail in time to see the fat anatomical silver tubes on the side of the engine, the silver disks masking the hub caps, the little fat squirrel tail whipping in circles on the tip of the steel aerial, and, behind the low rectangles of window glass, the two figures in the cut-down chariot for midnights under a full moon. It was traveling without lights.

"You see?" I said, "there she goes! And with Jomo—in Jomo's

hot rod, Miranda—not with Bub. Who's the old maid now, Miranda?"

Old Grand-Dad flat on the floor. Kitchen tumbler sailing out and smashing, splintering, on the roof of the kennel. And I was off the porch and once more running after my destiny which always seemed to be racing ahead of me on black tires.

"Wait a minute, Skip," she cried then, "I'm coming with you!"

So once again with Miranda I entrusted myself to the other hot rod that was still behind her house—orange and white and blue and bearing the number five in a circle on the hood—but this time I myself sat at the wheel and this time, thanks to Bub who had worked on the car as Miranda had said he would, this time that hot rod was a racing vehicle with a full tank of high-octane gasoline, and this time it was spring and the tires were pumped up tight and the fresh paint was bright and tacky.

"Now, Cicisbeo," I muttered, and we swung out onto Poor House Road, took up the chase.

No lights. No muffler. No windshield, no glass in the windows, and I was low in the driver's seat with my foot pushed to the hot floor and my fat hands slick and white on the smooth black steering wheel. Miranda crouched beside me, long hair snapping out on the wind and white skirt bunching and struggling in her powerful arms.

"If they gave us the slip," I shouted, "good-by everything! I hope you're glad. . . ."

Moonlight. Black shadows. Soft silk of the dirt road around the island, and larches, uncut brambles at the side of the road and a dead net hanging down from a luminous branch, and the occasional scent of brine and charcoal smoke on the breakneck wind, and every few hundred feet a water rat leapt from some hollow log or half-buried conduit, dashed under our wheels.

"It's all your doing," I shouted. "I hope you're glad!"

Shaking loose her hair and bunching the white foam of the ruffled skirt up to her breasts, Miranda was larger and whiter and more Venus-like than ever that night, and as we accelerated suddenly onto the silver flats of one of my favorite cow pastures—cows dead and gone, of course, but an open stubbled place in sight of the sea—I knew that in Miranda's eyes I was not the man to win a hot rod race. So I swerved a couple of times and gunned her, set my jaw. I had taken my chances in this very car before, and Miranda or no Miranda, now I would have my moment of inspired revenge. As we thundered across the bumpy moonlit field I made up my mind: the sea. The black sea. Nothing to do but run the one-handed lecherous Jomo into the black sea.

The road, the wash of stubble, the moonlit mounds of powdered shells, the prow of a beached dory, and off to the right the lighthouse and straight ahead a glimpse of the black-lacquered cut-down car we were chasing. I felt relentless.

"Come on, Skip, do your stuff! Good God!" Somehow she had gotten her enormous legs onto the seat and was kneeling and holding the skirt above her belly with one hand and with the other was clutching me around the shoulders. Her hot breath was in my ear, I heard the rising and falling roar of the beehives that were laboring away inside her enormous chest.

"No!" I cried, "Stop! You'll kill us both, Miranda!"

But she hung on, tightened her grip and snuggled her great black and white head down onto my shoulder. Her hair flew into my eyes and even into my open mouth. And tongue, teeth, hair, I was trying to breathe through my nose and gagging, choking, but somehow keeping my grip on the wheel and driving on. But was she trying to comfort me, encourage me, even love me, at least urge me to great daring after all? Had I been wrong about Miranda?

I knew the answer of course. And yet before I could spare a hand off the wheel or risk a glance in her direction, the other car had come into view again and was heading not for the dunes as I had expected but down toward the hard dark sand of Dog's Head beach which stretched northward about a mile and a half from the abandoned light. I saw him, swung the wheel in time, and followed him, tried to catch him midway between the Poor House Road and the beach. But I had no such luck.

The black car turned northward away from the empty lighthouse on Dog's Head beach, and for a moment we were close enough to see the silver disks on the wheels, the two silhouetted heads, the aerial in its whip position. Hot rod, driver, passenger, they seemed to crawl for a moment in a slow fanning geyser of packed sand, and I stuck my fist out of the window. "Beware, Cicisbeo!" I shouted this time, and stepped on the gas.

Off again, the black car leading up the wide wet stretch of deserted beach, black car racing close to the dark water's edge and filling the air with spray, flecks of foam, exhaust, a screen of burning sand. The aluminum exhaust pipes curving out of the lacquered hood were loud, musical, three or four bright pipes of power. Even Miranda lifted her head, leaned forward now and fought the driving wind to see.

"Faster, Skip!" she shouted, and despite winds, sand, uncertain motion, she bounced up and down on the edge of the seat, whacked me rhythmically on fat arm, knee, shoulder.

Two unlighted hammerheaded cars on a moonlit beach, and three times we raced up and down that beach which had been exposed only hours before by a choppy sea, three times up and down from the north end of low boulders to the south end of tall grass and broken faces of cliff and abandoned lighthouse, and three times he tricked me with his sudden and skillful turns, three times he made his turn and left me driving flat out toward disaster among the sleeping boulders or a crash against the cliff. And wasn't he leading me on? Leading me toward a night-consuming accident on the lonely beach?

But I got the hang of it then, so to speak, and made a short turn and cut him off. A surprise blow. Simple maneuver but effective. Quick action of a dangerous mind.

"Got him now, Miranda," I shouted. "Rapacious devil!"

And we were drifting together, that black hot rod and mine, and I was inching in closer to him and then ahead, fighting for the position from which I would cut him off, sailing out now to the left, now to the right on the treacherous sand and giving her the gun again. Side by side in the sound of speed. Shadows cast by the moon were scudding ahead of us, and there were sharp rocks waiting for us in the cold sea and I could make out the dark slippery festoons of kelp.

"Hold on, Cassandra," I shouted out of the window, "it won't be long!" I smelled the night, the salt, the armies of mussels and clams ground under our wheels and the dense smoke of our high-octane fuel. And the excitement touched the backs of my hands, told me the time was near, and I wondered how he could have been foolish enough to trap himself here on Dog's Head beach, how foolish enough to underestimate my courage, the strength of my love. I was half a radiator length ahead of him and Miranda might have touched that black-lacquered car had she held out her hand.

"Now!" I shouted, "Now!" and swung down on the wheel and smelled the rank sizzling cremation of the brake bands as we stopped short of the moonlit choppy waters—half-spin in the sand but safe, dry, coming to a sudden and miraculous stand-still—while the black car went pitching in. It pitched headlong into the rising tide and rocked, floundered, stalled. Smacked one of the rocks.

I fumbled for the ignition and fought the door, using fist, shoulder, heels of both palms. "Get your hook ready," I cried, "I'm coming after you!" And once more I was running until I too hit the shock of the cold water and suddenly found myself knee-deep in it but running in slow motion, still running toward the half-submerged black-lacquered hot rod wrecked on this bitter shore. Already it was bound in kelp, already the cold waters were wallowing above the crankcase, already the thick white salt was sealing up forever those twin silver carburetors which Jomo had buffed, polished, installed, adjusted beside the battered gas pump in front of Red's shack. Half-sunken now, wet and black and pointing out to sea in the moonlight.

"Game's up, Jomo, don't try anything. . . ."

And my two hands went under water and gripped the door handle. My soggy foot was raised high and thrust flat against the side of the car. And then I pulled and there was the suck of the yielding door, the black flood and, baseball cap and all, I dragged him out by the arm and shook him, wrestled with him, until I slipped and we both went under.

And then up again and, "You!" I cried, "It's you!" and I

threw him off his feet again and lunged into the car just as Miranda began laughing her breasty deep Old Grand-Dad laugh at the edge of the beach. I lunged into the car and reached out my hand and stopped, because it was not Cassandra. Because it was nothing. Nobody at all. A mere device, a laundry bag for a torso, something white rolled up for a head. Oh, it was Bub all right, Bub wearing Jomo's cap and driving Jomo's car. Bub's trick. Bub's decoy. And it had worked. Oh, it had worked all right, and while I was risking my neck in Miranda's blue and white and orange hot rod and making my foolish laps on Dog's Head beach or standing hip-deep in the biting black waters of the Atlantic, my Cassandra was lying after all in the arms I had tried to save her from, and falling, fading, swooning, going fast.

So I plunged both hands down and collared Bub, held him, dragged the streaming and spitting and frothy face up close to mine. He had a nosebleed and a little finger-thick abrasion on his upper lip and terror on the narrow sea-white boyish face beneath the dripping duck bill of the baseball cap.

"Where is she," I said. "Where's Cassandra?"

And choked and high-pitched and faint but still querulous, still mean: "Him and her is at the lighthouse. Been up there to the lighthouse since sundown. You old fool. . . ."

So for the first and only time in all my lifelong experience with treachery, deception and Death in his nakedness or in his several disguises, I gave way at last to my impulse and put Tremlow's teaching to the test, allowed myself the small brutal pleasure of drawing blood and forcing flesh on flesh, inflicting pain. Yes, I stood in the choppy and freezing darkness of that black water and contemplated the precise spot where I would punch the child. Because I had gone too far. And Bub had gone too far. The long duck bill of the cap, the cruel tone of his island voice and the saliva awash on his thin white face and even the faint suggestion of tender sideburns creeping down the skin in front of each malformed ear, by all this I was moved, not justified but merely moved, to hit Bub then and there in the face with all my strength.

"Hold still," I muttered, and took a better grip with my left hand, "hold still if you know what's good for you," I said and, keeping my eyes on the little bloody beak in the center of his white face I pulled back my arm and made a fist and drove it as hard as I could into Bub's nose. I held him close for a moment and then pushed him away, let him go, left him rolling over in the cold black water where he could fend for himself.

I left him, rinsed my fist, staggered up into the moonlight and shouted, "No, no, Miranda, wait!" Once more I broke into my sloshing dogtrot on Dog's Head beach, because Miranda was in the hot rod and shifting, throwing the blue and white and orange demon into gear, and waving, driving away. So I was alone once more and desperate and running as fast as I could toward the lighthouse. What heavy steps I took in the sand, how deep those footprints that trailed behind me as I took my slow-motion way down that desolate beach toward the lighthouse.

Slow-motion, yes, and a slogging and painful trot, but after a while I could see that the abandoned white tower of Dog's Head lighthouse was coming down the beach to meet me, was moving, black cliff and all, in my direction. And crab grass, pools of slime, the rusted flukes of a lost anchor, and then the rotted wooden stairs up the side of the cliff and a bright empty Orange Crush bottle gleaming on the tenth step and then the railing gave way under my hand on the head of the cliff and the wind caught hold of me and the lighthouse went up and up above my craning head. The lighthouse. The enormous overgrown moonlit base of it. The tower that had fought the storms, the odor of high waves in the empty doorway, the terrible height of the unlighted eye—I wanted nothing more than to turn my back on it and flee.

But I cupped my hands and raised my mouth aloft and shouted: "Cassandra? In the name of God, Cassandra, are you there?"

No answer, of course. Still no word for her father. Only the brittle feet of the luminous crabs, the cough and lap and barest moan of the slick black tide rising now at the bottom of the cliff and working loose the periwinkles, wearing away the stone, only the darkness inside the tower and, outside, the moonlight and the heavy unfaithful wind that was beating me across the shoulders, making my trousers luff. But of course she was there, of course she was. And had she climbed the circular iron staircase knowing she would never set foot on it again? Or, as in the case of my poor father, was I myself the unwitting tinder that started the blaze? Could she really have intended to spend the last six or eight hours of her life with Jomo in Dog's Head light? My own Cassandra? My proud and fastidious Cassandra? I thought she had. Even as I approached the black doorless opening in the base of the tower I was quite certain that she had planned it all, had intended it all, knowing that I would come and call to her and force myself to climb that tower, climb every one of those iron steps on my hands and knees, and for nothing, all for nothing. Even as I thrust one foot into the darkness of Dog's Head light I knew that I could not possibly be in time.

"Cassandra? Don't play games with me, Cassandra. Please...."

Proud and fastidious, yes, but also like a bird, a very small gray bird that could make no sound. And now she was crouching somewhere in Dog's Head light—at the top, it would be at the top if I knew Cassandra—or lying in Jomo's thin brown abrasive arms in the Dog's Head light. What a bad end for time. What a bad end for the BVM.

"Cassandra? In the name of God, answer me now . . . Please. . . ."

Iron steps. All those iron steps and on my hands and knees. Bareheaded, sopping wet, afraid of finding her but afraid too of losing her, I started up then and with each step I found it increasingly difficult to pull my fingers loose from the iron steps and to haul the dead weight of my nerveless feet behind me. Up it went, that tower, straight to the top, and the center was empty, the circular iron steps were narrow, there was no rail. Cracks in the wall, certain vibrations in the rusted iron, it was like climbing up the interior of some monstrous and abandoned boiler, and it was not for me, this misery of the slow ascent, this caterpillar action up the winding iron stairway to the unknown.

But taking deep dark breaths and bracing myself now and again and glancing up and at the moonlight fluttering in the smashed head of the light, I persevered until suddenly, and as if in answer to my clenched jaw and all the sweeping sensations in my poor spine, the whole thing began to shake and sway and ring, and I clenched my fists, tucked in my fingers, bruised my head, hung on.

A long soft cry of the wind—or was it the wind?—and footsteps. Heavy mindless footsteps crashing down, spiraling down from above, heavy shoes trembling and clattering and banging down the iron stairway, and behind the terrible swaying rhythm in the iron and the racket of the shoes I could hear the click, click, click of the flashing mechanical hand as he swung it against the wall with each step he took.

He passed me. He had already passed me—Jomo without his cap, poor Jomo who must have thought Salerno was nothing compared to what he had gotten himself into now—when I heard the breathing beside my ear and then the toneless bell-strokes of catastrophe fading away below in the darkness.

The iron gut of the tower remained intact, and I crawled to the top and crawled back down again without mishap, without a fall. But the damage was done. I knew it was done before I reached the top, and I began to hurry and began to whisper: "Cassandra? He's gone now, Cassandra, it's all right now. . . you'll see. . . ." I heard nothing but the echoing black sky and tiny skin-crawling sounds above me and the small splash, the eternal picking fingers of wave on rock below. "Cassandra?" I whispered, tried to pull myself up the last few shaky steps, tried to fight down dizziness, tried to see, "you're not crying, are you, Cassandra? Please don't. . . ."

But the damage was done and I was only an old bird in an empty nest. I rolled up onto the iron floor in the smashed head of the lighthouse and crawled into the lee of the low wall and pulled myself into a half-sitting position and waited for the moment when Dog's Head light must tremble and topple forward into the black scum of the rising tide far below.

"Gone, Cassandra? Gone so soon?" I whispered. "Gone with Gertrude, Cassandra? Gone to Papa? But you shouldn't have, Cassandra. You should have thought of me. . . ."

The neat pile of clothing was fluttering a little in the moonlight and it was damp to the touch. I could not make myself look down. But I felt that I had seen her already and there was no reason to look down again. So I half-sat, half-lay there in the cold, the moonlight, the wind, stretched myself out amidst the broken glass and debris and thought about Cassandra and was unable to distinguish between her small white oval face—it was up there with me as well as below on the black rocks—and the small white plastic face of the BVM.

"I won't ask why, Cassandra. Something must have spoken to you, something must have happened. But I don't want to know, Cassandra. So I won't ask. . . ."

I clutched a couple of the thin rusted stanchions and in the gray moonlight stared out to sea. The shoals were miles long and black and sharp, long serrated tentacles that began at the base of the promontory and radiated out to sea, mile after square mile of intricate useless channels and breaking waves and sharp-backed lacerating shoals and spiny reefs. Mile after square mile of ocean cemetery that wasn't even true to its dead but kept flushing itself out on the flood tide. No wonder the poor devils wanted a lighthouse here. No wonder.

I turned again, crept back from the edge and started down. I had climbed to the top of the lighthouse and I was able to climb back down again, feet first. It was a matter of holding tight and feeling my way with my feet and dropping down with little terrible free falls through that tower of darkness. But I managed it. I reached the bottom after all, and I sat on a concrete block in the empty doorway with my head in my hands. I sat there with the lighthouse on my shoulders. And somewhere the tide was rising, the moon was going down, the clouds were scudding. And I sat there while the damp grass sang at my feet and the white tower listed in the indifferent wind.

Ducks in June. Baby ducks in June. I could hear them, Miranda's brood of little three-day-old cheese-colored ducklings, hear them waddling behind the house on this bright early dawn in the first week in June, hear them talking to each other and doing their little Hitler march step as I stood by the bright black stove and coaxed the coffee to reach its rich dark aromatic climax so I could sit down to an early breakfast with Pixie. It was a chilly dawn, but outside the sun was out, and inside Miranda's kitchen the wood-burning stove was as rosy as a hot brick.

"Hear the ducklings, Pixie? You like the little ducklings, don't you, Pixie?"

She looked up at me from where she sat on the wide soft boards of the wooden floor—bright pudding face, bright platinum hair, on her finger a little tin ring that I had found in a Cracker Jack box—and opened her mouth for me and kicked her little dirty white calfskin shoes and gave the rolling pin a quick push. I smiled. Pixie always enjoyed the game with the rolling pin.

"Shall we go out and play with the ducklings after breakfast, Pixie? Would you like that?"

Fresh white apron, fresh white shirt, fresh creamy taste of the toothpaste in my mouth, and Miranda's old tin clock said that it was six o'clock in the morning and already I had ground the coffee in the coffee grinder and put the cereal bowls on the table and finished off Pixie's cold orange juice. And now the sun was shooting golden arrows through the blistered glass in the kitchen window and the stove was warm. The coffee smelled like the new day and was beginning to bubble up into the little myopic eye of the old percolator.

"Where's the corn flakes, Pixie? Go find the corn flakes. . . ."

Big square whitewashed kitchen, sharp golden arrows of the new sun quivering on the white walls and on the table set for two, old tin clock pattering and twisting and clicking in the throes of the hour, little ducks marching around and around outside and the light frost was beginning to disappear. I dangled a quilted pot holder from my fingers and tended the stove and glanced every once in a while at the waiting table. Because instead of the usual unopened fifth of Old Grand-Dad on the breakfast table for Miranda, there was a package wrapped in white tissue paper and done up in red, white and blue ribbons and so placed on the table that it could have been meant only for me.

"What do you think is in the package, Pixie? Something for Grandpa? A present for your grandfather, eh, Pixie? Shall we open it after breakfast and then go play with the ducks?"

There was a card tucked under the ribbon and I had already allowed myself a look at the card—*For Skip*—in a bold black handwriting, nothing more—while Pixie was busy with the rolling pin I had slipped it out of the envelope and read it and then put it back where I had found it in such a way that not even Miranda could tell the difference. A quick look at the card was one thing, but the present itself, I knew, would have to wait. Perhaps I could even hold off until I had done the dishes though I suspected not.

Corn flakes and cold milk and the bowl of sugar. And then the usual fight with Pixie until I made her drop the rolling pin and was able to pick her up and strap her into the pink enamel chair and give her the jam jar and little silver spoon to play with. And then the coffee. The heat of the spicy beans. The first heat of the day. Better than bacon. But just as I was pouring the coffee and sniffing it and watching the sensual brown meta-morphosis in my thin cup, just as I was smiling and getting ready to sit down to breakfast with Pixie, I smelled the sudden odor of a lighted cigarette and felt a movement at the door. I waited and then raised my eyes.

"Miranda," I said. "Good morning! Have some coffee?"

At six-fifteen in the morning she was standing in the doorway with her long legs crossed and her shoulder leaning against the jamb. Black eyes and sockets, uncombed hair, white face. And after all these months she was wearing the canary yellow slacks again.

"Come on," I said, "have some coffee. First pot's the best, isn't it, Miranda?"

She puffed on her cigarette, exhaled, shook her head.

"Well, Miranda," and I was stooping, still holding the pot, smiling up at her, "there seems to be some sort of present on the table. We don't have so many presents around here, do we?"

And then: "That one's got your name on it, Skip."

"Really?" I said. "Well, come on, Miranda, tell me. What is it?"

And slowly and keeping the big formless black eyes on mine and sucking the gray smoke back into her nostrils: "Fetus," she said, and the big mouth slid down a little as if it might smile.

I turned, set the coffee pot on the edge of the stove, faced her again, took hold of the back of the chair with both my hands. The arrows were quivering on the walls but she was watching me.

"What did you say, Miranda?"

"Fetus. Two-months-old fetus in a fruit jar, Skip."

I pulled out the chair then, slowly, and sat down. I pushed away the corn flakes, folded my hands. Miranda was smoking more quickly now, was taking deep rapid puffs. And she was wheezing now. There was a little grease on her face but no lipstick, powder, rouge. Only the uncombed hair and spreading black stains of the eyes.

"I don't understand you," I said at last, watching her, smelling the smoke, noticing that under the blouse she was naked. "I really don't know what you mean, Miranda. What kind of fetus?"

"Just a fetus, Skip. Two months old. Human."

Pixie, I saw, was holding the jam jar on its side and had given up the spoon and had thrust her little hand into the neck of the jar. Strawberry jam. Coffee fast cooling off. Baby ducks still marching. And the white tissue and the card and the ribbon. Red, white and blue ribbon. And I wondered, asked myself, if it could possibly be true. How could it possibly be true? Wasn't it only Miranda's whim? Knowing full well that I would never open it, wasn't it only Miranda's cruelest way of tormenting me at six-fifteen on a morning in the first week in June? But why? What was she trying to tell me? And then suddenly I knew the first thing I had to do, and I did it. I simply reached out my hand, picked up the package, put it to my ear and shook it. But there was no sound. And I could tell nothing by the weight. It was a fruit jar, just as she said, but whether it contained anything or was empty, I did not know.

"All right, Miranda," I said, still holding and weighing the jar and looking at her and seeing the mouth slide down deeper, seeing the breasts heave, "all right, Miranda. What is it?"

She waited. The cigarette was a white butt pinched between her two long fingers. Her legs were crossed. And then her lips moved, her mouth became a large quivering lopsided square: "I mean it, Skip. And just as I said, it's got your name on it. And it's hers," throwing the butt on the kitchen floor where it lay burning out and smoking, "Candy's, I tell you. Why do you think she jumped, you old fool?"

I looked at the mouth, the shadows that were her eyes, I looked at the bright package in my hand. Slowly, slowly I shook it again. Nothing. Full or empty, did it matter? There were tiny arrows of sunlight now on the backs of my hands and Pixie had her mouth full of strawberry jam.

"Cassandra's?" I said then. "You mean it was Cassandra's? But surely that was no reason for Cassandra to kill herself?"

And thrusting her head at me and slowly shaking the black tangled hair and with both hands clutching her enormous white throat: "Reason or no reason," she said, "there it is. Good God!" And she was laughing, wheezing, exhaling dead smoke from the rigid lopsided square of her mouth, "Good God, I thought you'd like to have it! Sort of makes you a grandfather for the second time, doesn't it?"

I waited. And then slowly I stood up and unfastened the strap and gathered Pixie into one arm—Pixie covered with strawberry jam—and in my other hand took up the package again and slowly, gently, pushed past Miranda in the doorway.

"I think you're right, Miranda," I said as softly as I could. "I'm sure you're right. But, Miranda," gently, softly, "you better step on the cigarette. Please."

And I knew then exactly what I had to do, and I did it. I went upstairs and took my white officer's cap off the dummy and put it on my head where it belonged and packed up our tattered flight bag. And with my arms loaded—Pixie hanging from one, bag from the other, bright smeared package in my right hand—I went back down to the kitchen and asked Miranda for a serving spoon. I asked Miranda to take a serving spoon out of the drawer and slip it into my pocket.

"Well," she said, "you're leaving."

"Yes, Miranda," I said. "I'm going to the cemetery first, and then Pixie and I are leaving."

"Good riddance," she said and grinned at me, fumbled for the cigarettes, struck a match. "Good riddance, Skip. . . ."

I smiled.

So I carried Pixie and the flight bag and the present from Miranda out to the cemetery, carried them past the sepulchral barn of the Poor House and down the deeply rutted lane and through the grove of pines and onto the yellow promontory where the expressionless old gray lichen-covered monuments rose up together in sight of the sea. Yellow stubble, crumbling iron enclosure, tall white grizzled stones and names and dates creeping with yellow fungus. And the sky was like the stroke of a brush. And of course the wind was only the sun's chariot and the spray was only a veil of mist at the end of land.

I kicked open the gate and let Pixie crawl around in the stubble between the stones while on my hands and knees once more at the side of the fresh mound I dug a little hole at the top of Cassandra's grave with the serving spoon and stuffed the package in, covered it over. Empty or not it was a part of me somehow and belonged with her. Under a last handful of loose black earth I hid the ribbons—red, white and blue ribbons— and stood up, brushed off my pants. Even from here, and standing in the windy glare of that little Atlantic cemetery, I could smell the pines, feel the pine roots working their way down to the things of the sea.

I threw the spoon out onto the black rocks.

Then off we went, Pixie and I, and I smiled at the thought that the night I found Fernandez on Second Avenue was the first night after the day they stopped the war, and that all my casualties, so to speak, were only accidents that came when the wave of wrath was past. But how can I forget what lies out there in that distant part of my kingdom?

The Golden Fleas

So I had my small quiet victory over Miranda after all, and had my victory over Cassandra too, since there are always faces, strange or familiar, young or old, waiting to kiss me in the dark, and since now there is one more little dark brown face that will soon be waiting like the others. My shades, my children, my memories, my time of no time, and I thank God for wandering islands and invisible shores.

But one more face. Yes, there is one more face because the mountain fell, the flesh went down, they soaked up the blood with coconut fibers, they washed the baby as I told them to, Kate smiled. A big success. And wasn't it the day, the very hour, even the sex I had decided on? And weren't we flourishing together, Kate and I, finishing up our little jobs together on a flourish of love? And didn't Sister Josie and Big Bertha pitch right in and help? Down on their hands and knees with the coconut fibers? And didn't I forbid Kate to have our baby in the swamp, and didn't Kate, young Catalina Kate, bear the baby on the floor of my own room in Plantation House and sleep with the sweat and pleasure of this her first attempt at bearing a baby for me—for Sonny and me—in my own swaying hammock filled with flowers? Didn't Sonny and I wait out in the barn with Oscar until they called us back to the house to see the baby? And didn't I spend the rest of that afternoon—just yesterday, just yesterday afternoon—sitting beside her on a little empty vinegar barrel and giving the hammock a push whenever the wind died down? What more could she ask? What more could I?

But there was last night too, of course, last night when I broke out the French wine and long cigars and took the three of them—Sonny and Kate and little black fuzzy baby in the strip of muslin—down to the cemetery to have a fete with the dead. In the afternoon I rocked Kate and little child in the hammock while the sun hung over us and grew fat and yellow in the leaves and vines outside and the hummingbirds sucked their tiny drams of honey at my still window. But with the coming of night and while Josie and Big Bertha softly clapped their black hands and sang to us outside the window, suddenly I felt like taking a long walk and laughing and eating a good meal and drinking the wine and smoking. So I leaned over Kate and shook her gently and told her it was time to get up because the moon was rising and they were already lighting the candles in the graveyard.

"Come on, Kate," I whispered, "time to go." Slumberous. The shadowy color of cinnamon and rouge. Bright and naked and smiling, softly smiling, in my old hammock full of flowers. Her hair was down and hanging in a single black shank over the side of the hammock, was hanging, swaying, brushing the floor. And even in the shadows I could see how full she was and see that already she had regained her shape and that her naked waist was once more like the little belly of the queen bee.

"Time now, Kate," I said, "give me your hand."

So I helped her out of the hammock and helped guide her head and arms through the hole of the dress, garment, rag, whatever it was, and fixed the muslin around the baby, held it out to her. A bunch of homemade candles; the old broken wicker basket filled with blood sausage, pawpaws, the bottle of wine; white cap on my head and baby in Kate's arms, and we were ready to go then and I shouted to Sonny, led the way.

"Go on, Kate," I said, "take one. . . ." And she smiled and did what I told her, and the coals of our three long slim cigars were as bright as the little red eyes of foraging pigs as we puffed away together down the dark path toward our festive hours among the slabs and crosses and shallow mounds in the sunken cemetery. I could smell the three of us in the darkness—rancid smoke, long hair, wet skin, newborn child—smell our invisible lives in the darkness, and I walked with a bounce and swung the basket to and fro and watched for the glow of the candles.

And then: "You hear what I hears, Skipper?"

"I think so, Sonny. Do you mean the birds?"

"That's it, Skipper. Birds. But birds don't sing in the dark. Does they, Skipper?"

"It's a special night, Sonny, a special night. That's all. They're singing for us."

"Oh. I see. Well. So we got the night angels with us, is that it?"

"Sure, Sonny," I said. "That's it. But how's the cigar? Burning OK?"

"She's burning just fine, Skipper, just fine."

Darkness. Shadows. Heavy dissolving moon. And it was the Night of All Saints as I knew it would be, and somewhere ahead I heard the soft voices in the cemetery and smelled the wax. And above us and hopping, fluttering, singing from branch to branch, Sonny's night angels were keeping pace with us toward the heavy uncertain field of light that was hanging, suddenly, about knee-level beyond the vines, trees, velvet silhouettes of the banana leaves. We were the last to arrive, Sonny and Catalina Kate and myself and the baby, and standing together on the lip of that soft bowl and smiling, waiting, peering down at the illuminated graves—candles were already lit and flickering on most of those old graves—and at the shades of soft fat women and squatting men and children who were lighting candles, eating, laughing—the laughter was as soft as the song of the ground doves—it was hard to know whether all those shades were celebrants honoring the dead or the dead themselves preparing a little fete for Kate's new child.

"Look at that grave, there, Sonny," I whispered. "Looks like a birthday cake, doesn't it, Sonny?"

We laughed then, Sonny and I, softly and gently laughed, and then we helped Kate and baby down the steep path into the sunken cemetery and the artificial day that was flickering and shifting in the heavy familiar darkness of our peaceful night. The floor of the cemetery was covered with sand, crushed shells, tall weeds. And all about us were the old graves that had settled long ago at steep angles into the powdery sand. And the homemade candles, the mere waxen stubs and living remnants of dull yellow light—I took a deep breath of tallow, smoke, spice, the wicks going down, and took in the shades and graves and little yellow teeth of light.

"Now, Catalina Kate," I said quietly, "the choice is yours. Do you think you can pick us out a nice grave?"

In the heavy light of the artificial day our birds were crowding around the edge of the bowl, crowding around the lip of the bowl, and were singing, flitting, sighing with their little wings. Our night angels, as Sonny said. Our invisible chorus.

"That's a beauty, Kate," I murmured, "a marvelous choice." And kneeling, shoving the cap to the back of my head, resting a hand on the raw stone: "OK, Sonny? If this one's OK with you, let's have the candles."

It was an out-of-the-way grave at the far edge of the cemetery, a massive untended affair in the shadow of the trees that leaned down from the top of the bowl. No name. No dates. Long and broad and canted into the sandy earth and half-covered with weeds. A bottomless stone box driven into the sand among the little roots of the weeds, great monumental outline of old stone that had survived grief and that had no need of identity. I knelt there in the darkness and quickly swept the little lizards off the rim of it.

"More, Sonny, more," I cried, "let's give him a big light!" And listening to the birds, the women, the soft sound of Kate talking to the baby—Kate was sitting in the crook of an exposed

tree root and guarding the baby, guarding the basket—Sonny
and I, on hands and knees, inched our way together around the
stone perimeter of that old grave, and one by one the gems of
the crude diadem took fire, swayed, gave off their yellow light
and the long black rising tails of candle smoke. We melted wax
and stuck candles everywhere we could on the dark stone, I
jammed lighted candles among the weeds in the center of that
listing shape. The little flames were popping up all over the
grave and suddenly the unknown soul was lighting up Sonny's
smile and mine and Kate's, was glowing in Kate's eyes and in
the soft sweat on her brow.

So the three of us and the baby sat at the foot of the old dazzling grave, and Catalina Kate tore into the bread and cut the
blood sausage into edible lengths while I broke open the French
wine. Thick bread. Black blood sausage. White wine. And I
propped myself up on Kate's smooth dark rouge-colored young
knee and ate, drank, felt the light of the candles on our cheeks.
And then I asked Kate for a look at the baby, and there it was,
the new face about half the size of her breast and three times as
black and squeezed shut in a lovely little grimace of deep sleep.

"Who do you think it looks like, Kate? Sonny or me?"

And smiling down, tangling her shank of hair into the muslin
and studying the small candlelit sheen of her first child: "Yes,
sir. Him look like the fella in the grave."

"Of course, Kate," I said then, and laughed. "But just think
of it. We can start you off on another little baby in a few
weeks. Would you like that, Kate? But of course you would,"
I said. Kate nodded, smiled, held the baby tight. And we finished the wine, packed the basket, waited for the moon to suck
the last light of our candles into the new day. When we started
back to Plantation House in the morning—this morning—I carried the baby in my own arms. Light as a feather, that baby.
Good as gold.

So yesterday the birth, last night the grave, this morning the
baby in my arms—I gave Uncle Billy's crucifix to Kate this
morning, I thought she deserved it—and this afternoon another
trip to the field because Gloria was calling, calling for me. And

now? Now I sit at my long table in the middle of my loud wandering night and by the light of a candle—one half-burned candle saved from last night's spectacle—I watch this final flourish of my own hand and muse and blow away the ashes and listen to the breathing among the rubbery leaves and the insects sweating out the night. Because now I am fifty-nine years old and I knew I would be, and now there is the sun in the evening, the moon at dawn, the still voice. That's it. The sun in the evening. The moon at dawn. The still voice.

New Directions Paperbooks

Y. Mishima, *Death in Midsummer*. NDP215.
  Confessions of a Mask. NDP253.
Eugenio Montale, *Selected Poems*.† NDP193.
Vladimir Nabokov, *Nikolai Gogol*. NDP78.
New Directions 17. (Anthology) NDP103.
New Directions 18. (Anthology) NDP163.
New Directions 19. (Anthology) NDP214.
New Directions 20. (Anthology) NDP248.
New Directions 21. (Anthology) NDP277.
Charles Olson, *Selected Writings*. NDP231.
George Oppen, *The Materials*. NDP122.
  Of Being Numerous. NDP245.
  This In Which. NDP201.
Wilfred Owen, *Collected Poems*. NDP210.
Nicanor Parra,
  Poems and Antipoems.† NDP242.
Boris Pasternak, *Safe Conduct*. NDP77.
Kenneth Patchen, *Because It Is*. NDP83.
  But Even So. NDP265.
  Collected Poems. NDP284.
  Doubleheader. NDP211.
  Hallelujah Anyway. NDP219.
  The Journal of Albion Moonlight. NDP99.
  Memoirs of a Shy Pornographer. NDP205.
  Selected Poems. NDP160.
  Sleepers Awake. NDP286.
Plays for a New Theater. (Anth.) NDP216.
Ezra Pound, *ABC of Reading*. NDP89.
  Classic Noh Theatre of Japan. NDP79.
  The Confucian Odes. NDP81.
  Confucius. NDP285.
  Confucius to Cummings. (Anth) NDP126.
  Guide to Kulchur. NDP257.
  Literary Essays. NDP250.
  Love Poems of Ancient Egypt. Gift Edition.
    NDP178.
  Selected Poems. NDP66.
  The Spirit of Romance. NDP266.
  Translations.† (Enlarged Edition) NDP145.
Philip Rahv, *Image and Idea*. NDP67.
Carl Rakosi, *Amulet*. NDP234.
Raja Rao, *Kanthapura*. NDP224.
Herbert Read, *The Green Child*. NDP208.
Jesse Reichek, *Etcetera*. NDP196.
Kenneth Rexroth, *Assays*. NDP113.
  An Autobiographical Novel. NDP281.
  Bird in the Bush. NDP80
  Collected Shorter Poems. NDP243.
  100 Poems from the Chinese. NDP192.
  100 Poems from the Japanese.† NDP147.
Charles Reznikoff, *By the Waters of Manhattan*.
  NDP121.
  Testimony: The United States 1885–1890.
    NDP200.
Arthur Rimbaud, *Illuminations*.† NDP56.
  Season in Hell & Drunken Boat.† NDP97.

Saikaku Ihara, *The Life of an Amorous
  Woman*. NDP270.
Jean-Paul Sartre, *Baudelaire*. NDP233.
  Nausea. NDP82.
  The Wall (Intimacy). NDP272.
Delmore Schwartz, *Selected Poems*. NDP241.
Stevie Smith, *Selected Poems*. NDP159.
Gary Snyder, *The Back Country*. NDP249.
  Earth House Hold. NDP267.
Enid Starkie, *Arthur Rimbaud*. NDP254.
Stendhal, *Lucien Leuwen*.
  Book I: *The Green Huntsman*. NDP107.
  Book II: *The Telegraph*. NDP108.
Jules Supervielle, *Selected Writings*.† NDP209.
Dylan Thomas, *Adventures in the Skin Trade*.
  NDP183.
  A Child's Christmas in Wales. Gift Edition.
    NDP181.
  Portrait of the Artist as a Young Dog.
    NDP51.
  Quite Early One Morning. NDP90.
  Under Milk Wood. NDP73.
Lionel Trilling, *E. M. Forster*. NDP189.
Martin Turnell, *Art of French Fiction*. NDP251.
Paul Valéry, *Selected Writings*.† NDP184.
Vernon Watkins, *Selected Poems*. NDP221.
Nathanael West, *Miss Lonelyhearts &
  Day of the Locust*. NDP125.
George F. Whicher, tr.,
  The Goliard Poets.† NDP206.
J. Willett, *Theatre of Bertolt Brecht*. NDP244.
Tennessee Williams, *Hard Candy*. NDP225.
  The Glass Menagerie. NDP218.
  In the Bar of a Tokyo Hotel & Other Plays.
    NDP287.
  In the Winter of Cities. NDP154.
  One Arm & Other Stories. NDP237.
  The Roman Spring of Mrs. Stone. NDP271.
  27 Wagons Full of Cotton. NDP217.
William Carlos Williams,
  The William Carlos Williams Reader.
    NDP282.
  The Autobiography. NDP223.
  The Build-up. NDP259.
  The Farmers' Daughters. NDP106.
  In the American Grain. NDP53.
  In the Money. NDP240.
  Many Loves. NDP191.
  Paterson. Complete. NDP152.
  Pictures from Brueghel. NDP118.
  The Selected Essays. NDP273.
  Selected Poems. NDP131.
  White Mule. NDP226.
John D. Yohannan,
  Joseph and Potiphar's Wife. NDP262.

**Complete descriptive catalog available free on request from
New Directions, 333 Sixth Avenue, New York 10014.**   † Bilingual.